CW00811018

Star
of
hope

Part III of The Sun Trilogy

Moira McPartlin

STAR OF HOPE
Moira McPartlin
© Moira McPartlin 2019

The author asserts the moral right to be identified
as the author of the work in accordance with the
Copyright, Designs and Patents Act, 1988

All rights reserved. No part of this publication may be reproduced,
stored in a retrieval system or transmitted in any form
or by any means, electronic, mechanical, photocopying,
recording or otherwise, without the prior permission of
Fledgling Press Ltd,

Cover illustration: Graeme Clarke
Published by:

Fledgling Press Ltd,
1 Milton Road West
Edinburgh
EH15 1LA
www.fledglingpress.co.uk

ISBN 9781912280247
Printed and bound by:

Martins the Printers, Berwick-upon-Tweed

For Colin

ACKNOWLEDGEMENTS

Writing a full trilogy is a hard task. It would not have been possible without the help of many generous, talented people.

I am especially grateful to my regular early readers Frances Wright and Colin Baird. To Rachel Davidson, Claire Watts and Miranda Moore who read the full manuscript and scrutinised every word. Thanks also to the rest of my YA crit group who have encouraged and supported me throughout the writing of these books and to everyone in the SCBWI network who have helped me along the way. I would also like to thank my adult crit group, FK8, for venturing into my future world to give some insightful feedback.

Many thanks are due to everyone at Fledgling, in particular Clare Cain who took this project under her wing at a particularly difficult time.

Lastly I would like to thank my family for their constant support. And of course love and thanks to my husband Colin. Without his expert knowledge and truthful comments none of this would have happened.

Steadie Reservation, Year 2089

Sorlie

It was like watching a toddler walk on glass. Pa on blades. Plastic straps tied them to what was left of his legs. He wore shorts and I saw where the blade fixings pressed and cut. The pain on his face tore at my gut. I wished I could go through it for him but he was the one who got blown apart. All I could do was help him recover.

'Come on Pa, just three more steps and you can rest.'

Harkin should be at his side but Reinya, so close to her birth date, needed Harkin more. So I was stuck with Pa in his rehabilitation. Not that I minded or anything.

I propped him up under his good arm, s'truth, his only arm. 'That's it, Pa.'

His teeth ground and not just from pain. He hated me helping him. He'd almost reached his goal when the siren began to WAH.

'What the snaf, that's the third time this week.'

'Leave me here,' Pa said. 'I'm not going in there again.'

'You have to.'

'No.' But he was defenceless as I hoisted him into a piggyback.

Even though his blades were plastic he was still pretty heavy. His limbs hung and rattled against my legs, almost tripping me up. The specials silent-screamed and flapped as the oldies huckled them towards the hothouse. Despite their fear, as they rushed by us, they gave Pa, their Prince and saviour, a wide berth and a respectful bow.

I ran with him past Harkin's infirmary tent.

'Harkin, quick,' I hollered. Reinya appeared in the doorway, her face sweaty, her bloated belly ready to pop.

'She's not 'ere,' she said.

'Where is she?'

'Don' know.'

I searched through the chaos hoping to see a glimpse of her black curls.

'Sorlie, get yur Pa out of 'ere, thur comin,' Reinya shouted before retreating into the tent. I heard the Military trucks trundling into Steadie. They'd soon be on us like flies to shite. She was right, I needed to get Pa to safety.

The door to the hothouse was closed. Locked. I hammered. 'I have The Prince. Let us in,' I screamed.

Pa breathed hot on my neck. 'They're just frightened.'

I turned back to face Steadie, using my heel to kick the door.

'Open up, Betty. Are you in there?'

The trucks stopped by the canteen. Bio-suited Military poured onto the duckboards, tearing open the container homes, searching for the specials and oldies they knew were here somewhere. One Jeep kept on, closer to the hothouse than they'd ever dared to come in the past. At the helm was a brute of a man I'd never seen before, his armour and mask terrifying with scales, grey-harled like the destroyer in the vid game I'd played at home. He held out a sabre, a copy of my game avatar's favourite weapon. Games Wall for real. What the snaf?

'You!' He pointed it at me, or maybe Pa.

Behind me the door opened. A hand reached out and grabbed us. I stumbled back through the opening but before it closed on me I heard the voice roar again. 'Sorlie Mayben, I'm coming to get you.'

Time, shielding, distance. That was the secret to staying safe in the hothouse.

Inside the specials were already in their penguin formations.

The shuffling huddled mass that ensured those on the inside of the huddle were protected from the radiation. Those on the outside take it for as long as their monitors stay quiet then the positions are changed. Harkin explained it to me the first time I had to hide in here with the oldies and specials. The building was highly radioactive which was why it remained safe from the Military. Once inside we needed to make sure we minimised our own damage. The rules, she told me, time, shielding, distance and the specials knew those rules.

I kept Pa strapped to my back while I moved into the safe penguin huddle with the specials, but their huddle seemed more erratic today. They bumped and shoved and girned at being put out of step and I realised it was our uneven shape – me with the hump of Pa on my back. I could feel him stiffen in pain every time a special touched him. He never uttered a word but his agony seeped into me.

'We'll go into the corner.'

'No Sorlie, you must keep safe.'

'It's OK, we won't be here long. They were here a couple of days ago. There isn't anything for them to find and most of the disarray they caused then has still to be mended.'

I gently eased Pa into the corner beside Betty. He slumped, head on chest. She gave him a small pat and moved to give him space. She chewed her lip. 'These raids sap his energy and it's not good that he's more exposed.' I checked his bar badge – amber, shit.

She held out a worried hand to me. 'Where's Harkin, Sorlie?'

'I couldn't find her.'

'This is bad.'

'She'll be fine.'

Betty shook her head. 'We don't know that.'

Ever since they closed the hothouse door I'd been pushing back the thought that Harkin maybe wouldn't be fine. She didn't look

3

special. The first time I met her, when she tended to my injuries after Vanora's kidnap, I thought of her as just a girl. Then, during that first raid, I noticed her difference, her exotic looks, her strange wanderings and the fact that the normally silent specials talked with her. And now she was out there while the Military rampaged through the camp, finding mischief.

'Raids are not so frequent but three in the last week. This is bad Sorlie.' She tapped the bar badge stapled to my lapel – amber.

Betty was a wise oldie. I had to believe her. Was the increase in frequency anything to do with the new leader heading up the raids? That roar, so alien and yet there was something familiar about it. Who was he? He knew me and he wanted to harm me.

Betty passed round the hard sweets, the pacifiers to keep the specials from worrying too much about yet another raid and what was happening outside.

She handed the poke to me. Pa took one with his good hand. I handed them back and waved her away.

'Suit yourself,' she snipped.

We sat quiet, listening to the shuffling specials. I wondered if Pa too was thinking about Harkin, she was his healer after all. But I was wrong. After a while he spat the sweet into his hand and tucked it in the gutter behind him.

'Sorlie, it will soon be time to act.' I looked at Pa, a remnant of the man I remembered. He was The Prince, the saviour who was to lead the natives from slavery.

He nodded. 'I know what you think. How can I lead? But I won't always be like this. Just you wait and see.'

'You need to get strong.' I didn't say whole but that's what I meant.

'There's no time for that. The Eastern Zone has been quiet for too long. There have been developments on the Bieberville border.'

'What do you mean?'

'I've had reports. Some of the TEX disciples have been organising themselves, or are being organised. TEX disciples are idiots, empty grabbers, wanting something for nothing, can't do anything for themselves. But they are up to something. We need to get to the source first.'

'I don't know what you mean. What TEX disciples? What source?'

Pa began to slide over. He pushed back to sitting, sweat washed his face. I moved to his battered side and let him rest on me. I could smell his torn flesh.

'Why can't they do more for you?'

'Harkin is trying,' he sighed. 'But things are so primitive here. Another reason to find the source.'

'Pa, stop talking in riddles.'

'Sorry, it's just before the Switch-Off my recovery could have been different by now. Cyborg technology.'

'What Switch-Off?'

'The internet. Switched off, supposedly to stop terrorists.'

I signed. 'Come on Pa, you're talking cyber-attacks, everyone knows that.'

'It wasn't just that.'

'That's what we were taught.'

He snorted and my face whooshed with stupidity.

'Yep OK,' I said. 'Taught History is a joke.' For sure. It was debunked for me at Black Rock when I read the real books in my grandfather's library. The Purist uprising, their right wing elitism and cruel purges, followed a few years later by the Land Reclaimists' fight back; their crippling environmental policies making natives' lives even more miserable. Even now I can't tell which was worse.

'We need a revolution, Sorlie.'

Just then a scuffle broke out in the huddle. I couldn't see, the huddle was a mess, specials stumbling everywhere. I watched, still stunned by Pa's words, trying to make sense of his riddles.

'Sorlie!' Betty roared.

I jumped, letting Pa slip to the floor. I elbowed my way into the melee. The group parted. A young boy was on his knees, choking. An old man held onto a walking frame with one hand and made feeble attempts to thump the boy's back. I grabbed the boy and hauled him to his feet, grasped him round the waist and jerked my arms under his rib cage. I felt him go limp, I jerked again, this time a sweet shot from his mouth and landed on the floor. One of the other specials moved to pick it up. 'No,' Betty snapped. The special shoved his hand in his pocket instead. The boy gulped in hoops of breath and leaned his head on my shoulder. I patted his back, I didn't know what else to do. Betty rubbed my arm. 'Thank you, Sorlie. What will we do when you are gone?'

'Gone? Where am I going?'

I turned back to ask Pa, but his spot was empty. The door lay open, the raid over with the specials starting their trail back to their jobs and ransacked homes. We were met by the usual mayhem; natives putting their homes to right and tending to the injuries sustained through Military brutality.

Harkin. I rushed to the infirmary. She was nowhere in sight. Reinya paced the floor, her swollen belly seemed to pull her frame over like a half shut knife. She had both hands pressed into the small of her back as if pushing herself straight.

'Have you seen her?'

'Cool yur jets Sorlie – she's around.'

'But have you seen her since the raid?'

Reinya pringled her brows. 'Now you come to mention it.'

'Did they take her?'

She shook her head. 'Word is they found nothin this time. Con reckons they'll give up altogether soon and leave us the 'ell in peace.'

'Where is Con? He's chief elder. He should be out there sorting this out.'

''e just popped his 'ead round the door lookin for 'arkin.'

'I knew it, she's missing. Where the snaf is she?'

'Where the snaf is who?'

The tent flap pulled back and there she was. Her curls tumbled around her cheeks and clung in little wisps to her forehead, like she'd been running.

'Where the snaf have you been?' I took a step towards her then stopped. I wanted to hug her, I wanted to shake her for making me worried.

She dumped an armful of vegetation on the floor. 'I was out foraging on the high top. I heard the siren so I had a little stravaig.'

'Stravaig?' Con had warned me her dangerous habit of wandering aimlessly would get her in trouble but this time it had saved her.

She moved toward Reinya. 'Is it bad?'

'Not too bad.'

Harkin wiped Reinya's forehead. 'You are too brave for your own good, let it go.' She took her arm and walked with her. 'Walking is the best thing.' Harkin looked at me. 'How's The Prince?'

I burled round expecting him to be there. 'Someone must have taken him back. He's in a lot of pain. When can you help him?' Harkin avoided my eyes. 'He said in the time before the Switch-Off he would have been whole by now.'

She laughed, something rare and eerie.

'What's so funny?'

'How many times have I heard that from the oldies? "Before the Switch-Off things were better", blah, blah.'

'What is it then? This Switch-Off?'

'Ask your Pa, he's the historian.'

'An' ma grandda,' Reinya said. ''e'll know.'

I found him in a wheelbarrow, left like a sack of potatoes, his head flung back, looking at the sky and letting rain drop on his face. A special came by and pulled up the hood of the barrow. It was a mix of blue and green tarp welded together in a plastic crimp. Pa peeked out and smiled when he saw me.

'Lovely day.'

'You are joking, right?'

'No I'm not. Look over there – white cloud, I think we may actually see blue later.'

I'd forgotten his maddening optimism. He hadn't shown much of it in the last few years after Ma had been given her Hero in Death status. After all, how could you be optimistic when your wife was ordered to be a suicide bomber?

'Take me to the beach, Sorlie. Remember that last time I took you?'

How could I forget? It was just before Ma fulfilled her status and blew herself up. Back where it all began and my life changed forever. The time he told me about that catastrophic change that was about to take place. About my grandfather Davie, and Black Rock Penitentiary. I now knew he had been preparing me to meet him. To live with him on that prison island.

As if he read my mind, Pa said. 'So many disasters in your life, Sorlie, but there was so much more.' I placed him on the sand, propped back against the barrow. His limbs straight out in front of him. I could see him move to scratch the space below, then stop. He let out a sigh, almost a shudder. 'Give me a moment,' was all he said.

We sat in silence looking towards the sea. The broken turbines out there baring their toothy girns. Despite his optimism, malevolent grey clouds hung on the horizon promising a storm later but for now I could sense we had a precious few hours of dry.

Pa pointed to the turbines. He hated them.

'Yes, I know,' I said. 'The money men running to the sun.'

'It wasn't just that. Energy and technology is the key to our survival and yet they spoiled it. It all got out of hand. The tech revolution.'

I held my wheesht. I felt a boring lecture coming on. Why hadn't I noticed this before? Pa was a typical teacher.

'Politicians didn't keep up.'

Here we go.

'You've heard of the internet?'

'The thing before FuB? Yeah, Scud told me. The governments wanted to take back control of the information. Stop terrorism. Gave us FuB. Fake information.'

'Fake news.' Pa started to laugh. 'There was a man once who obsessed with this, but I'm afraid to admit he might have had a point.' Pa began to draw a diagram in the sand with his finger, a circle with lots of branches sprouting from it. 'Did Scud tell you about artificial intelligence?'

'He said they switched the internet off. But he couldn't say any more. The surveillance, you know, on Black Rock.'

'It was because the machines were taking over. There was a group called TEX. They were once so powerful, so rich, they had the whole world in their grasp. They took the jobs of almost everyone and gave them to robots and algorithms.'

I thought of the specials sifting through the piles of radioactive rubbish and wondered how this was a bad thing.

'They treated poor people like slaves.'

'The way the Privileged treat natives?'

'Worse than that.'

'How can it be worse than that?'

'There was more contempt. They could choose who ate and who starved.' Pa gulped, and I saw the passion blaze in his eyes. 'They held governments to ransom. They controlled even the WMDs. They could destroy us all at a whim. They were kings. The politicians were old school, bickering like children. Couldn't agree. Didn't see it coming. It got out of control. Governments held secret meetings but of course the TEX knew. You think surveillance is bad now with the chips. Before the Switch-Off, TEX knew everything, every movement we made. The governments were lost. Then one maverick TEX did the honourable thing for the planet and the survival of homo sapiens.'

'How?'

'He pulled the plug on everything and sent the world back to the dark ages.'

'But how?'

'I don't know, but he did. And when he did, all hell broke loose. Everyone thinks this period began with the Purists' uprising. That was bad enough. But after the Switch-Off chaos reigned and, of course, the Purists took full advantage.'

'Who was he? This TEX who pulled the plug?'

'You mean who is he? He's still alive and living near the Bieberville border.'

'What's his name?

'Skelf. And I'm sending Ishbel's men in to find him.'

Ishbel

The harbour lights flickered on in the early afternoon and, for the millionth time since Ishbel's arrival on Freedom all those months ago, she wondered why Vanora insisted on burning so many lights during the day. They were on an island in the northern seas, many kiloms from the nearest civilisation, why waste precious generator fuel? Still, she shouldn't complain, it allowed her to sit longer on the damp hillside and watch the comings and goings. Seabirds whirled above her, oblivious to the strong cold wind that blew from the north. Somewhere on the shoreline a curlew's lonely call reached out to its near-extinct family. Broad streaks of rain slashed the sky in the south before disappearing into the black sea; they never break their promise of a storm, she knew that now.

On the quayside she watched a group of dissidents Sorlie had helped escape from Black Rock. They had a well-established routine now that The Prince's Blue Pearl brigade had taken control of Vanora's army. The Blue Pearl flag cracked in the stiff north wind, reminding everyone that they were now in charge, and they would lead the revolution to free the natives from the State.

Ishbel lay back, allowing her elbows to sink into the soft moss and, not for the first time recently, she wondered what Sorlie and the others were up to in Steadie. As the months passed she had begun to get used to the idea that she could spend the rest of her life here, oblivious to the suffering of the rest of the Esperaneo natives. And then the order had come through from The Prince two days ago, she was to prepare for action.

She spied her brother Kenneth on the quay, a guard by his side. This was his daily walk, always guarded since his vicious attack on Vanora. Poor Kenneth. They said he was mad beyond help, but it was grief. Ishbel couldn't blame him for hating Vanora and attempting matricide. Kenneth had loved the guard Ridgeway and Vanora had been careless with his life and death.

At the time of Kenneth's attack, Vanora, although shaken, had put up a brave front and tried to resume her role as empress and all round deluded despot. But that time had long disappeared and as the months went by Ishbel witnessed that behind all the bluster, Vanora had shrunk into the old woman she was. Her only ally now was Monsieur Jacques, the elderly Noiri king. Two aging has-beens propping each other's armies up like a house of cards.

Ishbel watched Kenneth retrace his steps back to his quarters in Freedom's infirmary. A whistle escaped through the gap in her front teeth before she sucked in her courage. She couldn't put it off any longer.

The infirmary orderly was a stern man given to staring past Ishbel as if she didn't exist. He was of a generation that still found face to face interaction threatening, and who found native women even more threatening. Ishbel thought she must terrify him. A whole two generations of natives brought up to interact only with their friends in a virtual world – friends real and not so real. Vanora had told her that before the Switch-Off, children were introduced to extra Tactical Social Classes to teach them how to interact with other humans. How could it have grown so bad? The damage had been done decades before. The faceless generations out there. And Ishbel loathed having to deal with them.

Kenneth smiled at her entry. 'Come to rattle my cage have you?'

'That's unfair and you know it.'

He held his hands out to Ishbel. 'Come talk to me. You are my sister, and yet I've never really spoken to you. Never got to know you.' He chuckled and she knew why. 'Except through your fine fare, that is.' Ishbel had been one of the domestic's natives who had fed Vanora's clandestine army. She had grown extra fruit and vegetables in the Mayben garden. Pickled them and sent them, via Dawdle's Noiri network, to Kenneth's hideout as well as two other coverts.

'You kept me alive, Ishbel.'

'If I hadn't someone else would have.'

He stroked his well-trimmed beard and glowered at his feet.

'What are you going to do with me?'

'I'm going to give you a project to keep you from trying to kill Vanora again.'

'What? Not execute me for insubordination?'

Ishbel laughed. 'Oh, Vanora is baying for your blood but there isn't anything she can do to you anymore.'

'Why?'

'It was agreed at Black Rock, after you'd tried to kill her. You'd be my responsibility.' He put his head down and she knew what he was thinking. He started to cry.

'Ridgeway and I had only just found each other again,' he said, choking on his tears.

Ishbel wanted to put her arm around him but found she couldn't. The emotional repression of her upbringing was too strong.

'I know,' she said. 'Ridgeway was a good man.' Ishbel also knew that Vanora hadn't needed to take Ridgeway with her on the mission where he perished. She only did it to deny Kenneth his company.

Kenneth sniffed loudly and cleared his throat. 'I miss him so much.'

'I know, he served us well.' She saw Kenneth's shoulders stiffen. 'He was a good man,' she said again, biting her stupid tongue. She placed her hands on his shoulders and forced him to face her. 'Look Kenneth, we are going to win this fight. We will conquer Esperaneo Major. The Prince has it all worked out. But we need good people back here to build a strong society. What's the use of taking control if we are left with a heap of uneducated natives who can't even communicate with each other?' Kenneth lowered his sad eyes, but she lifted his chin again with a gentle hand. 'You are useful. Scud has history, you have science.' She clicked her comms and scrolled through some screens. 'Look, remember, Davie's library at Black Rock.' He peered at the screen with his old watery eyes and failed to keep the interest from his face.

'We have saved the books. They're back where they belong on Black Rock. We have the old knowledge, true knowledge. Knowledge we thought we had lost after the Switch-Off. You and Scud are going to set up our education programme.'

He dry sobbed and took in a great breath. 'Ishbel, I want to fight in the revolution.'

'You are too old to fight.'

His eyes became fierce. 'I will never be too old to fight.'

'I'm sorry,' Ishbel said.

He sat down wearily. 'When are you going on your first mission?'

'Soon.'

'I'm coming with you.'

'The Prince will never agree.'

'Then don't tell him.'

He stood up and walked towards her and she could see his past still blazing in his eyes.

'You owe me, Ishbel. All those years Vanora had me ensconced in that cave for nothing. You expect me to retire to a cosy school room.' He thumped the wall. 'No, I fight.' He pointed at her. 'And, and I tell you, if Scud wants to fight, you let him. We might be old men but we have been in this mess a lot longer than you.'

'I hear rumours that Scud is not well. He wants to go back to Black Rock.'

'Rumours,' he shouted at her. 'From that Noiri scoundrel, Dawdle, no doubt. No wonder Scud's not well. You didn't have to go through the purge – see your career thrown out as useless. You didn't have your loved ones ripped from you.' Spittle flew with each passionate word.

She put her hands up against this onslaught, looking round for the emergency bell. She'd call to sedate him soon if this kept up.

'Kenneth, I am leaving you now,' she said, drawing herself to her full height. 'You will be kept under lock and key until we can place you outside the toxic range of Vanora. You can't come with me and I think you know that too. You are a scientist first and foremost. Think that over and think what good you can do the cause with that knowledge.'

The day before Ishbel was due to leave on her mission Kenneth asked to see her. She expected another plea to allow him to fight so she was surprised to find him in calm mode, sitting at his work bench.

'Kenneth.'

As she approached he held up a vial.

'What is it?'

'A virus.'

Ishbel baulked. 'Have we not had enough manmade viruses in our lifetime? The population has been selected, and reduced to near extinction, we don't need any more killing.'

He shook his head. 'It isn't a virus for humans. It affects concrete.'

'Concrete?'

'You asked me to apply my brain to a solution. Well I did. I've actually been working on this all year. There's a waterborne virus that erodes concrete, so I asked myself, what if it were made airborne? Think how much concrete there is in the Capital.'

Ishbel examined the innocent-looking vial. 'Has it been tested?'

'Sort of,' he said, his eyes to the floor, and she knew he was lying. 'There is only one way to find out. We could test it in Beckham City first. What harm can happen there? I've heard the place is a dump. If it works then take it forward.'

'What if it gets out of control?'

'We have to take that chance, Ishbel.'

'No, absolutely not. I forbid it.'

Kenneth glowered at her below his busy brows. 'You asked me to apply my knowledge and now that I have you reject it.'

'It's untested, Kenneth. If you can show me test results on how it works, how it is controlled and contained, I will consider it when I come back from my mission. Not until.'

'But...'

'No!' She held her hand out for him to shake a goodbye but he stared at it like a petulant child.

'Bon voyage, Kenneth, you will be going to Black Rock tomorrow. I will ensure your lab equipment follows you and you can perfect your virus when not helping with the education programme.' He stared at the wall, his eyes glazed over with indifference.

'I will fight one way or the other. I will fight.'

Ishbel whistled through the gap in her teeth. She'd be glad when he was safely ensconced on Black Rock.

Sorlie

Pa was wrong about the good weather to come. Rain plashed down heavier than normal for the PM. I lifted him back into the barrow and wheeled him to his container. I was just helping him up the duckboard step when Reinya's screams tore through the whole camp. Scud rushed from the canteen tent, his face paler than normal, his mutant expression, soapy and weak.

'What are they doin tae her? Make them stop,' Scud moaned, his hands over his damaged ears. Tears started in his walnut eyes. His Privileged looks meant he didn't have to hide from the raid. He'd have stayed out, working in the plastic reprocessing plant when the raid started.

He grabbed my free hand. 'You go Sorlie, see what's happenin. They'll no let me near.'

As I looked at the beseeching face of my friend I recognised an expression I'd seen in him many times before. In danger, in hope and in pain, he had asked for my help, the help of a mere boy but in his eyes still a Privileged, superior. But this time it was different. Our roles were more equal.

'OK.' I said as I let him take the burden of Pa.

I stepped out into the busy streets of Steadie where natives and specials continued to clear up the mess. Could no one else hear her? I hopped along the ridged plastic duckboard, jumping over broken sections, skiting round those now sunk in the mud. Relentless rain had battered this area in the last two months. In the old days this fourth quarter had been called Winter and was reputed to have brought a coldness so cold it burned; ice and snow and clean air. Not in my lifetime, so I was doubtful for a rain check any time soon. Ice was something the State President put in his Mash.

Another scream ripped through the camp. The door to the infirmary tent was pulled tight shut. As I bounded the steps two at a time I heard a slap then silence. Another scream issued from Reinya, just as painful but different. This scream held the hurt of nations.

A native woman pulled the flap open and almost fell over me. 'It's a boy,' she said through her gummy oldie grimace.

Betty moved out behind her and stared at me with worried eyes.

'What? What is it? Is Reinya OK?'

She shook her head. 'Go and see for yourself.'

'I'll get Scud.'

'No. Sorlie, you go first.'

I hesitated at her worried look. A cold thread plumbed my spine as I remembered Reinya's story. This child was the result of violence done to her on the Prison Ship. I didn't want to find out what was in there. Before I ducked into the tent I turned to survey Steadie. There were the specials, protected from the State in this radioactive haven. They would have been destroyed during the early purges for their flaws. Deemed a burden to our cleansed society. The result of nature or too much tampering with nature. They chose to be silent because society had shunned them. Both Privileged and native did not want to hear what they had to say. And now this baby. What if? But the what if didn't matter when I saw Reinya propped up in bed, her rusty hair spread out against the pillow, dampened round the edges.

''e's beautiful,' she said, smiling down at the bundle she held. This fierce girl who never smiled, always angry at a world who robbed her of her childhood. ''e's beautiful,' she said again. The room seemed to be holding its breath and cold air curled around us. I stepped up beside her and looked down at the baby so pale it was almost translucent. His eyes were cold, his lips blue.

''e'll never be able to leave 'ere as long as thurs no freedom. 'e'll always be in the middle of the pack 'idden. But 'e is the most beautiful baby uh've ever seen and uh'm goin to make 'is life worth livin if it's the last thing uh do.'

I touched his forehead. It was warm but cooling fast. The baby was dead.

''is name is Kooki,' Reinya said, her lips trembled. 'It means Star of 'ope.'

Betty went to Reinya and placed her arm across her back. 'Let me take him.'

Reinya hugged the bundle closer. How could she not feel the cold from him? She stared at us, one after the other. The smile on her face started to slide. She pulled the blanket tighter around him. ''e's gettin cold, uh must warm 'im up.'

Betty nudged me. 'Do something, Sorlie,' she whispered.

I looked at Harkin, who stood in the corner, watching us, her arms crossed over her chest. Her face blank of emotion.

'Harkin?' I said but it was Scud who stepped up. He'd been standing in the doorway watching the scene. I don't know how long he had been there but it was enough to know the score. He walked to the bedside and knelt down. Since our arrival in Steadie, Reinya had worked hard to rid herself of her revulsion at her mutant grandfather. In the past months they had even sometimes shared a meal. She now turned her head to Scud. Her lips twisted, there was a tear on her lower lid.

'It's this place,' she whispered. 'Uh should never 'ave brought 'im 'ere.'

Scud touched the baby's head. 'He would have been ma great grandson.'

Reinya's mouth hung open and a line of spittle dribbled from it.

With the back of one hand Scud wiped it clear, with the other he eased the tiny bundle from her grasp. Tears streamed down her face, her mouth forming an ugly gape.

'Please,' she whispered, trying to keep hold.

'Reinya, he's gone. Let him go,' Scud rasped.

As Scud removed the baby from her bedside, Harkin moved in and hugged Reinya close to smother the heart-breaking gasps. My chest was tight and a hard lump lodged in my throat. I stood helpless like a tube. As I turned to go I clocked Betty's normally jolly face grim with disappointment.

I followed Scud into the grey morning. 'What do we do now, Scud?'

He remained silent as he walked serenely towards one of the outer tents.

'Scud,' Betty hailed. 'Wait up.'

When he turned I noticed tears rolling down his face. We waited as she hirpled along the duckboard.

'Our death dealer will take care of him.'

'How?'

'There will be a cremation.' She pointed to a small building beside the hothouse. 'In there. Let me take care of it, Scud.'

He handed the baby to Betty. 'Make sure Reinya gets tae see him before he goes.'

'What if she wants to hold on to it again?' I asked.

Scud looked at me as if I were mad. 'She won't,' he said. 'And it's 'him' not 'it'.' He walked away. I ran after him.

'Scud, wait up.' I grabbed his sleeve but he shook off my grip. 'Scud?' I ran round him and stood to block his way.

'Let me go, Sorlie.'

'Where?'

'Anywhere away from here,' he gasped. 'Ah can't bear tae see her pain. Ah can't take this anymore. All those years in prison, workin as an agent for Vanora. Twenty-odd years. Ah always had hope. But the pain just keeps on happenin. The needless sufferin.' He cast his arm around the site. 'Look at this place. The specials, the oldies, forced tae live in this hell-hole because the alternative is death. Why did we have tae bring her here?'

'Because we thought she would be safe.'

'We should have taken her tae Freedom.'

'There's no place for her there, you know that. The Prince was clear, it was for warriors only.' I felt a chill as I thought about that order. No one questioned it at the time, but Scud was right. Reinya should have been taken to Freedom. 'Ishbel returned there because she was useful to the cause,' I continued. 'The Prince and Reinya would go to Steadie to recover.'

'Mebbes sometimes The Prince is wrong.'

'How can you say that? Only a few months ago you told me he was the best person to lead this fight.'

Scud stopped. 'And what fight is this? When will this revolution start?'

I squared my shoulders. We were both small but I tried to grow taller in defence of Pa. 'These things take time to organise.'

'Organise!' he spat the words. 'He needs tae act now. These people need tae get out o here before they all die.'

I tapped the bar badge on my overalls.

'They know how to live here, Scud. They know when they've had enough and get moved to the perimeter and those at the perimeter move in a bit.'

He took hold of his own badge, and ripped it from his jacket. 'And who told ye that?'

'Con did.'

'And did the great elder, Con, tell ye how many specials they have carted off tae that incinerator over there?' He pointed but he couldn't look. 'The Death Dealer has his work cut out for him here.'

'Scud, you're upset.'

'Upset!' he screamed. 'Snafin right ah'm upset. My wife died o a broken heart, my daughter was forced into being an addict and ended her days dyin a horrible death on a prison ship. My granddaughter suffered unimaginable horrors there too and that baby, the one good thing tae come from all that violence, is dead.'

'You can't blame Steadie for that.'

His eyes blazed at me. 'Ah can blame whoever ah like.' He took a step towards me, his finger jabbed my chest. 'And what about you? The great Privileged hope.' His face was right in my mug. His breath rank with years of decay. 'Get it sorted, Sorlie. Now get out o my way. Ah'm goin tae spend some time wi Reinya before ah leave.'

Ishbel

Ishbel loved this bleak landscape she now knew so well. The treeless wasteland scoured by the fierce winds and relentless rain had washed the weariness from her soul. She wanted to roam free on the hillside and take a small sailing boat out to the bay to harvest some precious fish. But she knew this wish was futile. Tomorrow she would leave to whatever her fate would bring her but she knew the memory of the place would remain with her and she would return.

As Ishbel made her way back to the control centre she heard rich laughter coming from the boathouse that sat back from the quay. She saw Huxton back out, his arms full of some booty. His laughter caught her unawares. He was normally so solemn. Which she was glad of. It was one of the reasons she'd appointed him her right hand man after she'd taken control. Also he was the most chemically stable.

She had learned that when the Black Rock prisoners had first arrived on Freedom, some had been ill with chemical withdrawal, in the same manner as Scud. But many had been immune to the DNA dilution they had been subjected to while on Black Rock. Perhaps this was due to a higher concentration of Privileged genes in their original make up. These men had stature and confidence. Many had been freedom fighters after the Purist purge until their eventual incarceration.

One such prisoner was Huxton, a tall thin man, with premature grey hair and of undiscernible age. He had a permanent look of concern on his face which Ishbel had always suspected hid his true nature. She had observed that men did what he wanted before he even asked. Ask him if he wanted a cup of brew and he would answer with a look that might be interpreted as telling you, 'yes a brew is acceptable but please beware, it might be poisoned'.

After her arrival at Freedom Ishbel had walked among the men as an invisible woman until she donned her Blue Pearl Commander uniform, so different from the ragged second-hand one of Vanora's army. Vanora's army was no more since The Prince's Blue Pearl marched in, took control and organised operations to their standards. Ishbel touched the fabric of recycled fibre and remembered Vanora's smirk the first time she saw Ishbel in her new uniform.

'Green. Just your colour,' Vanora had quipped.

'That's kind of you, although it is the same colour as domestic natives.'

'Well you can thank The Prince for that.'

When Huxton first saw her as Commander, he'd looked almost relieved and had readily agreed to assist her. She'd heard rumblings of unrest around the base. It wasn't going to be easy.

Upon her appointment The Prince had advised Freedom to watch all news reports coming out of The State news agency, as if this was something Ishbel hadn't already thought of. She had set one operator with the sole job of monitoring all new incidents where insurgents' attacks took place and then ranking them as fake news or genuine based on footage matching.

She knew she'd done a good job at the control centre but the flutter of excitement she felt in her belly when the latest instruction came through awoke her inner desire.

Ishbel was to assemble a team of men and send them on a mission. Men, she thought, always men. But she knew why. All the escaped prisoners from Black Rock were men. If she wanted an army of women she would need to orchestrate another prison break in another sector where only women were held. But there were fewer female political prisoners because The State still held the archaic belief that women were not worth bothering about.

She'd read through the plans for Freedom. She organised the rota of work that needed to be done around Freedom and she'd looked forward to the long dark months of quarter four and the tedium that went with it. She knew there were a few prisoners who were good leaders, good organisers. But she knew she could lead this mission. When she confided in Huxton that she was taking charge of the mission, he shrugged.

'I don't blame you.'

'Will you stay and take command here?' This was a request not an order.

'I'd rather not. See, I've been stuck in prison for ten years. Sometimes this island feels like a prison too. I want to be free of Freedom. I'd rather come.'

'OK, then you pick the men we take. You know them better than me.'

Ishbel considered her available options and chose a man who looked like a toad to manage the control centre. His name was Henny and his eyes nearly popped from his head when she asked him to take charge.

'Vanora will try to interfere,' she'd told him. 'If she does, don't try to fight her. Let her have her way for a while, then reverse everything she does. Her engineers know the score. They won't let her do much harm.'

He swallowed hard. 'You'll be fine,' she said, resisting the urge to give him a reassuring pat.

'OK,' was the short reply delivered to her shoulder, his eyes shifting everywhere but to her face. He certainly wasn't the most confident cracker in the box but was the best of the bunch.

Before final preparations began she visited the dentist and had her suicide pill reinstated. Another bone she had to pick with

Dawdle. Even though his ripping her last pill out her mouth had probably saved her life, she still resented his interference.

Ishbel faced the coming storm and let the rain scour her face before pulling her snood over her head. Tomorrow they would leave and when they did she'd instruct the harbourmaster to extinguish all but the lighthouse lamp.

Sorlie

'Grow up, Sorlie,' Scud said, creeping up behind me as I was leaving Pa's tent after taking him some grub.

'I thought you'd gone.' I don't know why Scud had turned all aggressive. His face, normally peely wally, was blotched with spots of rage.

'Ah've one more thing tae say tae you before ah go.' He stood with hands clenched. This wee wily man who'd been my native on Black Rock, had risked his life for me and all natives, now stood as if to knock my lights out. He'd had his DNA diluted, but that had been stabilised. Apparently some souterrain community knew how to do that. Was this aggression a side effect?

'Ah've watched you wi your Pa. All you see is a cripple.'

'Not true.'

He took a step towards me, invading my space as natives sometimes do.

'Aye, true. Ah see you watch him move, put a hand out tae catch him, steady, even when Dougie didn't need help. Every time you're near him your expression fills with horror lines.'

I could feel my face pink at his words. He wasn't finished.

'Your generation grew up in a world cleansed of disability. The fact Steadie is filled wi specials seems tae have bypassed your notice. Shows your Privileged disregard for what is unimportant tae you.'

'That's a lie.' It was my turn to step into his space but he stood his ground.

'This is personal. Your Pa was once the strong Military leader, now he's a broken man that a young girl has been tasked tae fix.' A small bead of spittle formed at his mouth. 'Don't you see?'

'See what?'

'The cut o his jaw when you're near him. Are you blind tae it? Too many times ah've had tae walk away because ah can't bear tae watch father and son play the part in this gruesome charade. He's your Pa for snaf sake. Have you forgotten what he is capable of?'

'I think you need to calm down, Scud. Too much has happened to you. Why don't you stay here a while longer. Harkin will make you a tonic.' He punched me in the mouth. My head snapped back and I tasted iron. I grabbed him round the neck and threw him to the ground then sat on him. His breath laboured, his eyes stared at me.

'What's wrong with you, Scud?' Tears sprang in his eyes. He gritted his teeth.

'Get off me.'

I released my grip. A group of specials gathered round, showing curious frowns but silent. Harkin grabbed my shoulder.

'Get off him.'

'He punched me.' I said but did as she bid.

'You probably deserved it.'

Scud rolled onto his knees and twisted his head to watch me rise. 'Just grow up Sorlie and get this sorted.' He struggled to his feet and hunched into Pa's tent.

'What's wrong with him?' I asked Harkin.

'Don't you know?' She shook her head. 'Incarcerated for years, betrayed by Vanora, finding a granddaughter then losing her child. Is it any wonder he is mad at you?'

'It's not my fault.'

'You and your kind.' And she left me to follow Scud into the tent of a Privileged who was also one of my kind. Why don't they blame him too?

When I thought back to our return from Black Rock the signs of Scud's unrest were there all along. Dawdle's sub, Peedle, coughed and spluttered all the way to Steadie and each time it stopped Scud scuttled into a corner and wrapped himself in a blanket. I had to stop myself scratching my wrists with the worry of what we might find back at Steadie, but that was nothing compared to the worry on Scud's brow.

'How do you think Pa'll be when we get there?' I'd asked Scud. He shrugged but stayed quiet.

'The note Pa left in the cave was a deliberate clue to his whereabouts. He must have known I'd have come after him.'

'Dougie's a lot craftier than he looks,' Scud had said. What the snaf did that mean?

Dawdle had been intent on his driving but his usual good humour was missing. Was it his touching parting from Ishbel that dampened his spirit? It was such a shame he was so wired for profit he couldn't see what he was letting slip from his grasp.

'Ah've met his type before,' Scud had said nodding towards Dawdle. Scud watched him with suspicious eyes from the corner. 'Driven by one thing and no deviatin fae it.' And then we reverted to normal. He told me about Reinya and the souterrain folk. Of the cloth they wove from the recyk fibres supplied by Steadie and of how they had helped him. He had seemed enthusiastic almost.

That behaviour changed again when we arrived into the chaos of Steadie during a raid. And the first sight of my injured Pa. Scud had been kind to me, as if he felt my pain, but then he got tough and ordered me to man up. Well I did and I'd been manning up ever since.

Maybe it was his reunion with Reinya and the death of her child that tipped Scud over the edge. Whatever it was, there was no denying, Scud had changed. It was good he was going back to Black Rock to focus on the education programme. I knew from my experience as his pupil that it was a task he could excel in.

Ishbel

They arrived in darkness. The moorloggers had legitimate business in the North Sea, trawling for wood. They'd been betrayed on recent missions for Vanora's Native Freedom Fighters and lost boat and crew as a result. Sven, the skipper of the *Amber Sky* had been reluctant to take Ishbel and her carefully picked band of men, but he knew he had no choice when she handed him the Blue Pearl badge. The NFF was history and the reputation of the might of the Blue Pearl Army had preceded her.

Ishbel clung to the bridge, fighting back her quease.

'I'm sorry for your loss,' she said to Sven, realising he must have known the crew of the destroyed moorlogger.

'Should have thought of that before you thrust the Blue Pearl threat in my face.'

'The Blue Pearl isn't a threat, it's our only chance to deal with the State and free the natives.'

'I've been trawling these waters for twenty years, ever since the purge. Boat's been in my family for decades before the fishing ban. I don't need no threat to help.' He stared out at the grey wall of sea mist. 'Should never have got involved with you lot.'

The Amber Sky had picked her party of six from the top corner of Freedom Island. Being the fourth quarter of the year, night-time came early, but so did the gales.

The boat rose and pitched into waves as high as the Capital's tower before they came crashing down to be swallowed by another wave. Ishbel wondered how the small vessel could survive such punishment. Each time they were engulfed she expected to drop to the depths of the ocean but the waves washed off the deck.

'We still don't know who betrayed us.'

'No,' Ishbel said and looked behind her as if the traitor might have followed her on board. At first she had suspected her old rival Merj, but he was trusted by The Prince and had obviously been in his pay all along.

The boat engine screamed again in protest at the battering sea. They wore life jackets, but these looked useless. Anyone overboard would be consumed. Because all her men had been prisoners they were in greater danger. After the establishment of the prison islands all prisoners had had part of their brains altered to disable their swimming ability. Scud had had his disabilty repaired but these men, now clinging to the boat and spewing on the floor, were still impaired, although she doubted being able to swim would help in these atrocious conditions.

From the depths of the murk she spotted a ship.

'What's that?'

'Don't worry 'bout that,' Sven said. 'Rusty old battleship that should have been retired long ago. The State, huh, they think they are the force they once were.' He shook his head. 'Show, all show. They are harmless, we go to this port many times. They will not bother us. The captain? He sits with his feet up drinking illegal Mash.'

At last the sea flattened out enough for them to see a light in the distance.

'Land,' Sven said. 'These people, they have wood of their own. The lungs of Esperaneo, but they make us welcome.' He grinned wickedly. 'Quality Noiri contra there.'

Despite his boasts of a grand welcome, they tracked round a small island and waited in a secluded natural harbour until Sven was happy all was clear. The waters calmed as they approached and the men, still grey with sickness, sank down in relief and sipped some soup.

One of the moorlogger crew – an old man with a face of crumpled rubber, grumbled about cleaning up the sickness, sluiced the decks with troughs of salt water not caring who got in his way.

Sven beamed nav-charts to Ishbel's communicator.

'Open the file,' he said.

She booted her comms and a holo hovered above the table.

'You see this bay here.' He pointed through the holo to a small heart-shaped bay deep in a fjord. 'This is where I drop you. The Prince already has men in the area.' He pointed to a dark mass with no detail like someone had rubbed it out. 'We guess this is a Military base.' She could see a dense feature just before a jagged mountain range. 'And this?' she asked.

He nodded 'A protected forest. This is where you rendezvous. Once you make contact you head south east towards the Bieberville border. Here.' He pointed to a blank featureless landscape, marked with scattered dwellings and a border line.

'Should we destroy these maps?'

Sven shook his head. 'These are basic maps. If the Military capture you they will not think it strange you have a map.' He tapped his mouth. 'And anyway, take the pill.'

Ishbel pushed down the panic bubbling in her stomach. At times like these she remembered she was just a simple native.

All her life her mother had convinced her she was capable of great things, even if Vanora did not always show that confidence in her. She knew she was strong but up until last year Ishbel had been a domestic native caring for her sister's privileged son, Sorlie. All that had changed when her sister died and fulfilled her status as a Hero in Death. Ishbel looked at the men in the boat waiting for her to lead them. What was she doing here? Why had she taken the responsibility to lead such an important mission on Esperaneo Major? If she failed the whole Blue Pearl campaign to free the natives from their slave state would fail. She couldn't let that happen.

They motored in a cloak of darkness into the fjord. The noise of the engine seemed to rattle off colossal cliffs like a ball bearing in a tin lid. Sven lifted his shoulders in a sorry shrug. There was a small inflatable that the crew lowered into the water. Ishbel and her five men climbed into the boat. Deep into the night they could see bouncing lights alone on the shoreline. Something was coming and it didn't care if it was seen. Distant but growing closer. Military trucks.

'Hurry,' Sven said.

As the smaller boat moved off, the moorlooger gunned its engines and began a wide curve away from them. The wake tossed the little boat towards the shore. The lights of trucks ranged on the water. From the shore an engine kicked off, a motor boat rocketed from a boatyard. Ishbel didn't think they had been spotted because the boat headed toward the moorlogger. She was wrong. Shots fired into the water, Huxton yelped and collapsed over the side. Ishbel grabbed for his jacket but he had drifted too far.

'Turn around,' someone shouted.

'Keep going,' Ishbel roared as she dived into the water to catch Huxton. The freezing sting took her breath away. She reached for Huxton who was thrashing in panic. 'Your jacket keeps you up,' she said as she grabbed his collar. She watched their small boat retreat from the hunter's light and disappear round the headland into safety.

'They left us.' Huxton said.

'Yes. But they'll come back. We'll head for shore.'

She saw a small wooded island, no bigger than a soccer pitch, separated from the mainland by a pebble causeway. She kicked off with one eye still on the wake of the departing boat. Suddenly the sky filled with a bright light and the sound of the boat cut. As she and Huxton lay on the beach snorting seawater from their noses, they watched their small boat being towed to the shore. Four of her men were led at gun point onto the far shore, prisoners yet again. They did not know the plan but that wouldn't stop the Military from torturing them. They'd been betrayed again.

'We have to get them back,' she said to Huxton, but he lay unconscious on the sand. First she had to get help for him.

Sorlie

'Go on son, you must do it.' Pa sat in his tent, seemingly oblivious to the stench that had been building in there over the past few days. I held my cuff up to my nose to block it out but couldn't block from the mind the cause of the stench.

'No way Pa – you're The Prince. You do it.'

Pa swept his hand down his body, striking out with one of his plastic legs.

'It needs to be you.'

I craned my neck round the tent door at the gathering crowd and remembered the oldie movie-caster that featured a girl, super strong and sexy, as the only one able to save her tribe. She was the emblem of the revolution. She had a salute and sarcastic bow everyone copied. They listened to her but that was stupid fiction. This was real life. No one really believed a kid could lead a revolution. Pa had me dress in the uniform of the Blue Pearl. The serge material made from the recyk fibre produced here in Steadie and woven by the souterrain community. It scratched and stifled me with its formality. I now craved the hateful black prison garb like a comfort blanket.

The speech Pa instructed me to perform was to be transmitted to native reservations and covert communities across Esperaneo Major and Lesser Esperaneo, using Vanora's unique comms. It had been a while since anyone had mentioned Vanora around here but it seemed that she still had her uses. I imagined her in her northern lair. The last time I'd seen her in Freedom she'd been majestic, but showing signs of unravelling. Through her neglect she'd allowed Pa's Blue Pearl to infiltrate that lair with ease and now she was just another deposed leader. An oldie thrown on the recyk midden. Somehow that thought troubled me.

And yet, as I walked towards the podium, it was Vanora's reaction to my speech I worried about most. I looked at the specials and oldies here at Steadie. Betty stationed herself in the front row of the crowd beaming encouragement to me. I searched for Harkin and found her hidden in the shadow of Con until he placed his huge paw on her shoulder and moved her forward. Drones flew overhead, capturing images of me from all angles and beaming them onto the sides of some of the containers and tarps hung up as makeshift screens. My face leapt out at me. I looked at my feet, I didn't want to see and yet I couldn't help it, there was no escape. There he was; boy, seventeen years old. Small for his age. He looked Privileged but he knew that was an illusion, there in that stance was a hint of native he knew he carried in his genes. That boy, me, Sorlie Mayben, was the answer; that's what Pa told me. A visible leader the native population needed to believe in, to give them the strength to fight. Something to replace the hardship of living. They needed the one thing they had never had before – hope.

But unlike Pa, I knew now that it was too hard for them to fight the State when every day was a fight for survival.

'Get out there and make them believe,' he had said.

I took another look at the boy, the unlikely warrior who straightened his spine to make himself appear taller, and he looked right at me as I stared into the drone's cold lens before me. I gulped back the fear and spied something in the corner of my eye. Projected back at me I saw Reinya move up to my shoulder. Her fiery hair shone bright on the screen against my dullness. Her eyes were red-rimmed. I turned to face her in real-time. She smiled a sad smile and even though her smile reached her eyes it didn't quite wash away her pain. She took my hand and squeezed it.

'Let's do this thegether. Boy un girl.'

Hand in hand we walked to stage front.

'Citizens of Esperaneo,' I began. 'The end of your suffering is near. It is in your hands.' Jupe sake, it sounded like a movie-caster script. 'In the past year we have released the political prisoners from Black Rock. These men, both Priviledged and native, have joined the cause for freedom. And what have the Military been doing? Very little. They spend their time harassing poor natives.' I saw the specials and Steadie natives take notice, they knew I was talking about them. 'All citizens of Esperaneo are sick of suffering, sick of scraping food from this damaged earth, sick of hunger and disease.' A few were nodding, the others looked bored. 'The Prince has a plan and we are about to execute that plan, but we need your help. We need you to keep strong, to envisage your future, free of the shackles imposed by a brutal regime. We need you to be ready and willing to build our new society. To resist the Military. We need you to believe.'

There was some polite applause. This was no good. Then I heard a murmur in the crowd.

'Privileged.'

I scanned the faces to see who had spoken. Most looked embarrassed. My throat turned to ash. I stared straight at the drone and tried to still my heart. It was time to admit the truth. I took a step away from Reinya.

'Look at me.' I thumped my breast. 'I look Privileged, but I am part native, part Privileged.' That got their attention. 'My native genes may be hidden but they are in me.' It was as if my words had ripped the breath from the crowd.

'Now look to yourselves.' I spread my arms wide to sweep the width of Steadie and include the watchers of the transmission. 'You have been told all your lives natives are inferior.' I thumped my chest again. 'When I learned I was part native, I believed I was inferior.' I took a breath.

'We are not inferior.'

37

'We may be poor, we may be starving, we may be uneducated, but we are not inferior. Together we have power, together we have hope. And together we must believe in our future.'

I paused and as if we had rehearsed it, Reinya took up the call and stepped up beside me. She made a fist and shook it at the drone.

'Citizens, freedom is within our grasp.' She pointed at me. 'We know many Privileged can no longer stand by and witness your torture.' She took my hand and we held them aloft.

'Together,' I shouted, 'Native and Privileged. We will be free.'

'Together we'll be free,' Reinya echoed.

My blood was bouncing through my veins. Maybe I'd watched too many scripts because I expected cheers. Instead we received a respectful clap from specials. The natives looked tired. They nodded and smiled. Some chatted with enthusiasm but I feared the hope they needed had to come from another direction. I saw in the image the triumphant smile slip from my face and I wondered again at Vanora. What I didn't realise then was that it shouldn't have been Vanora I was worried about.

There had been no more raids in the last part of the quarter, yet a niggly pinge tweaked my gut with the thought that a brute in armour was out there somewhere thirsting for my blood. Reinya and I had been summoned to the canteen tent after the crowds dispersed and we dutifully assembled in time to see Pa's great entrance. Harkin walked at his side as he teetered on new blades, her hand held up tentatively at his back, ready enough to catch if he fell but discreet enough for him not to notice.

Her hair was wet as if from a wash, but this was mid-week and washing was restricted to the weekend here at Steadie. She must have been out in the morning mizzle helping the specials. Pa waited for us to take our places. Con leaned his butt on a table so

I joined him for a seat. Reinya skulked in the shadows behind the serving counter. It was as if the effort of being brave had sapped her of all energy. If this tent had corners I'm sure she would have preferred to be there. For the first time she reminded me of Scud. She had been magnificent at the crowd share but despite that, since Kooki's cremation, she kept out of everyone's way. I saw her straighten when Pa walked in then her thumb went to her mouth and she nibbled the nail. Around us the tent flapped with the growing storm, an occasional gust whacked the sides. When the patter of rain rose to full pelt no one looked up – this tent was well weathered.

As Pa passed my spot he stopped. 'You were right to tell them of your native genes,' he said. I looked around. Betty smiled, Harkin nodded. It was as if everyone had known all along.

At last Pa got to his chair: The Prince on his throne. He beckoned to Con and I and searched the space with his eyes.

'Reinya, come out wherever you are,' he hailed. She crept from the shadows but still stood a couple of steps away from me. He beckoned to us both.

'Your mission is called The Star of Hope.' I heard Reinya gasp.

'Yes Reinya – your baby's name. He would have been our future, this mission will be our future. It is a fitting legacy for him.'

A track of tears trickled down Reinya's face but a small smile twitched at her mouth.

'When do we start?' she whispered.

'Soon,' Pa said. 'Hold out your wrist, Sorlie, and receive the plans onto your communicator.' When it was done he held up four fingers. 'Four steps. You will do them in sequence. The most important is the last and for that you must make sure you reach the source by day four of the first quarter. There is much to achieve before that. Cover your tracks. We will not go over all plans. You will receive instructions for each task in turn. You will not receive the next instruction until the task you are on is complete. You will know nothing of the future for your own good. If you fall into enemy hands you will be innocent.' He frowned. 'If the Military torture you, you will only know what has passed. But be assured that this mission, if successful, will save the natives and make their lives worth living. Ishbel will meet you for the final part of the plan.'

'Ishbel? But what happens at the final part?' I asked. 'You said it was the most important. If we are captured...' My mouth was dusty at the thought.

'Make sure you don't get caught, but if you do I would hope at least one of you will be able to continue. Or escape. But I can tell you this. If your comms are destroyed or taken from you, you must make your way to Sector V in mid Esperaneo. Someone will help you there. If this information falls into the wrong hands it is meaningless to the Military.' He paused. 'And there is another arm to this mission. One of you will get through. We must not fail.'

'What is The Star of Hope?' To hear the name spoken sparked a tingle in my belly.

Pa arched his eyebrow at my persistence. 'Were you not listening, Sorlie? You will find out in time. Now prepare to go.'

We turned to leave. 'Sorlie.' Pa called me back to his side. 'Trust in your strength. You can do this.' He took my hand in his. 'Your mother would have been proud of you.'

Ishbel

Someone had betrayed them again. If she didn't find help soon for Huxton he would bleed to death. She peeled her sodden rucksack from her back and dug out the first aid kit. She tore off a strip and applied congealant but it wouldn't hold for ever, what she needed was a graft patch to stop the blood completely.

She stayed on the bank and studied the place where her men had been led away. She was sure the Military had not picked up the external intelligence about them from Vanora's frequency. Vanora had the best brains in the world working for her and her frequency was even more secure than the Military's own systems.

She checked on Huxton again. She really should leave him and rescue the other men before they talked, that's what her training told her to do. The prisoners would be questioned. She should have eliminated them when they were taken but that was Vanora's way, not hers. She might be Vanora's daughter but she was sick of all the killing and hardship doled out to natives. It was time to do things right. The landing party knew little of the mission; all they knew was that they were headed to Northern Esperaneo Major but didn't know why. If anything had happened to Ishbel they knew how to get out. They were to make their way to the emergency drop point and send a signal to Freedom. That was all. They didn't even know where Freedom was. They'd arrived there in a submarine and had travelled from Freedom to here in the dark. They weren't sailors so could only guess the direction of travel. Their brains were so mashed up from years of incarceration and DNA dilution, she doubted they could even describe the landscape and layout if they tried.

They had been kept in discreet smaller bases for training. No, they didn't know much. Vanora had seen to that. Ishbel guessed she should get to the drop point before the Military got there first, but she had a rendezvous to reach. Her men would have to tough it out. They knew what they were getting into and they had their pills if things became too bad. They might try to send an encryption to Freedom but she had to take a chance that they wouldn't succeed.

The Prince had promised them a peaceful and bloodless solution. Ishbel now doubted that was possible but it might be less brutal than Vanora's way.

'Come on, we need to find you some help.' Huxton was the colour of chalk. She gave him a vit-pill and a sip of puri water.

'Can you walk?'

He nodded. Despite the freezing wind howling off the water she stripped off her jacket and shirt then replaced the jacket against her bare skin. She used the shirt to try to stop the bleeding. As gently as she could she lifted him to his feet. She was taller than he and because he'd been one of the Black Rock prisoners, he was still pretty emaciated. She lifted him with ease. When she looked into his vulnerable face, despite his silver hair she could see he was quite young, twenty five years, maybe, same age as Dawdle. Only a few years older than she was. She could tell by the beads of sweat that studded his forehead that he was in pain, and he was quiet. Too quiet.

Ishbel debated on booting up her communicator to check their position. She knew the Military would be scanning the area for unusual waves so she pulled an ancient parchment from her pocket.

'What's that?' Huxton asked.

'A proper paper map.'

'I've never seen one before.'

It was shiny and waterproof but cracked in many places where the folds were. With the small light and compass in her comms she worked out their position. The coastline had changed through years of erosion but this beach was still recognisable as the cove Sven showed her from his chart. She pointed to where they were on the map.

'Maps like this are old-fashioned but they never run out of power and can't be detected by Military.'

She ran her finger along the wiggly lines close together and the widening contours. Hidden between some crags was a natural bowl with a stream running off a nearby mountain.

'I bet there's a community here,' she stabbed at a stream junction. 'It's a perfect spot. It's pretty close by, do you think you can manage it?'

He nodded but remained quiet.

She calculated it should take them half an hour to reach the spot. But Huxton was slow and it was after at least an hour's walking when Ishbel detected a change in the air. She stopped then and lifted her head to the elements. The clouds were clearing in the south and they were sheltered now from the coastal gusts. She sniffed the air. Forest. Not the usual lung forests, planted solely to protect the earth, heavily guarded and regulated. No, these forest smells were more like the forests of her home in the Northern Territories.

'Come on, we're nearly there.' She half-dragged Huxton forward, praying to her ancestors that she was right. They soon stumbled upon a small indigenous forest which had signs of coppicing, well cultivated and well-tended. She was right.

'There must be a community near,' she encouraged Huxton but he was staggering like a mash-head.

An old pine left growing too long looked ready to topple. She sat Huxton by it and scouted round. A massive root, its timber long gone, and left to rot was just the right size for her to manage. She dragged it to the tree.

'Crawl under here and wait.' He looked relieved and ready to sleep for a hundred years in the land of trolls.

Ishbel crept into the forest. She closed her eyes and let her instincts move her forward. It wasn't long before her instincts were screaming at her. Sixth sense told her to draw her stun and shrink her body into the smallest space she could find. On a tree to her right she detected movement. A boy, a sentry posted. He hadn't seen her. She could stun him but he would be sure to fall and hurt himself. She heard voices – baby whispers, unconcerned with danger. She heard an infant whimper and a soft lullaby that soon stopped the baby's cry. She smelled something strange and guessed it was food by the way her belly rumbled in response. She held her hand against it, afraid the noises would alert the camp.

As she crept nearer she wondered how she would announce her arrival without being killed first. Should she whistle? She felt in her pocket. The clicker was there, a crude u-shaped metal clip, no bigger than her thumb. When depressed the metal sent out a loud click that proved a very effective communication tool. This was her signalling device to alert the rebels. First used over a century and a half ago by the French Resistance, it still worked. But this community was not rebel, it was too early, too close to the coast. Would they recognise this ancient signal for what it was?

The decision was taken from her. A rope grabbed her ankle, hoisted her skyward. Air whipped from her lungs, she cried out. She lost the stun. Her stomach somersaulted as the rope bounced then settled, spinning her round in slow gentle circles. When she opened her eyes she met the stares of a small group of children, dirty, ragged and hungry for blood.

Sorlie

Harkin never told me why but it was decided that Con would use his boat to take Pa with Scud back to Black Rock. I suspected that smell still lingering about Pa was part of the reason. No one said and I wasn't going to ask. Betty had prepared painkillers but it wasn't enough to wipe the agony off his face. Pa said he had been at Steadie long enough. The frequent raids were a danger, his bar badge was showing constant amber levels of radiation. His body needed a break. Scud would travel with him. Not as his native but as his aide. Scud had cooled his jets since his go at me and was glad of the chance to get away after he'd failed to persuade Con to take him earlier. That was his excuse anyway and he was sticking to it. Together they would set up the command centre and the learning hub.

'Why Black Rock?' I asked Pa. 'How do you know you'll be safe?'

We were in the big top tent. Scud had his fat history book laid out in front of them. Apparently Scud had written it years ago, before the Purists purged the ethnos, before the Separation of the Classes into Privileged and native. Before Scud was locked up in Black Rock. I still couldn't quite believe Scud chose to go back. Every now and then he looked up and grinned at me. I wondered at his mind's stability. Should I be trusting Pa into his care?

Pa sat back, he rubbed his thighs, he smiled but there was a grimace of pain, like a thread tugging one corner of his mouth and he couldn't quite hide it.

'There is an infirmary there.'

'Yes, but no one there to heal you. Harkin can go with you. She's looked after you well here.'

'Harkin can't leave here, and I'm not going to ask her to.'

'Why don't you go to that souterrain community, where they make the cloth? They helped Scud.'

Pa shook his head. 'We can have a healer sent from Freedom. The Blue Pearl have collected excellent healers. And as to safety, remember I told you I'd been there before.' I nodded. 'It used to be a Military base, before housing political prisoners.'

I remembered. That night on the beach, the day after my birthday. Before everything changed. Was that only a year ago? Pa had pointed out Black Rock to me then.

'Below the cell where you slept there's another installation. A bunker installed by the generals of the Purist regime.'

'Won't they reclaim it when the Purists regain power?'

'The Purists aren't going to regain power. That's what we'll prevent. Anyway, those generals have been displaced. I doubt anyone in the current regime knows of its existence. And they didn't find it after the prison escape, when the Military sent a small team out to clean and clear it.'

'They didn't clean my cell.' I remember the obsolete computer Scud had tried to tutor me on still lay abandoned.

'Who could blame them,' Scud quipped. 'A pure tip it was.'

'Maybe they had a mind to turn it into a museum or reinstate it as a prison,' Pa said.

'It would make a good museum,' Scud agreed.

'Look, Sorlie, the point is everyone believes the Military is an all-powerful machine but the truth is it's a shambles in Esperaneo Lesser. It's been left to fend for itself by the State. Esperaneo Major can't be bothered with us. So I doubt if they'll use Black Rock again. And if they do come, we'll have plenty warning.'

'Why can't you go to Freedom?'

'That's still Vanora's kingdom. She hasn't quite forgiven me for taking her army. She'll come round but in the meantime I'll stay out of her way.'

'What about me, what about Reinya?'

'You have your orders.'

As if on cue Reinya walked into the tent. It was only a few weeks since Kooki's stillbirth; physically, she seemed to have recovered, but her gnawed fingernails and forced cheerfulness told another story. She was dressed in loose work clothes, her hair tied up, her cheeks pink. She took the drink a special handed her and came to join us.

'Uh've just been for mu usual run along the beach.'

Scud beamed at her. He and his granddaughter seemed to have a love-hate relationship and this week it was good. Just before Kooki was born they had been hurling insults at each other.

She looked at Pa. 'So when do we fight?'

'We don't fight if we can help it, Reinya. I told you yesterday, we wait for word from Jacques' Noiri operations. Dawdle should be back any day to escort you on your mission.'

'At last,' I said. 'We've been kicking our heels for aeons.'

'Yes. Well some things can't be rushed. You better make the most of your time here.'

Harkin had stayed elusive since Kooki's birth. I found her in the infirmary tent reading a big tattered book that lay open in front of her.

She hadn't heard me come in so I watched for a while. It was so peaceful in here. Her hair had grown since the last time I saw her. It sprang from her head like she'd been caught up in a mad experiment gone wrong. She had tried to tame it with colourful bands but clumps escaped like stuffing from a mattress waiting for mending.

She stopped reading and stared at the tent wall for a few nanos. She frowned, nodded then blinked.

'You can come in if you like,' she said to the wall before turning. 'Thanks for looking after Pa.'

She nodded again, 'It's what I do.'

'You once told me the healer was visiting the northern reservation but he never came back.'

'He was taken by a rogue community and decided to stay and help. I'm the only healer here.'

'Is that why you can't leave?'

'You know why I can't leave, why all the specials and second gen can't leave.'

'Because the radiation withdrawal will make you sick?'

She nodded.

'But you know that's not true, that's only in your head, Con said so. It isn't physiological. Anyway you do leave. You followed us to the tower.'

'That was only for a short while. No, I cannot leave.'

'I need you to go with Pa.'

She put her head down, chin to chest. 'I can't leave. Ever.'

I moved to take her hand but she shrank from me and my hand was left hanging mid-air. 'Please, I'm begging you. He needs you.'

An expression passed across her face . She put her hand up and touched my lips with one finger. A heat whooshed through me.

'I care for the specials. They need me. You and your Pa do not need me. There are plenty out there can do my job.'

'What about me?' Jupes, the shit whiney voice was back, where'd that come from? A burn in my thrapple blocked my next words.

Her chin lifted and she held my gaze. 'You will always be OK, you have kin who love you. I saw your address to the people. Everyone is talking about it – about you. No-one else has given them hope before.'

'I doubt that. What about The Prince? When I arrived here everyone was whispering about him.'

'But he was only a myth, you are real. Sorlie, you might not realise this but your Pa has passed this fight to you.'

She took my hand then and traced my lifeline. The touch of her finger sparked a sensation in me so strong I had to sit down to hide.

'Look,' she said. 'Look how long your lifeline is. You are strong, brave. You will do as your father wishes and be a great warrior. Believe in yourself, Sorlie.'

'I don't want to be a warrior.'

That seemed to be my new mantra, but even as the words left my mouth they fell lame. This is not what I told Ishbel when she had doubts and wanted to return to Freedom. Our fate had been chosen for us and I must fight this fight to the end.

'I'll be leaving with Reinya as soon as Dawdle arrives.'

I wanted a reaction but all she said was, 'We should say goodbye then.'

'What about you?'

'I will be fine, this is my home.' She smiled then. 'And remember you can always come back to Steadie.'

'I will always remember you.'

'And I you, Sorlie.'

I hugged her tight, I moved to kiss her lips but she turned from me.

'Memories are the one thing the State cannot take from you.'

'What?' I grabbed her shoulders, she looked confused but I didn't care. 'That was my mother's mantra, and her father's before. Where did you hear it?'

Her faced flushed. 'You're hurting me.'

'I asked you, where?'

'I picked it up somewhere.' She paused and bit her lip.

'Where?'

She stared at me, then nodded as if making a pact with herself. 'From you. When you were ill. I stayed with you. Many nights.'

'How many?'

'Many...' Her face darkened with embarrassment. 'You repeated it over and over. It is a good mantra.'

She stepped forward and kissed me full on the lips. She tasted of the mint she grew in her herb garden, cool and tingly. I placed my hand around her back and tried to hold her close.

'Go now,' she whispered. And with one hand placed on my chest she pushed me away. I could hear Con hailing me from outside.

'Sorlie, come, we must leave before it gets light and your Pa wants to see you before we go.'

Harkin turned and sat back to her reading.

As I left the tent, I touched my hand to the lips she had kissed; from where I had held the small of her back came the faint smell of lavender. The smell of my mother, the smell of Vanora.

Three women and two men were our transformation team. The women were Privileged and the men native but they worked as a unit, quite extraordinary. The senior woman, Eloise, was to rig Reinya and me with travel clothes. It would be a relief to shed the scratchy, strangling uniform. Since Reinya's rescue from the prison ship she'd worn a mishmash of castoffs. Her latest garb was the drab red uniform of a field native. I laughed when I saw what Eloise produced. I was given the uniform of a military cadet and Reinya the green of a domestic native. When Reinya saw the combo she threw me a spectacular look.

'I think our roles have been clearly laid out.' I said with a laugh.

'Uh don't know what's so funny. It makes sense.'

Next in line to help us transform was a native man. He was one of the generation who never quite met your eye. The goggle-gen some called them. He squinted at us and pressed a device into our chip area.

'Hey, what are you doing?'

'Reprogramming,' he said above my head. 'New identity, see.'

My communicator and Reinya's command band were also to be reprogrammed. My communicator would be easy to do because the good people of Steadie had already wiped it clean first time I arrived here. All it held now was Pa's plan. The native asked for Reinya's command band.

'Uh don't 'ave one.' She flushed but stayed quiet.

'She's been on a prison ship,' I explained.

The native stepped back at my words. 'No, she wasn't an addict,' I added.

'They're just for addicts,' he said holding his ground.

'Uh went wi mu mum.' Reinya was retreating into the corner of the room. The native looked sceptical. 'She died,' Reinya mumbled then she took a deep breath. 'Uh'm goin to blow that prison ship up one day.'

The google-gen started back.

'She's only kidding,' I joshed. 'Can we please get on with this?' I glowered at Reinya but she was back chewing her fingers.

He handed a command band to Reinya. 'These programmes are different,' the goggle-gen told us. 'You can override them. Reinya can use her command band as a comms and vice versa.'

I'd reprogrammed as a newly qualified teen from Urban A.

'I thought Urban A was a myth,' I said. The native shrugged. 'Maybe it's not,' I told Reinya trying to draw her out. 'It's reputed to have been set up in the eastern corner of Esperaneo Major for teaching gifted Privileged. Because of the nature of the Urban its output tended to be vague, cerebral and preoccupied. Apparently they had been studied and the Military found the students to be the most harmless citizens.' Sakes, I sounded like a tutor.

'They wouldn't make you one if it's u myth,' she said.

'You're to be my native, Reinya. You'll need to look after me.' With her rust hair and green eyes she couldn't look more native if she tried.

When we were ready to go and I inspected our transformation a bubbling started in my stomach. Sure, I'd been through a lot in the past year but somehow, no matter how difficult the task had been there had always been an adult there, now we were just two kids out on our own. Dawdle would only escort us as far as the boundary to Beckham City.

We ran through the pelters of rain to reach the pier, expecting to find a newly refurbished Peedle waiting for us. Instead we were greeted by Dawdle sitting in a rusty old van. My distrust of him returned the minute he grinned but I suppose he was the best of a bad bunch.

'Where's the sub?' I asked.

'We go overland, so the quicker yer in the quicker we're away.'

Once we were settled in our seats he turned and grinned again. 'So, ma young pretenders, we'll head south through the wetlands, then east and all goan well we'll be in Beckham City by night fall. Ah'll give ye a lift tae the native shanty reservation that serves BC. Then yer on yer own.'

He turned to Reinya. 'So how are you wee hen? Still moping about?' he said with a wink. I could have kicked him. He must have heard about Kooki.

'Shut it you. Uh nevur mope.'

'Jump in the back if ye like, it's safer and mair comfortable.'

'We're fine here,' I said.

Reinya snuggled into her seat next to me, pulled her jacket tight round and stuck her thumb in her mouth.

'You OK?' I asked.

'Yeah!' came the bristly reply. After a couple of minutes she said. 'If somethin 'appens to me, tell Scud uh love 'im.'

A chill dragged my spine. 'Nothing's going to happen to you.'

She narrowed her eyes. 'You don't know nuthin.'

'Nothing's going to happen to you, Reinya.' Trying to convince myself as much as her. She stuck her thumb back in her mouth and for the first time I had a minute to wonder whether Pa had been wrong to ask her to come along. She was a child, sucking her thumb for snaf's sake. And yet I knew how she felt. I'd never been to Beckham City before. I'd been cosseted in a Military base. When I was small sometimes Ishbel would take me to our local market. I remember it being busy with natives who always teased me. The only Privileged I'd encountered had been Military.

'Act naive,' Pa said at our briefing with no clue there would be no acting required. I'd memorised our first objective. Tucked into the thick folds of Reinya's hair was a clip of glass baubles. Each ball contained the new 'toy' Kenneth had been working on. Pa told us it was top secret. It came direct from the Blue Pearl. We were not to mention it to Vanora, if we happened to cross her path.

'Why would we?' I asked.

'Just don't mention it to anyone,' he said.

Pa assured us it would revolutionise the way we fight from now on but he refused to tell us what it did because if we were caught we might give the game away. If we were searched it was unlikely they'd find such a small thing in that mass of red hair. This was phase one of our mission.

Rain plashed on the roof of the cab. The roads were rough and rocked us from side to side. Gales had been fierce so far in the fourth quarter and there'd been a particularly bad spell of rain, worse than usual, and all the flood defences had been breached. Every now and again Dawdle would stop the van. It lifted on hydraulics and then the movement would shift from bump to float, thanks to some sort of amphibious device fitted to the van. Once across a stretch of water he switched back to road mode.

After the first exchanges in the cab Dawdle stayed quiet. Every now and then I'd look at him and wonder what made him tick. It couldn't all be about profit. But as he put his hand out to shift gear I noticed his communicator was studded with one precious stone. Subtle, but there on show for anyone with the energy to look. That stone probably had enough worth to feed a reservation for a week.

Ishbel

She must have lost consciousness. She lay on her back on the forest floor. Her big toes and hands felt like blocks of wood. She'd lost all feeling. Her head pounded and something soft and cold freckled her face, transporting her back to her home in the Northern Territories. Snow.

Her feet were still bound by the rope but her hands were free so she propped herself up to sitting. Those grubby children were still there, hunkered in an orderly circle, staring at her. There weren't as many as she'd first thought – six or seven maybe. The cooking smells lingered in the air. It was getting dark again. It was nearly always dark here. She shivered.

Through the guddle of children she spied a settlement nestled in a clearing of trees. The homes were fabricated from wood and shingles like the houses on Freedom. But these houses were covered in camouflage nets. Hidden and therefore not an official reservation. Another hidden community. She hadn't realised until recently how shielded she'd been at the Base Camp Dalriada. Ishbel had no idea how many secret communities were hidden throughout the land mass of Esperaneo but she reckoned there were quite a few. She must remember to ask Dawdle next time she saw him. He'd know. The Noiri knew everything.

Ishbel tapped behind her ear to indicate the universal chipping spot and held up two fingers to form a cross. She wanted them to know she wasn't a threat, she wasn't the State. She pointed to them.

'No chip?' she said in Esperanto, hoping they had been trained in Esperaneo's designated language. One of the kids, a boy aged about fourteen stood up from the crouching crowd.

'We have no chips.' His language was good with only a slight northern clip.

'Good,' she said hoping they would understand her position. 'What is this place?' Ishbel asked. 'Where are your elders?'

The boy moved towards Ishbel. She smiled, a universal language that the State had never managed to eradicate, despite the population's deprivation and misery. At first she thought he was going to help her to stand but as she held out her hand he clamped hand cuffs on her. He grabbed the middle chain then hauled her to her feet with surprising ease.

'No, I'm no threat,' she said, biting her lip against the pain.

He nodded to one of the younger boys to release the rope around her legs. When he tugged on the chain again the bands bit into her wrists.

'There's no need. I'm no threat.'

He pulled again and Ishbel felt her anger rise.

'I can walk, show me where,' she said trying to keep the indignation out of her voice, but the boy kept hold of the chain.

Together they walked towards the clearing where a lone woman stood and watched their approach. Behind her two smaller children sat on mats working with vegetables. The woman reached out her hand to Ishbel in welcome but Ishbel merely held up bindings.

'What is this, Saul?' the woman said to the boy. 'Release her.'

'She might escape, she's my catch.'

'Release her I say.'

'No.'

Ishbel was astounded that this boy answered back to an elder in this way.

'Where are the men?' Ishbel asked. 'The other adults?'

'Gone,' the woman said.

'Gone where?'

She looked at Ishbel as if she were mad.

'To war of course. With The Prince.'

Ishbel felt her face flush. She didn't want them to know she knew The Prince and was his commander. Something was not right here.

'There's a man in the woods back there who's injured and needs help.'

The woman signalled to the boy to go and fetch him. And for once the boy did as he was bid.

'She'll need to come and help,' he said, pointing to Ishbel.

Sorlie

Beckham City was closer than I expected. The pink glow I'd spotted in the sky on our approach to the reservation was the light pollution from the wasteful illuminations of the administrative capital of Lesser Esperaneo. The reservation was grim and probably the reason Dawdle chose to take us round the outer fringes of the main camp. From what I could see, no gate or fence barred the way. There were no ordered streets of freight containers as we had in Steadie, only raggedy tents and ripple tin roofs. Some natives seemed to be living under scraps of tarps. Small grubby children with plastic bags tied onto their feet huddled in groups and stared at us with wide hungry eyes as we passed them by. There was no sign of camp fires and from what I could see no cooking area.

'How do they survive here?' I asked Dawdle, but he ignored me and continued to stare straight ahead, ignoring the suffering. The smell of sewage and rotten vegetables hung in the air like a putrid plague. This was nothing like the well-ordered neat reservation the Military Academy had taken us to for a cultural visit, where natives walked free and clean and smiled and waved as we passed through. But of course I already knew this to be a fabrication by the State. This was just further confirmation of the fake facts debunked during my time in the library at Black Rock.

We drew to a stop at the outer edge camp where a wasteland stretched between the reservation and Beckham City, now visible on the horizon. Dawdle stopped the van, jumped out and signalled for us to follow. He pulled backpacks from the cargo hold and threw them to the ground. I moved to pick up the largest sack and he pushed me away.

'That's fur Reinya, huv ye forgotten how tae act Privileged?'

He helped the biggest pack onto Reinya's back then said, 'Right, afore ye go, run roond the camp.'

'What? Why? We have a mission,' I couldn't believe he was serious but his face never cracked a cent .

'Yer too clean and shiny is why. Now git. Ah'll wait fur ye here.' He climbed into his van, rested his head back and closed his eyes.

It wasn't raining when we started but when we were halfway round it came on pelters. By the time we got back to the van we were both soaked and frozen.

Dawdle climbed down when we arrived. 'Ye'll do.' He took us to the main track that led to Beckham City. Many natives trudged towards us, returning from their work in the city, weary and defeated.

'OK,' Dawdle said. 'Got yer stories? Ye go through the scanner. The guards'll check yer chips and irises. The changes tae yer chips should get you through. Let's just hope they dinnae put a Geiger on ye, eh?'

'Shut up Dawds,' Reinya said. 'We were in the safe part o Steadie.'

'Aye, if there is such a place.' He shuffled his feet and if I didn't know him better I'd swear he was reluctant to let us go. 'Good luck,' he said and climbed back into the van.

The rain had stopped but the track was muddy. Reinya slithered about with the heavier pack and I couldn't do a thing about it. She soon found her feet and trailed behind me at the designated metre distance expected between natives and Privileged.

Beckham City was surrounded by twenty metre high walls and they loomed large as we approached.

'Have you ever been here before?' I asked Reinya.

'Nope.'

'Me neither.'

'Don't lose me.'

I didn't want to lose her either but kept that piece of shit-scared intel to myself.

'There are four ports,' Pa's instructions told us. 'Go to the western port but be sure to leave by the eastern port.'

A couple of guys stood at the western port, watching us approach. As we drew closer I recognised their bouncer-build. Necks thicker than heads, the types with pea brains and cauliflower ears. Same guard spec we had at Camp Dalriada. There must be a training camp somewhere in darkest Esperaneo Major, probably near Bieberville, that churns them out. For hire, wide-neck brawn – brain not included.

One neck-guy held a designer gun with another strung through his belt and hanging by his side like a gun slinger. Dolt. I walked ahead of Reinya.

We passed our bands over the first security and walked through a scanner corridor. My heart thumped hard enough to set off the earthquake alarm. A guard at the other end clicked his fingers at us.

'Papers.'

Papers! How old was he? They haven't called ID 'papers' for centuries.

We ran our bands over another scanner. Reinya's hand was shaking.

'Name.'

'Sorlie.'

'Not you, her.'

Reinya stiffened and said nothing. He clicked his fingers in her face.

'Wakey wakey.'

'It's on her band.' I said. 'Leave her alone, she's my property.'

'Bit young for having such a fiery bint, no?'

I pulled myself up as tall as I could muster and still only met his chin. 'My age is none of your concern. We're here to do a job, open the gate and let us through.'

He narrowed his eyes at me. I peeled my tongue from where it was wedged to the top of my mouth and roared, 'Now!'

I'd been among natives for so long I had forgotten how strong Privileged works. My ID stated I was a junior professor, and some of these dolts didn't even understand what that was but they knew it was important.

'Nice one Major,' Reinya whispered as they let us through to the next scanner without another word.

Our tatty bags scanned through no bother because we carried only spare rags, grainer bars and credit bits. The virus was still secure in Reinya's thick locks.

Once through they left us hanging between the outer and inner walls that towered above us. Smooth concrete panels, welded together with crimped seams and bolts, fierce barbed wire strung along the top, just in case anyone managed to scale their twenty metre height. At last a small door opened in the inner concrete expanse and we were ushered into the city proper.

I don't know what I expected. Some sort of shining palace. Beckham City had been the Capital of Lesser Esperaneo for decades. It was where the Ambassador stayed, where the High Heid Yins of society lived. But by the look of the stalls that hung around the city gates, the beggars and the lack of travellers, it looked like business in Beckham City was slow, almost dead already. Only the last few Privileged trying to hang onto their idea of the old rule of this land – the romantic notion that it could be great again, free from the might of Esperaneo Major. A few regional flags hung around expectantly waiting for the great nation to rise again. Reinya's mouth hung open as she gazed in wonder at this once great city.

Ordinary Privileged citizens wandered the streets without weapons, deluded into the belief they were behind a mighty wall and therefore safe.

'Uh'd expected neon signs, Transports,' Reinya whispered. 'Where are the super-rich?'

Buildings crumbled with peeled paint and broken masonry. Shattered windows outnumbered those in good repair. Gutters hung loose. The place was falling down despite the efforts of natives we witnessed carrying out maintenance work, cleaning, hammering, fixing what was past repair. Market stall holders called to each other and joked to hide the fact they had nothing to sell and no customers to serve. People laughed but there was fear in their eyes. Natives stopped their work and watched us pass with ambivalent stares before returning to their mundane tasks. The green-clad domestic natives gawped at Reinya's uniform, no doubt puzzled at why she was with a traveller.

A group of children, dressed in Academy greys marched towards us with their tutor in the lead. It was unusual for children to have direct contact with each other due to the high risk of infection so this group must be heading for their workplace selection. The time when they are pitted against each other to see who will come out on top for the best professional training and who would be suited for Military service, who for the service industry. I remembered how pleased I was when I was deemed unsuitable for combat. How ironic that my grandmother and Pa now called me their warrior. We were only a few years older than these passing students but still they did not acknowledge our existence. To them we had passed onto the realm of old teen and were not worth bothering about.

'D'you know where we're goin?' Reinya's whisper reached me from where she walked one metre behind me.

'Don't speak without being spoken to, native,' I hissed. I could feel her bristle from behind but still heard her 'sorry.'

At a junction I turned to wait for Reinya. She was dragging far behind under the weight of the pack, her feet scuffing the paving. Her fierceness hidden in her new identity. Since our early days together in Steadie we had both changed. In the first months I'd been concerned with Pa and nothing else. Reinya grew weary as her birth date approached and found it hard to walk the length of herself. I'd seen her a few times wandering the duckboards, talking to the children and playing with the wolf cub. Sometimes she walked and ran along the beach but not too often. I think she was always scared of Steadie and its radioactive reputation. She was so different from Harkin. Harkin helped her when she needed help but kept her distance as she did with me too. It was as if Harkin didn't want to know what was planned for us which was just as well. Her job was to care for Pa and with that task she'd become as silent as the other specials who remained calm as long as they were not threatened.

As soon as Kooki was born, Reinya seemed injected with new life, despite the baby's death. It was as if she wanted to forget the whole thing. She got her strength back, walked then ran around the camp, organised an exercise class for some of the more able specials. They grinned at her as she chivvied them along to do their squats and jumping jacks. She would make a good tutor.

Dawdle had a strange effect on Reinya. She became a different person whenever he turned up. Ishbel had explained to me that because of Reinya's treatment in the prison ship, she hated all men but Dawdle seemed to hold the exemption card. Maybe because he always brought some fresh food for her to eat. Maybe because he called her 'wee hen'. Maybe it was just because he made her smile. But she smiled at me now as she caught me up. Maybe Pa was right to send her on this mission after all.

Somehow my new identity infused me with added strength. Our comms led us across a major square. We didn't know where we were going but they did. When I reached an intersection my wrist pinged. The comm's compass told me to go right. We left the main thoroughfare to tread along smooth cobbled lanes, towered by rickety old buildings, as if straight out of some ancient text. My wrist buzzed again and we turned left. This continued until we arrived at a dead end. A wall at the end of the alley blocked our way. The air stank of pee and plague. I wanted to turn and run. I scanned the walls with my communicator.

'Look, no surveillance in here.'

'Wow, this place must be u gold mine for contra activity,' Reinya said after she had made her own check. 'What does yur comms say?'

'We make the drop here.'

I watched as she untangled the small baubles from her piled up hair.

'Break the top, it says. And shake the contents out into – wait a minute.' I searched the ground. I dragged a plastic crate from the wall. Underneath was a grill, also plastic, that covered the hole of a sewer gundy. 'There,' I pointed to the grill. 'Pour it down and throw the baubles in after it.'

'But there's nothin there, it's like an invisible formula.' I saw her point. The baubles seemed to be empty.

'What is it for? Is it goin to poison the water?' she asked.

'I doubt the water can be any more poisoned. No, this is the sewer. I can't hear any water, can you?' She shook her head.

'Then it's a dry sewer,' I said.

'So what is it then?'

'I don't know, a virus of some sort. Remember, Top Secret. We've been told not to question. I suppose we'll find out one day. Pa wouldn't have sent us here if it wasn't important.'

Reinya flung a bauble down the hole. We heard the satisfying sound of tinkling glass then each took it in turns to smash the others in the sewer. It was almost fun. When they were all used up Reinya hugged her arms round her shoulders.

'Let's get out o 'ere, it feels odd and wrong that there's no surveillance.'

We ran back to the main thoroughfare. Reinya resumed her position walking behind me.

'Where you goin?' I heard her say. 'Uh thought we were to 'ead for the east port?'

'My comms has gone blank.' I tapped it. There was nothing showing, it was blocked. Then it sparked again and told us to turn around.

When I turned she said, 'It's not right.' I continued walking. 'No, this is wrong,' she persisted.

'Don't disobey me.' I shouted to her, but with my eyes I tried to communicate my puzzle because we were back in the surveillance zone.

'What do we do?' I whispered, but before she had a chance to answer she flung herself at me and threw me to the ground. A missile flew past, slammed into a wall and exploded, showering us with plaster and plastic.

'What?' I raised my head just in time to see a figure run through the alley ahead of us and disappear. I pushed Reinya off and made to run after him but Reinya grabbed hold of me.

'No, we must go. The Military'll be 'ere any second to see what the commotion is. We 'ave to get out of 'ere.'

'Where?'

'Follow me.' And she led us back to the alley with the gundy.

'I'm not going down there. We don't know what we put down.'

'You're the one with total faith in yur Pa. We've no choice.'

'That was a virus. How do you know it won't kill us?'

'We'll be dead anyway if we stay 'ere.' She tugged at the lid. 'Come on Mr Warrior, 'elp me get this off.'

We searched through our bags for anything useful, mostly grainer bars, and stuffed them in our pockets before chucking the rucksacks into the corner of the alley. We stepped onto the ladder that led down the hole and pulled the cover back over the gundy. The smell made my head swim. It was worse than the open walkways in Steadie that ran with stale mud when the rains were too strong to drain. Worse than Betty's cabbage soup even.

It grew from grey to pitch dark the further into the sewer we went. I switched on my comms light and prayed it had enough charge to last.

'Your Pa wouldn't 'ave given us somethin that would kill us. We 'ave to believe it and just get on with it.'

I held my breath and pulled my t-shirt up over my nose just the same.

'What happened back there?' I asked her.

'Uh saw this guy come out from the shadows when you turned round. 'e carried a grenade gun. It was pointed right at you.'

A chill memory shivered through me. 'What did he look like?'

''e wasn't like Military. It might even 'ave been a woman.'

'How do you mean?'

'There was no uniform just a…uh don't know, it was a sort of armour. And a mask. Grey with scales. Weird.'

It was him. The one from the raid. The one who called me out by name. Who was he and if he knew we were here, how could we get out of Beckham City alive?

We crawled through that stinking hole for an age, using the comms torch to light the way. The smell grew unbearable and when we hit a T junction I knew the reason why. Behind us dry sewer, and flowing left to right ahead of us was a river of black putrid shite.

'We don't have a choice, we need to follow this river,' I said. 'At least there's a walkway.'

'Aye, a nano wide,' Reinya moaned, then shook herself. 'Right then, we follow the water.'

'Damn right, let's go.' I said, readjusting my t-shirt over my nose.

'Uh've another idea,' Reinya said, tugging at the shirt tucked into her trousers. She tore a strip off and tied it round her nose and mouth. 'You do it.'

But my shirt wasn't as long as hers and when I ripped it I was left with a bare midriff.

'Very sexy,' she said. I fastened my jacket tight.

We hugged the wall and sidestepped along the walkway that was indeed a nano wide.

'Jupes, this place is rank,' I said.

'Uh want this to end soon.'

'And not with us falling in.'

'At least we'll get to the outlet quicker if we fall in.' She was right, the river was flowing faster than our shuffling.

Because my hands were on the wall, the comms' light was intermittent, but at least that meant we didn't have to look at the putrid river at our toes.

'So who is 'e then?' Reinya asked after we had been teetering for too long.

'I've no idea, but he knows me.' I told her about the incident before the last Steadie raid.

'An enemy then – do you 'ave many enemies?'

'What, you mean apart from the whole Privileged tribe?'

'You know what uh mean.'

'I don't think I have an enemy, apart from Merj.'

'The guy with the eye?' She'd seen him at the souterrain where they fixed up Scud and also when he visited Pa at Steadie. He had only stayed around for a couple of days then disappeared again. But Merj was in Pa's pay so it couldn't be him.

'It might have been one of the men from the submarine.' I told her about the escape from Black Rock when I'd been holed up in a submarine with a bunch of restless natives. They'd been threatening towards Ridgeway the guard, so, being the only Privileged present, I'd taken charge and tried to get the men in order. It had all gone horribly wrong and I'd ended up being threatened by a thug with a smiley scar. The situation, and I, had been saved by the intervention of Vanora's commander, Arkle.

'You are such a dolt, Sorlie,' Reinya laughed. 'So this smiler guy might be your enemy.'

I shook my head. 'No, not him. Vanora blew his brains out for being cheeky to her.'

'Charmin.'

We fell silent for a while.

"ow did 'e know you were 'ere?' Reinya asked. 'Your enemy?'

'I don't know. Sometimes I think I have a secret tracker on me.'

'What's that smell? It's changed.' Reinya moved a little faster, bumping into me.

'The sea. I think it's the sea.' We rounded a corner and a pinhole of daylight showed ahead.

As we crept closer, the smell of the sea began to dilute the stench. At least we were heading for the coast, although I couldn't believe sewage went straight into the sea. That couldn't be right.

We stopped just before the opening.

'You wait here, I'll check it's OK.'

'Get real Sorlie, we go thegether.'

I stuck my head out the opening at the end of the walkway and grabbed a gulp of wind blowing off the sea.

'We're about five metres from the water but I don't know how shallow it is down there. We could break our necks.' I looked out at the sheer cliff face and almost swooned at the exposure. 'We don't have much choice, we can't climb down.' The channel carrying the sludge protruded from the cliff for another couple of metres. 'If we use that to get a run at it we'll have a better chance at reaching deep water.'

'Yur jokin, right?'

But I wasn't sitting around listening, I closed my eyes, my mouth, my nose and jumped in. It wasn't too deep, just above my ankles but the stench made my eyes water and the feel of the lumps bumping into my legs made me boak. When I tried to run, the thick sludge splashed up, threatening to hit me in the mouth so I was forced to walk. I felt the channel wobble as it left the security of the cliff face. I peered over the edge and froze, my fear of heights overpowering my fear of failure. Then I felt a boot on my back and I was kicked forward into the air. My ears whistled, I crashed on the sea's surface. Sludge engulfed me, I sank, my eyes still tight shut, no way of knowing what way was up. I touched something solid with my feet. I kicked and started to rise, then bobbed out on the surface just as a splash happened beside me.

Reinya surfaced a metre or so away.

'You kicked me!' I spat with words and sludge.

'You were faffin, Sorlie,' she said and struck out south, swimming strong and fast. I followed although I had no idea if it was the right direction. But at least it took us away from the stench. We swam well out from the shore until we were clear of the stinking debris then headed inland toward a small bay. Our clothes and body washed in the relatively clean water as we swam.

'How do we know it's not mined?' Warnings from my Academy days clanged my memory cells.

'D'you know 'ow long the coastline is these day wi aw the erosion? They gave up minin beaches decades ago.'

'How do you know all this stuff, Reinya?'

'Get real Sorlie.' I wished she would stop saying that but held my tongue.

We found a ring of rocks lower than the land but higher than the tideline and pulled ourselves free of the water.

'Uh can still smell it,' she said. 'It's imprinted in mu nose.'

'I know what you mean.' I tapped my comms. 'Is your comms working?'

'Yep, why?'

'Mine's still blocked, what does yours say? We were supposed to leave Beckham City by the east port.

'At least we're southeast,' she said.

'Only by chance.'

'No matter, chance works for me.'

'What do we do now?'

'It says we've to rendezvous at these coordinates.' She showed me the dial.

'How long?'

She tapped it again. 'Two 'ours walkin.'

'Are you tired?' I could see her panda eyes darkening, but they narrowed at me.

'Why d'you ask? Are you?'

'No,' even though I was. I wasn't going to let on.

'Let's go then.'

Ishbel

Huxton was where she'd left him but in a state of shock. His skin look like porridge and when Ishbel touched his neck to check for a pulse, he felt ice cold and his pulse was little more than a flutter.

As the boy picked him up, Ishbel tried to help but he brushed her aside.

'I can do it.'

'Then why ask me to come?'

'You're my catch,' was all he said.

To her astonishment the little fellow heaved Huxton onto his shoulder without so much as a grunt. Ishbel retrieved her bag and followed. They moved silently through the woods to the camp. Twilight glimmered on the snow and the sky lit up with a kaleidoscopic green light, streaking through the clouds like the tresses of some mythological goddess. The hair stood up on the back of Ishbel's neck. Such celestial occurrences were common in her homeland in the Northern Territory but only seen on clear nights when the rain clouds occasionally disappeared. It was always a thrill to stand with her mother and watch the sky. She wondered when Vanora lost that love of nature and became obsessed with war. The boy seemed oblivious to the spectacle and disappeared into the woods. She knew she should follow but couldn't help but watch the sky. Of course, this far north in Esperaneo would have the same phenomenon, she should have realised that.

Fires had been lit around the camp perimeter. Wooded huts of many shapes and sizes were erected under the tree canopy with a larger plastic panel block in the centre. She now suspected these woods were of designated status, the lungs of Esperaneo, protected for the sake of the planet and yet this community was burning them without conscience. It was to a plastic hut that the boy carried Huxton. Ishbel followed.

Inside, five beds fanned out in a circle and the woman waited by an operating table to receive the injured. Once Huxton was laid out on a slab he looked like a corpse. The boy took Ishbel's arm and tugged her away. She shook him off.

'You leave him here,' the woman said.

'No, I'll stay.'

The earlier benevolence in the woman's face slipped.

'No miss, you leave him here.'

The boy took her arm again, this time exerting some pressure. She remembered the ease with which he had lifted Huxton. She knew she was a warrior but guessed this boys' phenomenal strength was a match for her so she moved to the door.

'You'll let me know how he is?' The woman nodded, already cutting the trouser leg around his wound.

Outside the fires sputtered and raged with the occasional gust of wind fanning golden flames, igniting sparks and obscuring the spectacle in the sky.

'Why so many fires?'

'Wild beasts,' the boy told her. 'They are few but deadly. We have hunted most but there is one who steals our food. We cannot catch it.' He splayed out his arms to shoulder width. 'Its feet are this big.'

'Sounds like a legend.'

'No, it is real. I have seen the footprints myself.'

She let it drop, he was just a boy after all. Only a few years younger than Sorlie.

The camp seemed deserted but Ishbel could sense people behind doors, waiting perhaps for the mysterious beast.

'Where is everyone?'

'In bed.'

'How many in this camp?'

He looked around each hut in turn, as if counting. 'Thirty maybe.'

There were at least fifty dwellings. 'So many houses for so few people.'

The boy shrugged. 'People die, leave, are carried away by the beast.'

'Men go to war,' she added. He shrugged.

He showed her into a cabin of two rooms and four bunks. It was covered in dust and cobwebs as if it hadn't been used for a while.

'I'll bring you food later.'

Ishbel sat on one of the bunks and suddenly felt weary. How long had it been since they'd been wrecked? How could it have been just this morning? For the first time since then she wondered about the other men taken prisoner. Would they have given any intel over to the Military? She doubted it. She'd made sure they knew very little of her plan. She should leave now and try to find them. She had a mission to complete and if she didn't complete her part when Sorlie reached the goal then all would unravel. Huxton wouldn't be going anywhere soon and although this tribe were strange they were trying to help him.

She tried the door. It was locked as she expected it to be. She looked out the window. All was quiet. No, there was a movement over by the infirmary. It was the boy. He left the main door carrying a thick long parcel the length of a rifle. She watched him move to the outer rim of the camp. The fires still burned bright enough to show his shadow moving towards a stone building. It was quite different from the other shacks but she hadn't noticed it before. He propped the parcel against the wall and opened the door. He disappeared inside with the parcel then returned carrying something small in his hand. He placed this in a bucket by the door and pulled the door closed. He stood still for a minute. A small woman came out of the shadows carrying a tray. She gave him the tray in exchange for the bucket, then turned and disappeared into the dark. No words seemed to have been spoken. The boy watched her go. When Ishbel saw him turn in her direction she juked back into the room and crouched on a lower bunk. Her heart was thumping but she had no idea why.

The boy came in and placed the tray on the table. On it was a mug of brew and a bowl of steaming broth. The delicious aroma made Ishbel's belly rumble.

'Why am I locked in?'

'For your own protection.'

'From whom? The beast?'

A sly smile passed his face. 'From everyone.'

'So I'm not safe here.'

'You will not be harmed.'

'Then why lock me in?'

He pushed the tray towards her. 'Eat.'

'I need to speak to your elders. I need to move on and leave my friend in your care.'

Again that smile. 'That should not be a problem. You can see them in the morning. Now eat.'

He left her to her food. The bowl contained a broth of root stew but she knew by the film on top of the cooling liquid that this also contained the banned substance, meat. It seemed that sometimes the community hunted successfully because she doubted if the Noiri reached so far north with its famous contraband meat.

The food was minimal as she expected in such a remote community but delicious and enough to fill her belly. And yet when she sat to drink her brew she felt a clawing at her gullet

74

and a nausea bubbled in her. The brew was cold. The type that frothed with fermentation. It was strong and helped wash the nausea away. She tried the door again – locked. Something was wrong with this place. She would sleep with one eye to the door and in the morning she would leave Huxton behind and forget about this strange community.

Sorlie

When we arrived at the rendezvous point we found Dawdle sitting cross-legged on the nose of his mini sub, Peedle. His face was tripping him.

'What's wrong with you, not pleased to see us?'

He screwed up his nose. 'You stink.'

On the way the rain had stopped and we managed to dry off some, but the resulting damp, shite-splattered clothes were less than palatable.

'Nice to see you too.'

'Did ye make the drop?'

'Course,' said Reinya. 'Then we got chased into u sewer by u nuttur.'

We waited for his reaction but got nowhere.

'What is wrong with you?' I persisted.

'Look brat, ah prefer tae travel alone. Tae work alone. Now ah'm lumbered wi a couple o kids. There's nuthin wrong wi me. Ah should be askin what's wrong wi you.' This was directed at Reinya. She had been slow and struggling for the past hour but I hadn't really taken any notice. Now I could see by the way she held her arms across her chest she was in real discomfort.

'Uh'm sore is all.' She took her hands away from her front and looked at them. 'Uh'm leakin milk.'

'Aye? Ah could sell that fur ye.' Dawdle was only joking but I still punched him on the arm. He passed a hand over his face but his silence proved he knew his gaffe.

'Mu bairnie's dead.'

'Aye, sorry, oot ma mooth before ah thought.' He reached into the cab and threw her a towel.

'We dried off on the walk,' I said.

'It's no fur that. Tie it roond ye. It'll help the pain and the leakin.'

Reinya gawped at him. "ow do you know that'll work?'

'It will. But you suit yersel. If ye dinnae like ma advice ye should huv stayed back at Steadie and got that Harkin tae look efter ye.'

Reinya squared to him. 'Uh 'ave to fight.'

'Aye, well it'll be a while afore we see ony action. Yir no here tae fight. There's mair ways tae skin a cat ye ken.'

'What?' both Reinya and I said in unison.

'Look, just dae as ah say coz ah'm yer nursemaid.'

'We don't need any nursemaid,' I said, but Dawdle just sighed.

'Mebbes ye dae, mebbes ye don't, aw ah ken is ah've been ordered tae take ye tae Esperaneo Major.' He stood up. 'Hop aboard. It'll no take long.'

As soon as we were aboard and changed into dry, sweet-smelling clothes, Reinya crawled into the corner. Both Dawdle and I turned our backs on her thinking she would strip and tie the towel round her leaking breasts. Dawdle started the engine. It coughed and wheezed but after a final belch it kicked and he manoeuvred us out into the bay.

'We can stay on the surface fur a bit,' he said. 'We'll hug the coast south then cross tae mainland Esperaneo Major at the shortest stretch.'

'No we won't, we 'ead for sector W.'

Both Dawdle and I whipped round at Reinya's rough voice. She stood facing us holding something up in front of her face. And then I saw what it was.

'Fuck, it's a grenade.'

'Come on wee hen, put that down,' Dawdle sounded calm but I could smell the fear coming off him.

'Uh'm no your 'wee hen' and uh'm no puttin this grenade down.' And there she was, that fierce animal I first saw on the quayside in Ulapul, waiting to smuggle herself aboard Dead Man's Ferry with her addict mother. I had thought she was a boy then, not this young girl.

'Take us to Sector W. It's not far out o our way.'

'It's in the west.'

'Aye, but it's flooded from 'ere to there so we can go.'

'Got it aw worked out, huvn't ye?' Dawdle looked almost proud. 'Why dae ye want tae go there?' he asked, but I knew and so did he. Reinya's mother died weeks after landing on the prison ship at Sector W and Reinya had been forced to suffer unspeakable horrors. Ever since she'd been rescued she'd threatened to go back and blow the ship up.

'You know why.'

'Look hen, there's addicts on that ship. They're put there as a lesson tae society. They dinnae last long, you know that. Why blow them up?'

'Uh wasn't an addict. Uh was innocent.'

'Aye, but you chose tae go.'

'There was no choice. There's many innocent children on that ship who won't be rescued like me. Uh'm going to put thum out their mysery.' She still held the grenade at arm's length but I could see her hand was shaking. A trail of snot started to roll from one nostril down to her lip. She dashed it away with the heel of her free hand. I edged away from Dawdle.

'Aye, ah realise that, but why kill them? They dinnae deserve tae die,' Dawdle was trying to distract her, I could tell. I pressed my back against the hull. 'It's murder, Reinya,' he said.

'Don't move anuther inch, Sorlie.' She held the grenade higher, her other hand now on the pin.

I held my hands up. 'OK, OK. But you're not really going to blow us up?'

'Why not? What do uh 'ave to live for? As Dawdle reminded me, uh don't even 'ave a baby.'

'Ah said sorry.'

'Just get goin, Dawdle, let's get this done.'

Dawdle sighed and changed course. He looked over his shoulder at Reinya and I could tell he was thinking of a way out of this. It wasn't like him just to give in.

'And don't try any of that rockin. Or the 'Oh, we're under attack,' shite you pulled off before. Uh can read your coordinates and one slip out o course – boom!'

I stared at her. Her tears had been replaced by a sort of madness.

'We'll be there in under two hours. But ah might need tae let Peedle cool,' Dawdle said.

'No, the dials show un even temp. Keep goin.'

All three of us remained silent, counting those minutes. Silent that was, apart from Reinya's heavy breathing. Every time I so much as twitched she held her hand up, steady now, and glared at me.

'Dinnae antagonise her, Sorlie. She means what she says.' I could see the throb in Dawdle's temple.

'Right, we're here. We cannae get any closer or the guards'll open fire. OK, so Reinya, ah'm gonnae cut the engines, so dinnae freak, it's no a trick.' Dawdle turned round and faced her. 'But tell me. How dae ye intend tae blow it up?'

She reached behind her, while still threatening us with the grenade pin held to her teeth. From her back she pull out a bandolier of grenades.

'You hid them here, back after we left the souterrain community. Ah wondered where they'd disappeared tae.'

'Never know when you'll need somethin like this.' She glanced out the front screen.

'We're too far, Reinya. They'll pick us off afore we get close enough.'

'They won't be lookin fur a solo swimmer. It's what? Fifty

metres? Uh can swim that easy. She howked the bandolier over her head and shoulders. 'Aw my days on that 'ell 'ole wur no wasted. Uh know where to get on board without detection, Uh know the sweet spot. It won't take much. The whole lot'll gan up in seconds.'

'Aye and you with it,' I said. 'Please Reinya, don't do this.'

She narrowed her eyes at me. 'Uh've nothin to live for.'

'What about the revolution? I thought you wanted to fight.'

She pointed towards the ship. 'The sufferin's 'appenin now. They can't wait fur your revolution.'

'Let her go Sorlie, we cannae hang around here aw day, they'll huv a'ready seen us and will huv radioed their command.' Dawdle opened the hatch and let Reinya pass without even trying to stop her. We followed her up. The prison ship was indeed only fifty metres away. It wasn't as big as I'd expected, not much bigger than a sub and yet it was rumoured to house over a thousand addicts. They must be packed in like rats. Its grey, rusting hull lay lurched in the water, the bow dipped low as if waiting to nosedive.

Reinya turned, held up her hand in salute. 'Good luck with the revolution,' she said before launching herself into the water.

Ishbel

Ishbel felt someone in the room. The boy maybe, she could smell him. He stood over her. She could hear his breathing. She tried to control her own, fool him into thinking she still slept. She felt a touch on her arm, very light, then something like a feather landing on her leg, her thigh. She tried not to tense and yet still made ready to stop that hand if it crept higher up her leg. Instead it moved to her calf. She was being measured for something. A coffin?

She opened her eyes. It wasn't Saul but a small boy she had seen by the fires.

'What..?' But as soon as she spoke he whipped out the room leaving the door wide open, letting in pink tinges of daybreak. She checked her wrist, her communicator was still there but the unease she had felt the previous night returned. She dug into her sack she'd used as a pillow. Her map of the area showed her she still had many kiloms to cross to reach her rendezvous before Bieberville. But what about her men? She would need to come back for them. If she missed her rendezvous there was a three day hike ahead of her. And even if she did make Bieberville in time, she would be left with the problem of finding transport to get her prize out of there. There was no time to waste. She reassessed her original plan to leave Huxton. This place was wrong. She couldn't leave him. It was only a flesh wound, nothing to stop him recovering if he took it easy, but he would slow her down. If need be she could fashion a crutch and carry him part of the way.

She peered out into the camp, not knowing what to expect. Daylight was only just creeping in through the sparse gaps in the trees and the fires were embers. She saw small boys, dipped over in sleep, obviously set by each fire to keep them stoked. Ribbons of mists whispered into the trees. Across the yard lay the infirmary, its door open as if they were expecting her. She grabbed her bag and ran on tiptoe across the gap. As she slipped through the door, her hopes of seeing Huxton up and ready to go vanished.

He lay on his back, his face pale in the dawn light, his whole body soaked in sweat.

'Huxton.' She shook his shoulder. 'Come on, we need to go.'

'Eugh?'

He rolled his head and his face screwed up in pain.

'Come on, it was just a flesh wound, get up.'

She pulled the cover off his bed and fell back in horror. Huxton seemed unaware his leg was gone. The stump just below the hip was wrapped in blood-soaked cloth. His other leg lay bare, with a line tattooed around it at almost the exact spot of his amputation.

'What are you doing here?' Ishbel jumped at the voice. She hadn't heard the woman step into the tent, Saul lurked behind her, grinning, as if he was expecting some reward.

'What have you done to him?'

'His leg was infected, it had to come off.' Ishbel remembered the bundle the boy carried from this tent. No way, they couldn't have.

'It wasn't infected. It had only just happened, a flesh wound.' Ishbel couldn't hold back the panic in her voice.

'Are you a healer?'

'No but...'

'It was infected.'

Ishbel pointed to the other leg. 'Then what is that mark?'

The woman didn't flinch. 'It is for study purposes.'

She had to get out of here but she couldn't leave Huxton at their mercy.

'I need to move on.'

'Saul tells me you wish to leave him here.' She motioned towards Huxton. 'Under the circumstances I think that's wise. You can leave once you have eaten.' The woman nodded to the boy Saul. 'Breakfast is being prepared.'

Ishbel looked at Huxton. This fine soldier who had so much promise for the future of the revolution. She leaned down to speak to him. His laboured breath was rank on her face.

'I'll come back to say goodbye,' she whispered, but the man was past caring. Her back straightened and she turned to face them.

'I'll just go and perform my body management then leave.'

The woman pointed to the north of the camp. 'The latrine area is out there.'

Ishbel left them, but instead of heading for the latrines hurried back to her cabin. She watched from the door until the woman and boy left the infirmary then she slipped out the back.

In the shadows she slid past the catering tent, her back pressed to the wall. The smell of meat cooking made her puke so fast she almost soiled her boots. She gagged and spat in the snow.

The store had double doors made of plastic with two bolts threaded across. She carefully slid each bolt open. They worked smoothly as if well-oiled with fat. She gagged again. The snow outside was piled up around and packed hard against the stone walls, telling her it was an ice house. The door squeaked open and she slipped in, leaving it open a crack.

The room was perishing, her breath froze on her face. She pulled her snood up over her nose. It was dark with only a sliver of light stretching through the opening. She torched her communicator and saw a dark lump hanging in the corner, just as she had expected but not quite believed. She moved further in to the room just to make sure. The shelves were empty apart from Huxton's leg, the pepper shot removed, hanging in the corner to cure, all ready to be carved and served with two veg. Her heart sank. Is this what civilisation had become? A flutter of panic rose in her breast. She had to get out of here she told herself for the umpteenth time, but first there was something she must do. She turned and reached for the door but before she could get there it banged closed. She heard the bolts slam in place, one then the other.

Sorlie

I tried to catch her cuff as she leapt but my hand snatched at the air.

'Reinya,' I roared.

Dawdle grabbed my arm to stop me diving in after her. 'Don't – it's no like when ye rescued Ishbel. Reinya wants tae dae this.'

I couldn't believe she'd gone. What would I tell Scud? I remembered her words to me not that long ago. 'Tell him I love him.' She'd been planning this all along. And all I could do was watch.

She was a strong swimmer and a good way towards the ship when the roar came from a distance. A Military Transport appeared over the horizon. Dawdle dived below and whipped the sub forward and ninety degrees starboard at the same time, throwing me off my feet. I clung to the outboard ladder hanging over the side and saw the missile pass, missing us by a whisker. It carried on right under Reinya's thrashing legs. Fifty metres ahead the world exploded into a million pieces with only the bow of the prison ship showing seconds before it disappeared into the ocean's deep, leaving splinters as a trace of those poor helpless souls.

'Sorlie, get in here. We're goin down.' Dawdle roared.

'But Reinya.' I could see her treading water, staring into the space where her target had been.

'Reinya, quick.' She didn't have to be told twice and started back towards us.

'Sorlie.' There was more urgency in his roar and I knew why.

The Transport banked and headed back towards us. It flew low over the ship's debris, almost skimming the surface of the water. I could see the other missile hold, still loaded and pointing at us with deathly intent. I hooked my arm round the ladder and grabbed Reinya's collar with the other just as a rain of bullets puttered in the water beside us. A searing pain tore through my hooked arm. As the Transport passed and slowed it seemed to hover above us and I just had a glimpse of the armoured pilot. He was alone, with no crew waiting to pick us off. Time seemed to stand still as I looked into those blinkered eyes. It was him again. He was tracking me, no doubt about it. Reinya yanked me from my dwam, shoved me down the hatch, followed and slammed the lid tight.

The pressure to my ears was immense as we dived at speed. The sub rocked as something hit us. The engine screamed then settled to a disturbing clunk.

'Any damage?' I shouted above the clunking, trying not to think of the stounding pain in my arm.

'Hard tae tell, but it disnae sound good, eh?' He tapped a gauge. 'We're losing fuel. We'll need tae take it easy.' His face was grim. He beckoned me over. 'Take the controls a minute would ye.'

I could only hold on with one hand, leaving my other held high as I tried to halt the blood I could feel trickling from a wound.

Dawdle leaped over his chair and grabbed Reinya's bandolier, almost taking her ears off as he yanked it over her head.

'Oi!' she shouted.

'Ah'll oi ye.' He stowed the bandolier in a trunk, locked it and placed the key in his pocket.

Reinya slumped in the corner and stuck her thumb in her mouth.

'Aye. That's right hen, you sit still, content somebudy's done yer dirty work for ye.'

She ignored him. His fists were clenched and I could see by the way he stood he was itching to kill her.

'Peedle's damaged. We could aw huv been killed back there.' He looked at the dials, chewing his anger in his cheeks. 'We'll be lucky if we can limp tae port.' He took a breath and stepped closer to her but she seemed to be asleep. 'Aye that's right, you huv a wee greet about that.'

'Dawdle.'

'Not now Sorlie, Ah'm no hearin yer pleas fur mercy. As soon as we git tae port, ah'm handin her tae The Military. She's no fit tae be let loose.' He bent down and took a handful of her hair and pulled her head up to face him. Her eyes blazed with defiance. 'You can rot in prison. We should've left ye there tae begin wi.'

'Dawdle.' I said

'No the now, Sorlie.'

'Dawdle, do you have any bandages?' I held up my arm. My sleeve was drenched in blood and when I looked at it my head heaved. I slumped into the captain's seat. I never could stand the sight of my own blood.

The sub stuttered and coughed its way across the channel. Every hour required a sneaky emerge in the hostile waters and the risk of detection while Dawdle hammered and banged. We eventually lurched into an estuary ten hours after our unplanned diversion to the prison ship. Dawdle called ahead.

'We're sorted.' He patted the control panel of the sub. 'Sorry Peedle, old girl, but ah think this time we need tae part company fur good.' He turned to us. 'We'll transfer tae another vessel.'

'Not a van?'

He shook his head. 'No, we travel by boat. It's easier in this terrain. Monsieur Jacques' men here in Esperaneo Major have some quality gear.' He patted the control panel again. 'Ah've put up wi this piece o junk fur far too long. Time fur a shiny new Peedle.'

Tempers had cooled in those ten hours. Dawdle recognised that Reinya was cracked after her baby's death.

'Aye but she's said all along she wis going tae blow that ship up.'

'Well it's done now so she's no more to worry about.'

'She's unhinged, Sorlie.'

'We're all unhinged, Dawdle.' Dawdle raised his eyebrow at that. 'Aye, even you,' I said.

'Well what dae we dae wi her?'

I held out my injured arm. 'We take her with us as planned. We need all the help we can get.'

Dawdle turned to Reinya who sat cross-legged on the floor, calmly waiting her fate.

'What do you want, Reinya?' I asked. 'Was the only reason you came with us because you wanted to blow up the ship?'

She shook her head, then nodded. 'U bit, if uh'm honest. But when The Prince got you to stand up in front o that crowd and uh joined you, uh could see the 'ope in their eyes.' She rubbed her hands over her face. 'Look, uh'm sorry, Dawdle. Uh shouldn't 'uv. But you've no idea what it was like. No sleep coz yer scared the rats'll nibble ye or someone'll cut yer throat, or worse. And that's just the guards. You wouldn't put u wild animal through that.'

'Aw right, nae need tae bump yer gums aw ower again. Ah get the script. But we nearly got killed.'

'Uh never meant fur that tae 'appen.' She looked up at me. 'It was 'im again.'

'Who?' Dawdle asked.

'There's a warrior,' I said. 'Covered in armour. He was at Steadie, he chased us into the sewer in Beckham City. I think he was at the tower when the Transports blew up. I think he's trying to kill me.'

88

'Who is it?'

'No idea, but he knows me. He called me by my name at Steadie.' I looked at Reinya to back me. 'I think he has a tracker on me 'cause he always seems to know where I am.'

Dawdle ran his hand over his stubble chin. 'We'll get somebudy tae check that out when we disembark.'

'And what about me?' Reinya asked. Dawdle glared at her.

'OK, you can come. But step out o' line just once and ah'm gonnae kill ye.' And I knew by the set of his jaw and the throbbing in his temple that he meant what he said.

As soon as Dawdle opened the hatch a biting cold rushed in and nipped my nose.

We climbed out onto the rungs of a ladder leading to the quayside. It was broad daylight and yet a couple of white vans were parked at the end of the quay and a gaggle of Noiri ops huddled around a brazier, their hands cupped round mugs.

'Brilliant,' Dawdle said. 'Just in time fur a brew.'

A woman swaddled in scarves of pink and orange ran towards us.

'Shasta?' Reinya said. 'What's she doing here?'

'Who's Shasta?' I asked.

'She's from the souterrain community. She helped heal Scud.' Then in a whisper Reinya added. 'She's also Dawdle's bint.'

Dawdle daggered his eyes at Reinya. 'She works fur the resistance.'

Shasta stopped just short of us. 'Dawdle,' she said, breathless.

'Yeah, good,' Dawdle said as if she had asked how he was. 'Got the vessel?'

'It's just…'

'What? A good one ah hope. Ah'm no payin over the odds, mind.'

She shrugged and beckoned him to the other side of the quay and pointed downwards. Dawdle slapped his hand to his forehead and said something to her we couldn't hear, but by the look on her face it wasn't a pleasantry. We joined them and looked down.

'What the snaf?' I said.

'It's a fourman.' Shasta sounded so optimistic.

'It's a snaffin canoe,' Reinya said and burst out laughing.

'The canoe's big enough to take four,' Shasta repeated.

'Before you get in the boat go tae the second van on the left,' Dawdle told me.

'Why?'

'Tae get scanned, ya dolt. You're the one convinced o being followed.'

'You saw the Transport.'

'Aye, aye, haud yer wheesht, we'll get it fixed. So, second van, get it over with.'

I knocked on the van door and was admitted by a woman about the same age as Ishbel. She looked a bit like her too. Same red hair and amber eyes. I wondered how Ishbel was. Was she still in Freedom? Then quashed that thought. We'd a mission to do and Ishbel had another, so of course she wasn't still in Freedom.

The woman held the door wider to admit me. Inside was kitted out like a mini infirmary. A bed with blankets made from Steadie plastic fabric. A shiny plastic table, laid out with drawers and compartments below and in the wall next to the cab, a machine that hung from the ceiling, blinking a red dot, powered no doubt, from the van battery because the engine hummed in fine tune.

'Lie on bed,' she said with an accent very different from the ones I was used to hearing in Lesser Esperaneo. I did as she asked.

She pulled a canopy over my body and plugged the blinking machine into the hood hanging from the ceiling. It beeped steady then slowed and clicked to a stop. The woman examined the screen above my head.

'Well?'

'You've been bugged.'

'How?'

She shrugged. She came towards me with a pair of small pincers held between thumb and forefinger. I shuffled up the bed, backing away.

'You want this intrusion?'

'Course not.'

'Well stop babying – it won't hurt.'

'Where is it?'

'In belly button.'

'My belly button? How the snaf did it get there?'

'This I dont know. Lift t-shirt.'

I lifted my t-shirt, aware at how puny my chest looked. Not a hair and definitely piddling little abs. She went in with the tweezers. I closed my eyes. I felt a surge in my loins followed by a wave of nausea.

'Tell me when it's over.'

'Is over ages ago.'

I opened my eyes. She held up the tweezers but there was nothing to see.

'You need to clean belly button more often, amazing that fluffed up transmitter sent anything.' I felt my face pink.

'Never mind the fluff, what about the device?'

She placed it under a microscope.

'Look.' It was truly tiny. 'Is Military.'

'Military? How can that be?'

'I don't know.'

I racked my brain. How did it get there? Could someone on Steadie be the one? Did I pick it up during all the time I spent there? Harkin? No, that couldn't be possible. Where would she get her hands on Military gear? Con? I was unconscious for a while after all. Pa? No, why would he?

'How do you know it's Military?'

'Is very sophisticated.'

'Could the frequency be changed from Military to non-Military?'

'Is possible. Would need someone very clever. A tech maybe.'

'A tech. Is that the same as a TEX disciple? Pa, I mean The Prince told me about them.'

'Could be.'

When I told Dawdle the verdict he rubbed his chin with his hand but said nothing.

'Does this mean the armour guy won't be after you now?' Reinya said.

'Hopefully.'

'Uh wonder who it is.'

'I don't know, but it must be someone with connections to the Military.'

'And even though the tracker is gone, uh doubt they'll give up that easily.'

'Thanks Reinya, you're such a comfort.'

'Just sayin.'

Ishbel

She pushed. Had it been the breeze or had it been closed deliberately? No, she'd heard the bolt, it had definitely been deliberate. She looked at the leg and pictured herself, a carcass hung up for carving. She had been measured after all.

The door was stuck hard. She beamed the communicator torch and had another look round. She placed a hand on the wall and it almost stuck to it. She tugged and gave herself a freeze burn. She stuck her hand in her mouth to ease the pain. It was an ice house. She remembered her home in the North West Territories where they built such places. Even though they had electric power and white boxes called freezers, some villagers preferred to use the ice houses for preserving their food. The cement between the stone was cold and brittle and she wished she had Kenneth's virus with her. But that was stupid. It would take maybe weeks to work and by then she'd be dead and hacked up. The ground was freezing so she knelt rather than sat and switched the torch off to save power. She hadn't been out in the open for a while and had had no chance to recharge it and she would need it if she ever got out of here. In the dark she became aware of the smell. Not of rotting meat but of clean pure ice, tingling like a fresh mountain stream.

She couldn't believe how calm she was. In a movie-caster right now she would be freezing to death but some hero would come along to save her, just as Dawdle had saved her from Black Rock all those months ago. Just as Sorlie had saved her from the waters below Jacques' crumbling tower. Where were Dawdle and Sorlie now, when she needed them?

Maybe there would be a maverick in the tribe who didn't like the way things were going. But then she remembered the efficiency of the woman and the bloodthirsty eyes of the boy. Huxton was out of it. She was on her own.

She could try to send a comms but she daren't risk the signal being picked up by the nearby Military Base. A stray signal in this wasteland was bound to set alarms sounding, but she doubted a signal would penetrate these thick stone walls. She had to retain radio silence while her mission was still possible. And it was still possible, she believed that much.

As she knelt on the stone slab floor, she slapped the wall, groped around for the door again. She was sure it was plastic. Maybe she could try to melt it with her comms flint but the fumes would probably kill her, she doubted there was any ventilation in here. Two bolts, that's what was holding her in. A simple door. They didn't need high security out here, only a couple of bolts to stop the door being blown off its hinges by the fierce gales and flying over the border into the Eastern Zone. Two bolts.

She unhooked her comms from her wrist and using its strap, scraped the grout from between the slabs. Maybe she could lift one and dig, but her fingers were numb. Her bag was at her knee, she dragged out her hat and gloves, hugged her coat tighter and pulled the hood over her head. Her toes were beginning to freeze. The heat drained from her core. She started to shiver hard. She rummaged some more in her bag for something useful to help her but knew there was nothing. If she didn't get out soon they would have another frozen piece of meat. If she could dig it would warm her up.

A couple of her short nails snapped when she tried to hook them under the slab lip. She took a deep breath and heaved at the slab with all her strength. It wouldn't budge. This far north the ground was permafrost and of course the slabs were welded to it.

She stood up and did some jumping jacks. Her hand accidently touched Huxton's leg and she squealed.

'Stupid,' she said.

She shoved her hands under her oxters. Maybe that was the plan all along; to have her frozen. Could the hinges be blasted with her gun? But they would hear, and it might ricochet and she had to get back to Huxton before anyone was around. She fingered her communicator. There had to be something. It had a magnet which she'd not used and had no idea of its power. And she knew if she used it the battery would drain. But what choice did she have? So she groped her way back to the door.

She ran her hand over the surface with no clue where the bolts were situated. There was a slight bubble where the fixing had all but punctured the door. Working blind, she held the magnetic element to the bubble and down a couple of cents. She slowly dragged the magnet up, imagining the bolt's butterfly lift to horizontal. When she thought it was there, she slid the magnet across, seeing in her mind the bolt glide. There seemed to be a slight resistance or maybe that was wishful thinking. Her ear pressed to the door, there was no sound other than the magnet scraping across the surface of the door. When she guessed it was all the way across she pulled the magnet off the surface and heard a faint clunk from outside. She pushed the top of the door to test. It didn't budge.

'Damn.'

At the bottom of the door she felt for the same bubbles on the surface. These were more pronounced. Hardly breathing lest she slipped, and careful to take her time, she tried again. She was certain she felt a resistance in the drag of the magnet this time and quashed the thought of her battery charge draining, but she could almost taste the air filling with current. Slowly, slowly, catchy monkey. Then, she heard the clunk but it was more definite this time. She made a silent prayer to her ancestors and pushed the bottom of the door. It gave, it gave! And a tiny crack of daylight seeped in. She sat back on her heels and swayed in concentration for a couple of beats then moved the magnet back up to the top bubble. She closed her eyes and imagined it. She relived the act, sure that the bolt stuck halfway along. She dragged the magnet along the line of the bolt until she sensed it catching. She nodded, yes, this time. She tensed her shoulders and planked her feet solid, shoulder width apart. 'Now,' she whispered to herself. And it dragged along and then – clunk.

'Result!' She grabbed her bag, pushed open the door and sprinted into the woods. Her breathing thundered as she hunched behind a tree and watched the camp. The place seemed deserted, even the children were missing this morning. Where had all the people gone? Had they systematically eaten them? That's one way to solve diminished resources, she thought, feeling a bit sick at her own imagination. Or had they been carried off by the mysterious Big Foot animal the boy described? Everyone knew the story, details of it had even survived the info purge; the myth could be found in the State database, FuB.

She retraced her steps to the rear of the store and hugging the wall, she turned and checked the way was clear. She heard voices and dropped to the ground. Snow fringed the bottom of her coat. Her footprints led into the forest and back again. Stupid, stupid. She should have stuck to the slush path. The boy and the woman appeared from behind one of the cabins. They were deep in conversation but too far away for her to hear. She waited until they disappeared into one of the perimeter huts.

Crouched low as a hunting cat, Ishbel half crept, half ran for the infirmary.

Huxton was as she had left him the night before, in fact he

looked better. An IV had been hooked to his arm and Ishbel suspected it held some sort of saline to fatten him up.

She moved to lift him.

'No,' he said.

'We have to get out of here.'

'I can't.'

'You know what this is?'

He swallowed hard and nodded. 'Yes, I heard them discussing their next feast. But I'm too weak to go. The mission will be jeopardised.' He grabbed her arm. 'Kill me.'

'No,'

'They've taken my pill otherwise I'd do it myself.'

'I can't.'

'Please Ishbel. I don't want to be kept here like an animal being fattened for slaughter. Kill me.'

She shook her head, trying to cast off thoughts of his future.

'Call yourself a commander. Get it over with, let them have their fill and maybe they'll choke on me.' Tears welled in his eyes. 'Please Ishbel, I'm begging you. I'm no good to anyone now. Quickly before they come back…'

She sliced his throat before he could finish. He didn't even see the blade. His blood gushed warm and cooled over her hand. Her nostrils filled with the bitter smell of it, her lips tasted it. His eyes still held their pleading and she gently closed them so she couldn't see. She wiped the scalpel on the bed cover and replaced it on the tray behind her where she had lifted it on the way into the infirmary.

'Sorry, dear friend,' she whispered and felt the now familiar catch in the back of her thrapple but did not allow it to grow. Natives were not permitted to cry and she had been tempted, too many times recently. She fled the hateful place.

Sorlie

Shasta stood on the quay avoiding eye contact.

'The roads between the north and south have been eroded by constant floods,' she said. 'The first canal you will travel along was once part of a long gone rail network. Every kilom or so you will pass evidence of this. Run-down station yards abandoned when the power plants shut down. New waterways opened up and our Noiri operatives were the first to take advantage of them. In the wetlands our vans were useless but like rats, we Noiri adapt to any environment we find ourselves in.'

She sounded like some propaganda ad for the Noiri, but Dawdle let her ramble on as if we had all the time in the world.

'I thought she was resistance, not Noiri,' I whispered to Reinya.

'Maybe it's the same.' And maybe Reinya was right about Dawdle and Shasta having a relationship. If so, where did that leave Ishbel?

'The Military have given up on the water transport,' Shasta continued. 'But they can still be encountered when dry land crosses the wetlands. It will not be plain sailing.' She stood above where the green canoe bobbed. 'The canoes on Esperaneo Major are good, sturdy stock. You will not be disappointed.'

Dawdle didn't look convinced. He glowered at Reinya. 'Ah'd huv preferred tae huv Peedle.'

'The waterways are often too shallow in places and sometimes disappear altogether.' Shasta expanded. 'You might need to deploy portage.'

'What?' I asked.

'Carry the canoe overland.'

The canoe wobbled when Dawdle got in. 'Ah hate these snafin things.' He held his hand out for Reinya to take but she sniffed and stuck her nose in the air as if she was the one who had been wronged.

She boarded with ease and picked up a paddle as if she'd canoed all her life. My only experience of canoeing had been at the Academy field trip. I'd hated it. The Academy canoes were small and we were forced to do something called an Eskimo roll, which was to deliberately tip the boat upside down and try to right it again. I was surprised the Academy allowed it. The water was deeply polluted so when we got out, spitting and spewing, the nurse immediately injected us with something to make us 'safe'.

Shasta held Dawdle's bag while the supplies were being loaded. As he stretched out his hand to take it, she hugged it to her chest as if keeping it ransom.

'Will you return to the souterrain soon?' she asked him. His face pinked.

'Aye, aye. Ah'll see ye next quarter. Now. The bag,' He snapped his fingers at her and she threw the bag at him, her face as sour as sweat.

It took us a couple of turns round the estuary before we got the hang of us all paddling in the same direction, same pace and sequence. Although the wound on my arm wasn't too bad it tugged when I paddled.

Even though my secret tracker had been disabled, my eyes constantly searched the sky and the horizon, waiting for him to appear again. The countryside was flat apart from small hillocks with those church things perched on top and each settlement had a concrete water tower.

'Are they still in use?' I asked Dawdle.

'Probably – they collect rainwater – crazy not tae. But they'll have tae have some sort o puri filter workin.'

After a couple of kiloms Shasta's words about the shallow water materialised. The canal narrowed and the boat jammed in silt.

'We'll have to get out,' I said.

'Ye don't say.' Dawdle drawled.

Water seeped into my boots. 'We need wellies.'

'Ah'm surprised Steadie didn't issue ye wi them. They've enough plastic in that place.'

We hauled the boat onto a tow path and carried it between us. Although Dawdle was the tallest, we were all of similar height so the portage worked well with him at the front, me in the middle and Reinya at the back. I felt safe under the boat, less exposed to what was out to get me.

'You youngsters might look like wimps but ye're strong,' Dawdle said. Reinya and I looked at each other.

'You takin the piss?' Reinya said.

'Me? Never.'

'I wonder if we'll even get this running again,' I said. Dawdle looked puzzled. 'The railway. These used to be railway lines, didn't they?' I said, pointing to the channel of water we were just about to enter. 'It would be good if after the revolution we had trains again.'

Dawdle slapped his palm on his forehead. 'Don't be soft lad, they'd need tae take care o the water first. An what's wi aw this "we" jargon ?'

'Just thinking big.'

He snorted but kept quiet.

Once we returned to the waterway the kiloms splashed by. The sky turned pink and Dawdle suggest¬¬¬ed we think about stopping for the night.

'There's an emergency Noiri van parked near a high top settlement. Just round that bend, ye'll see a city rampart. We'll stop before that because ah heard reports o some new activity since the last time ah wis here.' He scanned the hillside. 'Aye, we'll just take it steady.'

As we turned for the shore the canoe started to drag.

'Pull harder,' Dawdle shouted from the back.

'I can't,' I shouted. 'Something's stuck at the front.

'Thur's a net slung across the river,' Reinya said, hanging over the bow, trying to tussle with something. Dawdle looked right and left to the natural escarpments that rose on either side.

'Ah kent this wis always goin tae be the trickiest part o the journey.'

'Can you cut the net, Reinya?' I could feel panic bubbling in the pit of my stomach. 'We're sitting ducks here.' My voice sounded screechy to my ears. Dawdle gave me a sharp look. I handed my little penknife to Reinya and she began hacking at the net.

'It's pretty perished. Uh nearly huv it.' I could see the muscles straining on her shoulder blades. And then we shot forwards – free.

We rounded the bend in the river and sure enough there was the rampart, but before that, across the river, a barricade had been built. A higgledy-piggledy conglomeration of plastic chairs, duckboards and boxes. On top of the barricade, beside a fluttering flag, stood a tousle-haired girl of about twelve years old with two younger kids on either side like gateposts. The two youngsters held bats.

'Baseball bats,' Dawdle informed us. 'The kind made fae reclaimed plastic. Tough, smooth and very, very hard.' The flag was white with a yellow circle crudely painted on its centre.

'What the snaf?' I said.

'Thur just kids,' Reinya snapped.

'Yeah,' Dawdle said, quickly stowing his bag in the provisions box below his seat. 'But we dinnae ken what's behind them.

'Maybe thur orphans.' Reinya's face was soft and I guessed she was thinking about Kooki.

'Who cares?' Dawdle reached down into the water and pulled the remnant of the net into the boat.

'Oi,' the girl said with a booming voice that belonged to someone much older. She pointed to the net. 'That property Sun Court.' The way she said it gave the words upper case status.

'Ah dinnae gie a snaf who it belongs tae,' Dawdle shouted. 'Let us through.'

'What's Sun Court?' I asked.

'We Sun Court.' The girl said, spreading her arms and twirling in a circle.

'Oh no. Look,' Reinya said pointing right and left to the escarpment. The skyline began to blot out as ragged children appeared. Hundreds of them aged between about four and twelve years of age. Each carried a crude weapon. Catapults, slings and more of those plastic bats.

'Jupe sake,' I said.

'Who's boss?' Reinya shouted to the girl.

'I boss,' the girl answered and her little bodyguards nodded in agreement.

'Who cares? Let us past.' Dawdle's face pulsed with boiled blood. He was beeling.

'No! Ransom,' the girl said rubbing her fingers together to denote the need for credit.

'We don't have anything to give you,' I said in the most reasoned voice I could muster.

'Liars,' said she of few words.

Dawdle looked at the bags under our seats that contained all the goods we had to last the journey.

'We've nuthin tae give,' he said. The girl narrowed her eyes at Dawdle. The kids on the ridge stretched their slings. 'Look, if ye let us past we won't tell anybudy yer here.'

Reinya sniffed. 'Yeah and that'll work. Look at thum, they don't care.'

'You're little kids, should be in a reservation,' I said. 'We can help you. We know a good one where you'll be safe.'

'What's wrong wi you two?' Reinya started. The girl moved down the barricade, held her hand up.

'No look…' Dawdle said holding up his hand in peace. The girl dropped her left arm and a rain of pebbles fell on us from the left flank. I cowered and held my arms over my head, but a rock the size of a builder's fist bounced off my shoulder and a searing pain shot through my wounded arm. I could hear Reinya yelp as she was being pepper-dashed by chuckies.

The girl held up her right arm. 'This side – boulders, rocks. Give us ransom.'

'Just give them the bloody stuff, Dawdle. You'll be able to get more,' I said, wiping blood from my hand. Dawdle stood up in the canoe, setting it rocking.

'Ah'm Noiri, nae kid's stealing fae me.'

The girl began to let her arm fall.

'Stop!' Reinya shouted. And miraculously she did. 'Dawdle, we won't tell. Just give thum the stuff.' His shoulders slumped. 'We've no choice,' she said.

'OK.' He turned to the girl who still had her arm ready to fall. 'You win, hen,' Dawdle said through gritted teeth. 'How bouts we gie ye half?'

The girl jumped onto the boat, rocking it violently.

'All,' she said.

The throb on Dawdle's neck bounced in jig time as he handed over the supplies. 'Know what, wee hen, ye'll come a cropper wan day.'

She spat in his face. 'Animal.'

'Cheers hen,' he said, wiping the gob off.

Reinya held her hand up as if asking permission to speak. ''ow long 'ave you been on your own?'

'Always,' the girl said.

She passed the bundles to the two small boys who now stood in the water at the canal edge, but after the first bundle they began to fight over a can of beans. The girl pulled a sling from her back pocket and with lightning speed fired a pebble into the older one's shoulder blade. The boy sank down and started to cry. The other went to pick up the bundle. 'Leave,' she shouted and signalled to another boy to come and help.

''ow many o you are thur?' Reinya really wouldn't let it go.

'Too many.'

Reinya turned to Dawdle. 'Can you not 'elp thum?'

'What? The thievin bint just spat on me.'

'They're starvin.'

'No charity, remember.'

'Can we at least tell The Prince about thum? Maybe we can get 'elp to thum.'

'Aye and maybe you can just blow them up.'

Reinya threw a discarded pebble at him. 'Unfair.'

'Aye, Dawdle,' I said. 'Can we please let it go?'

The girl finished unloading the loot and left them. She signalled to a couple of kids on the barricade who began to move some duckboards aside.

I pointed to them. 'Look Reinya. They're doing OK.'

'What if someone exploits thum?'

'That's life,' Dawdle said. His cruel sentiments stunned me but he was looking behind him so I couldn't see if he really meant his words.

Soon a small gap opened in the barricade and the girl was true to her word. 'Sun Court bids you farewell.' There was pomp in her words that definitely did not suit her rough exterior.

'Bloody highway men,' Dawdle said through gritted teeth.

We had only just passed through when the barricade closed behind us.

'It really is a clever structure. Resourceful.'

'Aye well, you tell yer Pa, Sorlie. Get him tae set up a school fur thieves here. Ah'm sure they'll serve him well.'

As we rounded the next bend I looked back and noticed the girl still stood watching us from the top of the barricade, a baseball bat in her hand and a weary look in her eye.

'They won't last long,' the prophet Dawdle said.

'Uh'm coming back to 'elp thum when this is over.'

'It'll never be ower enough fur them,' Dawdle said with something like regret in his voice.

A few kiloms further on we passed the ramparts of a ruined city where the same yellow sun flag tattered in the breeze. The Sun Court. This sun had rays coming from it like a child's picture.

'At least they're optimistic.'

'Uh wonder 'ow they survive.'

Dawdle pointed to the bank. 'There's yer answer.'

Along the canal bank crude plastic hutches held grey rabbits, crammed in with only a few cents living space each. 'Being fattened fur the pot. They must trap them.'

'I expected something more gruesome,' I said.

Dawdle stopped paddling. 'What dae ye mean?' he snapped.

'I don't know, what's wrong with you? What did you think I meant?'

'Nothin.' But it was obvious he'd been rattled.

'What did you mean, Sorlie?' Reinya asked.

'I don't know. Rats or something.' Why were they picking on me? Everyone knew the Noiri dealt in contra meat. What was the big deal? 'Sorry I mentioned it.'

The Noiri van was where Dawdle said it would be. Of course it had been ransacked but a secure floor compartment was still intact and soon we were tucking into tinned beans and oat crackers.

'It isn't right,' Reinya said with her mouth full.

'What?'

'We've so much and they've so little.'

'Oh here we go.' Dawdle sat back on his heels. 'We just gave them aw our stuff.'

'Still.' Was all she could reply.

'And how long ago was it you wur in a reservation wi yer junkie maw and then on a stinkin prison ship? Yer life's been shit so far, Reinya. Dinnae feel sorry fur them.'

'Uh can't 'elp it.'

'Let me tell ye. Ah've busted a gut fur this stuff here and that stuff back there that they stole. The Noiri is nae charity. They kids'll be aw right. Well, the lassie will onyway. Did ye no see her? Man, what a brute.'

'But still.'

'Nae buts, Reinya. That's the way o the world, wee hen. Always hus been, always will be, nae matter how many wars and revolutions there are tae change it. Survival o the fittest.'

'Then why are we embarking on this mission?' I had to ask.

Dawdle sat back and picked something out of his teeth with a splinter. 'Because sometimes the fittest aren't at the top tae begin wi. We're just gonnae change the stakes some.'

Ishbel

The forest was dense. She ran through already woven, well-trodden paths, to avoid breaking branches and giving away her route.

She didn't stop until her lungs felt as though they were bursting through her ribs and her head was dizzy from lack of oxygen. Before she checked her communicator for co-ordinates she sent out a silent prayer to her ancestors that they had sent her the right way.

She checked – they had. 'Thank you,' she whispered into the past.

She'd put twenty kiloms between her and the death camp. If she had gone wrong she would have had some catch up.

She climbed a tree and sat in the branches to plan her next move. She'd lost two days since landfall but she was now alone so reckoned she could travel quicker. The Prince had wanted a landing party, safety in numbers, but if she was honest she always worked best alone; all she needed was her communicator that was now recharging in the dim daylight. She'd find water and she could live off roots; she'd done it before. The thought of food cramped her stomach. She reached out her hand to the branch and grabbed a fistful of snow and sucked it. It nipped her nose and lips. She held it to her mouth, tingling her teeth especially around her new-filled molar where they had replaced the pill Dawdle had ripped from the mouth at the tower. She had wanted to punch him back then but if she had she might well have used it and wouldn't be here today. She hoped Dawdle was taking good care of Sorlie. She knew their mission was connected to hers, but

The Prince's paranoia had kept the details from her. She would find out soon enough.

She placed more snow on her tongue. Even though she knew the snowfall was not safe without purifying first she had no choice. Once in a while wouldn't do her much harm. She always reckoned the State propaganda machine pumped up the danger of rainwater ever since the tree-hugging Land Reclaimists got in power. More paranoia meant more for the people to worry about, which led to fewer protests about their lot and the State had a nice little earner on puri tabs.

She checked her pockets. She did have puri tabs but didn't want to waste them on a handful of snow. She also found her clicker. She used it now, just a couple of SOSs to try it out. In this wasteland anyone around would be either Resistance or local. Locals would probably think it was some weird birdcall. Only the Resistance knew the real call. There was no return. She took another handful of snow and sucked. Her head stabbed with brain freeze. This would have to do her for a while, she had too many kiloms to tramp. A clump of snow fell from the tree and dropped under her collar. The wind was picking up and her comms told her soon a gale would howl through the trees. At least the snow had ceased for once and a weak sun was struggling through white clouds; the light on the trees looked almost pretty. She heard a growling close by and thought again about the Big Foot. But the noise came from her belly and a cramp followed. Time to move.

Memories are the one thing the State cannot take from you. Her sister Kathleen's mantra ran through Ishbel's mind as she squatted in the snow to relieve herself for the fourth time in an hour. Eating snow was maybe not so good for her after all. She would squat for a bit longer just to make sure her bowels were completely empty. Memories are the one thing the State cannot take from you. Kathleen had instilled it in Sorlie's head as if that was all that mattered. And he believed her and carried the memory of his mother and her death like a badge of honour. But Kathleen had been wrong. There were other things the State couldn't take. Integrity, loyalty and love. Kathleen should never have allowed herself to be sacrificed in her Hero in Death suicide mission. Ishbel now knew that Kathleen and The Prince had been working, scheming, to take over Vanora's operation long before his disappearance. Why hadn't they taken Sorlie out of the Military Base before things had escalated to the point where he had to flee? There must have been somewhere safe. Ishbel felt her anger towards them bubble like the acid in her stomach. Maybe the State could take love from her after all because all she felt for Sorlie's parents at this point was hatred. Instead of protecting her son, Kathleen had allowed herself to be martyred and with The Prince's subsequent disappearance, Sorlie had believed himself orphaned. Ishbel had been left with no option but to take him to Black Rock and deposit him into the hands of his grandfather, Davie. But of course that had been in The Prince's plan all along. The poor boy had been yanked from his cosseted life, an innocent who spent his days working through his Academy lessons at breakneck speed so he could get to virtual wrestling with his pal, Jake. He became a man almost from the minute he heard of his mother's death.

Ishbel spat in the snow, trying to rid herself of the memories. The State could have them. She looked back at her tracks in the snow. She should have tried harder to muddy them to prevent the cannibals following her. The sky held no trace of a further snowfall that might help camouflage her footprints; soon they'd freeze and the trail would be etched onto the path. The sky, for once studded with stars and satellites, the clouds dispersed. She checked her compass and pulled herself to standing, fastened her breeches then set off east. As long as she kept to the bearing she knew she would eventually hit the Bieberville border. The wind gusted, picking up and throwing snow into her face. Good, she thought, some of that would obscure her tracks. She pulled her hood over her head. The wind tugged at it, trying to tear it from her. When she tightened the string the sounds from outside became muffled, like a cocoon. Something flapped by her head, made her jump. A goose flew across her path, inches from her face, warning her off its territory. She wished she had a net, she could do with some food. The thought of food made her stomach bubble again, she picked up a clean handful of snow and sucked it away knowing it was wrong.

She hit a wide track – a logger's trail – and was tempted to follow it to make the going easier. There were deep ruts and her footprints disappeared into them. She ran on the track for a couple of kiloms, south east. She would pick up her bearing further down the track, once she'd made up some lost time. Her breathing settled into a steady rhythm. She felt good running, despite her upset, better than she had in years. Her arms worked as pistons and with each stride she cast off another of the bitter memories that had claimed her. She wanted to run to the ends of the earth but knew there was no such thing and eventually she would need to stop and face her responsibilities.

A light flashed through the trees but she knew it wasn't a settlement. It moved, the track bent to the left. A vehicle was approaching. She ducked off the trail and climbed a tree. It was a Military Jeep. The cab light showed the driver. He was alone. Maybe she could ambush him, take the Jeep. He was just a boy, she could easily overpower him. There was something familiar about him. He reminded her of one of Sorlie's friends. Normally he hung out with his friends in a virtual world but now and again one would risk the Infections Avoidance Act and come visit in person. He was like the one who disappeared after he'd asked an awkward question of his tutor. She remembered Sorlie asking his parents and they had shut his question down in click time. The tutor had disappeared too.

As the Jeep crawled past, skidding in the deep rut, she managed a better look. It was so like him, but he was bound to be dead by now. Boys of that age all look the same.

The Jeep drove on and Ishbel suddenly felt weary. The tree she nestled in had wide branch junctions. It would be properly dark soon. The sweat she had worked up on her run now chilled her. She unclipped her belt and tied it around the trunk and then fastened it to her tunic buckle. It would hold her while she slept. She huddled into her jacket, trying to forget the cold. A power nap would be enough to give her the strength to get through her night journey. She would rest again at daybreak. She had a long way to go, she should pace herself.

She woke to the sound of the goose returning from its flight. It was still too dark to watch it settle on its feeding ground. It was not the season for breeding so she washed the pleasant thought of eggs from her mind. There would be no eggs.

Dark crept through the western forest. She'd slept too long. When she moved her limbs they were stiff. She was only twenty-one winters old and yet often these days she felt like an oldie. She unclipped her belt, swung down and walked off the track into the forest. Crusted snow was broken by prints. Huge distorted paws, twice the size of adult feet, bigger than the diameter of the huge Steadie porridge pot. The prints had a strange ridged pattern that ran from toe to heel. It was a most peculiar sight and like no animal she'd seen before. The sky clouded over again and she could smell fresh snow on the wind. The tracks led away from her in the direction she was heading. Could this be the Big Foot the boy told her of?

Far off in the distance she heard a roar like a bear from her homeland before they disappeared for good. A knot of bad told her to stay where she was but she had her mission and time was running out. Big Foot or bear would have to be faced if she was to get to Bieberville on time.

She buttoned up her courage and followed the ridged footprints. Her mouth blotted, she scooped another handful of unblemished snow into her mouth.

Was it her imagination or was the little pile of stones next to the tracks a mini cairn signalling a junction? The prints led purposely away from the track into the forest. She placed her feet in the larger plates lest someone followed her. Now and again she saw a snapped twig as if the beast was making a new trail. This was not a creature of habits.

She came upon a clearing, footprints stamped right over it, unconcerned with followers. But it was an exposed piece of ground so Ishbel skirted round, hugging the tree line until she picked up the prints on the other side.

She remembered the trap from before, so, with one eye on the prints and one on the lookout for traps it was impossible for her to watch her back.

In the distance she heard the rumble of a Transport, then the boom as it buzzed past overhead. She threw herself to the ground then cursed her stupidity. It was too high to see her in this light but it unnerved her just the same. She was days from the Bieberville border. Why were they flying over this Arctic wasteland?

A dark mass thickened the tree trunks, changing the shadows from within the forest. There was a familiarity about the shape and suddenly an image of Dawdle flashed in her mind. He infuriated her but oh, how she wished he was here right now. She crept closer and noticed the footprints stopped. She almost let out a laugh because there, propped up against a tree trunk, was a pair of snow shoes, webbed and roughly fashioned. Discarded and flattened plastic bottles threaded through with blue rope to form straps. She should have known what they were. Hadn't she worn them as a child in her northern homeland? She shook off the memory because the owner of the shoes was on the other side of the camouflaged structure. She crept nearer and detected a smell of wood smoke but it was stale, not from a burning fire but from the night before, perhaps.

She drew her battered gun from where it nestled beside her hip bone, always a reminder of her tyrant father. She hated him and his gun but often old technology was best for the kill.

She eased a branch aside and saw the rusted white paintwork of the van. Of course, that was what it was. A dead Noiri van left in some remote spot, to hold emergency supplies for Noiri operatives in danger. Dawdle had led her, with Scud and Reinya, to one near the souterrain community. It had saved their lives. And now someone was living in one out in the forgotten winterland.

She listened and through the yowling of the wind and the creaking of the trees she heard a song. A male voice, singing a song of her ancestors. Mouth music designed to help along the toil of life's labours.

The rear door was closed. She yanked it but it was stuck. Damn. The singing stopped. She scrambled round to the side and tried the door there. It opened first time. She pushed her gun in first. 'Hands up,' she said.

The cold of steel touched her ear followed by warm breath. 'No, Ishbel, you put your hands up.'

She dropped the gun and turned to face her daemon.

Sorlie

We slept in relays, taking turns at keeping watch, two hours each. We didn't know what else was out there and we didn't want the rest of our goods to disappear. I took the last watch, death of night before dawn. I climbed on the roof of the van and huddled into my blanket. It was fourth quarter, the dying season. Normal conditions in this part of Esperaneo were wet and windy but tonight it was clear and cold so at least I would be dry. I wondered how Ishbel was progressing with her mission. The little Pa had told me was that she was in the far north of Esperaneo, many hundreds of kiloms from us. It was cold enough here, it would be freezing where she was. And where were Pa and Scud? Would they be in Black Rock now? I'd been forbidden contact. I remembered the smell seeping from Pa's leg and prayed to my ancestors to send a decent healer to help him.

Through the black night I could just pick out the flickering from the kids' fires high on the rampart, burning brighter than they needed to keep wolves at bay. They kept burning all night as if the Military held no fear for them but some unknown bogeyman did. I suppose we're all afraid of some unknown in the dark. The smoke drifted towards me forming a spooky mist hovering just above ground level. It stank of melted plastic and mud.

I still couldn't work out how Pa managed to pull all the underground forces together in a common cause: Vanora's NFF, set up twenty-five years ago, supposedly to free the natives, but all it seemed to be was empire building for Vanora. It was easy to see how her devotees became disillusioned and willingly followed Pa. Monsieur Jacques' Noiri, I wasn't so sure about. The Noiri was a huge underground black market. Did Jacques maybe believe his profits would increase if the State was defeated? Whatever Pa promised Jacques, it was sure to involve profit. They were now all focused on this one campaign and yet each part had no idea what the other's part was leading to. It was like some ancient farce where actors moved in and out of scenes. I just hoped that it would all work out. The Star of Hope – if successful, Pa assured me, would crush the State for good. Easier said than done. And from what I'd gathered so far, The Blue Pearl army was the same ragtag bunch Vanora commanded, only bigger. And if that were true why was it just Ishbel and me heading these missions? What else was going on?

All was quiet but above the stench of burning plastic, the air still reeked of the perpetual sourness of our world. Water and mud everywhere, encroaching, suffocating and drowning all hope for the future. There must be a better future than this.

I heard Reinya turn in her sleep and give a sigh. She was bound to be still suffering over her baby's death. She'd never mentioned him since she flipped over the prison ship destruction. Harkin had predicted an illness might overwhelm Reinya, but didn't elaborate; something to do with hormones. It might take a while for her chemicals to stabilise, Harkin said. Harkin knew so much. No, best not to think of Harkin. But as I stared into the night I failed to put Harkin out of my mind. I wanted her to walk out of the mist towards me. And then Reinya climbed up beside me, handing over a brew.

'All quiet,' I said.

She smelled of rank milk and groaned as she eased herself down to perch beside me.

'Sore?'

'Uh hu.'

'Maybe you should have stayed behind in Steadie.'

'Don't start all yur Privileged shite, Sorlie. This needs sorted. What's the point in bringin the next generation into this chaos?' I could see tears stand on her lids. 'You saw those little kids back there. What future do they 'ave? They live like rats on a landfill.'

'I just want things to go back to the way they were before.'

'Before what? Thur lives 'ave always been like that.'

I knew what she meant. My life had been so different to hers. So cushy before Ma died and Pa disappeared. Reinya wasn't finished with me.

'Get real, Sorlie. We, the kids, 'ave to make up the rules now. You 'eard him.' She pointed to the cab where Dawdle slept. 'Survival o the fittest and he knows 'ow that's done. So let's get this done. My body wull 'eal.'

What about the mind? I thought but didn't voice these words.

Behind us in the camp a fire died from raging to flicker, to black. The silence was eerie. Hairs stood on my neck. The air so still. Suddenly a wail rose in the night that reminded me of the screams I heard in Black Rock that I now knew were the result of the DNA experiments.

'What..?'

'Probably an animal,' I said. But I knew that wasn't true.

'An animal?' Reinya asked. 'Sounds like it's comin from the kids' camp.'

'We should go.'

'Don't be soft Sorlie, not in the dark. Don't you know? This is cowboy country. What do you think we ur keepin guard for?'

Daylight crept into the sky and a faint glow of a hidden sun shimmered in the east. Dawdle climbed onto the roof, scratching his stubble chin, yawning.

'Whas happenin?'

'We need to go back. Something's up at the kid's camp,' I said.

'No way, son, we've a long way tae go.'

116

'Look.' Reinya said. 'We 'eard screams.'

'Nut! Let's get goin.'

'No Dawdle, look, there.' She pointed to the castle that now stood out in the growing light. The sun flag no longer flew.

'Means nothin. It's probably a trap tae get mair loot fae us.'

'You didn't 'ear the scream. They might need 'elp, they're just little kids.' I let Reinya go on. She had a better chance of persuading Dawdle.

'No.'

'Yes.'

'Enough,' I shouted and jumped to the ground. I ran to the canoe and struggled to pull it into the water.'

They both stood on the cab and watched me.

'We'd be quicker walkin thun tryin to paddle upstream,' Reinya said as she louped down to join me.

'OK.'

We left Dawdle foaming mad by the van and crept towards the castle.

The ground between the van and rampart was open with ruined buildings in the way so we juked from building to building, crouching low behind walls to make sure no one could see us.

We smelt it before we saw it. Piles of rubbish smouldering in a pit, which explained the raging fires. I saw a couple of baseball bats piled on the pyre like stacks of bones, the heavy fumes of the plastic polluting the air. The rabbit hutches lay open and empty. Not a kid in sight.

'Where are they?' I asked Reinya, not expecting an answer.

'Who knows? Now let's get the hell out o here.' It was Dawdle. He'd followed us after all.

'Maybe they moved to a better camp.' But even as I said it I knew it wasn't true.

We heard a booming to the south.

'Heavy artillery,' Dawdle said.

'What's that?'

'Weapons they used tae use before cyberattacks and short range missiles.' Dawdle said. 'There's a base near here and we better git.'

Reinya wandered about the scattered pieces of the little kid's lives, bending down now and then to pick up a fragment before throwing it on the embers. She rooted under the tattered flag lying trampled on the ground.

'Aw, look.' In her hand she held a rag doll. 'They 'ad so little.' Suddenly she jumped up. 'What's that?'

'Nothing, let's go.' Dawdle walked away, back towards the van.

'Uh 'eard somethin.' She dropped the doll and scrabbled up the wall and crawled out of sight like a lizard. A scream followed by Reinya's shout came from above.

'Stupid bitch,' Dawdle said.

Shoeless dirty soles wriggled through the gap in the wall then small legs in torn leggings appeared. The girl Dawdle had called a brute landed at our feet and Reinya followed by leaping off the wall like a ninja.

'Oww!' she said wrapping her arms around her chest.

The girl had lost her gallus air. Snot ran down her face into the corner of her mouth. When she licked it away I felt my stomach churn.

'Where did they go?' I asked her.

'Harvest.'

'That doesn't make sense, it's fourth quarter, the dying season.'

''arvest what?' Reinya asked. The girl pointed to herself. I noticed Dawdle backing away.

'Where did they take thum?' The girl stared at Reinya as she asked her question. She pointed south.

'Told ye,' Dawdle said from the side of the camp. 'Military'll have them at the base. They'll be safe.'

'But why 'arvest?' Reinya wasn't letting go.

'Search me,' he said.

'Well we're no leavin 'er.'

The girl clocked her kingdom and a tear rolled down her cheek. She looked just like a wee kid whose play den had been destroyed

'Let's see what we can salvage here and get on,' I said. 'Mon wee hen.' Reinya snorted. 'What?'

'You. Yur startin to sound like Dawdle. Uh thought the point o 'avin a Privileged with us was to make it easier to get past the guards. "Mon wee hen."'

Dawdle found this less funny. 'There's no enough room in the canoe,' he growled at us from the sidelines.

'That's rubbish and you know it,' I said.

He drew me aside. 'Can you no see?'

'See what?'

'Look at her, man.'

'All I see is a grubby kid. She looks a bit strange but some natives are like that.'

'Look at her hair, her eyes. The length o her arms. The way she speaks. She's no one o us.'

'What are you on about?' But I did look closer and he was right. Thoughts of Black Rock and the DNA experiments came whooshing back to me. Scud had become a mutant on Black Rock. His native alleles diluted out of him. The State's aim was to create a pure Privileged race but the experiments killed more natives than they turned. Word on the wire claimed the State had abandoned the experiments and were concentrating on something else.

But this girl was different. If she wasn't a special, if she wasn't a mutant, what was she?

'She looks like one o those Neanderthals,' Dawdle said as if tracking my thoughts.

Reinya gaped at us as if we were mad.

'Don't be soft,' she said. 'They died out with the dinosaurs.'

'Mebbes she's a throwback, a mutant.'

I moved to key my communicator to check the spec but Dawdle clasped my arm.

'No, no signal. We have tae go. And we leave that here.'

'No.' Reinya had the girl by the hand and was leading her towards the van and canoe.

The girl resisted and pushed Reinya over with ease. Her eyes were wild.

'No, stay, brothers, sisters…' She pointed south. 'Must save.'

'There, telt ye,' Dawdle said. 'That's whit she means by harvest. This isnae a camp, it's a nursery fur a new breed.'

But I knew Reinya was right, we couldn't leave her. Reinya handed her the doll.

'Was this yur sister's?' A tear rolled down the girl's cheek and she nodded. 'They've gone to the Military base. You must come with us,' Reinya told the girl. The girl shook her head. I crept behind her. Reinya could see that. I expected Dawdle to give the game away but something was stopping him. He stared at his boots. He knew he had lost.

'We'll come back for thum.' Reinya said, watching me approach from behind, her voice soft almost soporific. 'You 'elp us, we 'elp you.'

I pounced on the girl's back and wrestled her to the ground. The girl roared the scream I heard in the night. Reinya grabbed her arms while I tied her legs with the tattered flag.

Reinya said, 'Uh'm so sorry, so sorry. Uh promise we'll bring you back. Make it better.'

'Ye realise this is kidnappin.' Dawdle said as he walked away from us. His shoulders were slumped as if we'd punched the stuffing from him just by taking the kid. But it was more than that.

Ishbel

'Merj.'

Before her stood her former lover. The man who'd betrayed Vanora. The man Ishbel had blown up on Black Rock during his fight with Sorlie. She had left him for dead then, arm blown off, eye damaged. The last time she'd seen him was back at Black Rock when he had revealed The Prince to the players. Then he'd still showed signs of injury. Now, he appeared his old self. The surgeons had performed a miracle. He'd always been handsome but now he was beautiful. His eye and cheek were completely repaired and his skin held a lustre any movie star would die for.

He held up his arm. 'Good eh?' His hand was encased in a glove but he wiggled fingers. 'Of course it isn't as good as it could be. If we had old technology I could be rummaging my fingers through your hair.'

The image made Ishbel step back.

'What are you doing here, Merj?'

'We got word back at Freedom that you'd been betrayed and ambushed so I volunteered to help out.'

'You were at Freedom?'

Ishbel had left Freedom only a few days ago and saw no sign of Merj then. She'd assumed he had gone back to Steadie with his new master, The Prince.

'I've been to one of the other islands for reconstruction. The healer at the souterrain could only do so much in the primitive conditions and I knew Vanora had specialists working with new techniques on another island on the archipelago.'

'What other island? I know of no working island under Vanora's control.'

He grinned and part of his face did not move. Maybe the job wasn't so good after all.

'Oh, Vanora and her secrets. You know how I could always get around her. When she saw my damaged looks on Black Rock, she was only too happy to help. In return for certain favours, of course.'

Ishbel felt sick. Her mother was a stupid old woman when it came to pretty young men.

Merj looked behind her. 'All alone? I thought one other got out with you.'

She felt her face tingle with the memory of that scalpel.

'Huxton's dead.'

The moment she began to tell Merj about the cannibals the colour drained from his face.

'Enough. Don't tell me any more.'

'I had to kill him.'

'I said enough, Ishbel.' He turned from her and slammed his hand into the van panel, casting a heavy metal din round the forest she was sure they would hear in Bieberville. When she saw the indentation there she guessed it didn't hurt his prosthetic arm as much as it hurt the van. He swallowed hard then hunkered to revive the ashes of a fire lying by the van front grille.

'I'll make you some food.' His voice sounded choked.

Ishbel wasn't sure what just happened but this was a side to Merj she hadn't seen before.

'Did you know where the camp was? Have you been there before?'

He shook his head.

'I was locked in the store. It would have been good if you'd been around to rescue me.' He blew on the kindling. 'Imagine being locked in with Huxton's limb.' A vein throbbed in his neck.

'Well you obviously got out so, no more.' He spat into the fire and she heard its pathetic hiss.

'But the shoes.'

'What shoes?'

'The snow shoes, the camp was terrorised by a Big Foot, stealing their food.'

He shook his head. 'Not me. You know what it's like with these vans. They're for Noiri use. It must have been another Noiri Op who used it before me. It was in a pretty shocking mess when I got here but still some tins were left.' He disappeared into the van and returned with a tin and saucepan as if to prove the point.

'How did you know it was here?'

He glanced at her then attended to putting the pan of beans on the fire. 'Someone told me.'

'Someone in the Noiri? Dawdle?' She had suspected when she saw them together at the souterrain that these two men knew each other.

'There are more folk in the Noiri than your man Dawdle.'

'He's not my man.'

He grinned now. 'As you say, Ishbel.'

'How did you know I would come this way?

'The forest is pretty thick north of here, so I reckoned you would pick up the logging road. I left prints for you to follow. A good Celt like you can sense these things. I knew you would be after shelter and would find me.'

'I might have followed the logging road all the way south.'

'Why would you do that? You know the timetable. I knew you'd head east.' He tapped his communicator. 'Time's running out.'

They moved into the van to eat. The interior was basic with standard tattered sleeping bags that were surprisingly warm. The beans were good and made her feel sleepy.

'Go ahead and sleep,' Merj said.

'Are we safe here?'

'For now, but we need to move soon.' As she drifted off to sleep she felt a blanket laid over her. When her party was betrayed she first suspected Merj as traitor, now she wasn't sure, but she'd watch him just the same. For now she would sleep.

A gale blew out of nowhere, hurtling round the van like a banshee, punching it with gusts so it rocked violently. As Ishbel slept she dreamt she was in the bowels of a ship carrying her to Freedom. Something battered on the cab roof jerking her awake.

A flash lit the cab and she saw Merj hunkered in the corner, watching her. Thunder boomed and another flash illuminated the van.

'We should maybe move from under all these trees,' she said.

'No, we're safer here. The van still has rubber tyres. They'll keep us insulated. We're safer here.' Although she could detect hesitation in his voice.

Torrential rain dumped on the roof and drowned out the noise of the thunder. It was sure to wash the snow and their tracks. That's good, she thought.

Merj threw a pair of snow shoes across the van to her.

'You can fit these now, ready for when the storm ends,' he said.

They really were an ingenious thing. Lots of plastic bottles, caps still on, were welded together with one strap that crossed and overlapped the foot. Except Ishbel couldn't get it to wrap around and stay on her foot.

'I'll do without,' she said throwing them back at Merj.

'Don't be dumb.' He picked them up, bent down and took her foot. Ishbel's instincts kicked out, her foot contacted his face and bowled him back. He put a hand up to his mouth and checked for blood, there was none. He smoothed his hair and glared at her.

'That's not smart and you know it.' He was right so she let him take her foot. But still had to repress the feeling of kicking him again.

As he began to strap the bottles to her feet he avoided her eyes.

'If you don't use them you'll slow us down and what's the point of doing without just to prove a point?'

Right again, but she held her tongue. So much had passed between them. She knew she was responsible for his injuries after her butterfly bomb exploded near him. At the time she'd thought Sorlie was losing the bout. Once she and Merj had been lovers but she'd never trusted him. She couldn't let him kill Sorlie. His head was bent over her foot, the hair silky and white, so Privileged and she knew she still didn't trust him.

'Your mother did a good job of patching you up.'

He sat back on his heels, a puzzle on his perfect brow.

'How do you know my mother?'

'I met her, remember, when we brought Scud to her.'

'You brought Scud to the healer Llao.'

'Yes, and she told me she was your mother.'

'She should not have told you.'

'Why? She thought you had been injured by the Military, friendly fire. I didn't set her straight.'

'You want thanks for that?'

'No.'

'Anyway, I told you, she has her limits. Other healers did this work. I think you're fishing.'

They were silent for a few minutes.

'OK, I'm fishing. Are you Military, is that it? You're a double agent?'

'Don't be dumb.'

She tried to kick again but he held her foot too tightly.

'Stop calling me dumb, you know I'm not.' He didn't bite and went back to his binding task. 'Are you Military?'

'Is that what you think?' he said, tying off the straps and placing her foot on the floor.

'What are we to think? You appear in Vanora's Freedom and charm her into giving you First Lieutenant.'

'You really need to let that go, Ishbel.'

Yes, Ishbel knew this but sometimes she couldn't help herself.

'My mother has a blind spot when it comes to you.'

Merj gave her a twisted smile and that smile made her angry.

'You tried to kidnap Sorlie. Moorloggers were betrayed and now my men have been taken. The Military always seem to be one step ahead and you always appear on the scene at just the right moment. So, come on Merj, spill. Who are you, really, and where have you come from? Because I'm not going any further with you until I know.' He looked at her with narrowed eyes and that maddening smirk of his. At that moment she wanted to wipe it off his face for good.

'I have men to rescue and a mission to complete. And I can do it without your help.' She looked at her communicator. 'And as you say, time is running short on both counts.'

Merj eased himself from the floor but she noticed he used his good arm, keeping the repaired one limp. Maybe they hadn't done such a great job of patching him up as she'd first thought. And yet he had been able to tie her strap with both hands as if he had dexterity in his fingers but no strength in his arm. It was a mystery.

He sat on the metal box opposite her and rested both arms on his knees.

'Very well, Ishbel, I will tell you. My mother, Llao, you saw, is Privileged. My father was the great politician, Cato Flint.'

'Never heard of him.'

'He's been wiped from history. Ask Scud about him. He fought for democracy. The Purists were just coming into power. They won an election. A democratic election, but the people didn't know what they were voting for.' He shrugged. 'The people, mostly natives, voted them in to power.'

'How can that be? Natives are not permitted to vote.'

'Not now, but they could then.'

'How do you know this?'

'My mother told me. Stories get handed down. Did Vanora not tell you? Maybe she was too embarrassed.' There was a sneer in his voice. Despite his reasonable story, Ishbel could still see the old Merj under the veneer.

'Natives were responsible for their own demise,' he said.

Ishbel shook her head.

'Shake your head all you like, Ishbel, it's true. My father worked hard but he was middle ground between the hard right Purists and the tree-hugging Land Reclaimists. There was no room for middle ground in those days.' No expression passed over Merj's face. It was as if he was now reciting taught history. 'After the election my father was taken.'

'Taken where?'

He shrugged – a native shrug – so incongruous in this Privileged, as she could now see within him.

'Somewhere. Maybe Bieberville, most likely he's dead.'

'So is that why you're here? To make your mother proud, to find your father?'

'No. It was a long time ago. I can't even remember him. My mother brought me up Privileged. She believed that if I got into the Military I could infiltrate high echelons and find out what happened to him.'

'That's why she believed you were injured in the Military?'

'That's what I told her.'

'So why join Vanora?'

He gave a cold laugh. 'Why not? I knew I wasn't going to find my father. Why should I follow the path my mother laid out for me? I'd been under her will all my life. What I want is simple. I want what's best for Merj. No one has done me any favors. I wanted glamour, celebrity, power. Excitement, Ishbel. And that is what Vanora offered in her revolutionary army.'

'So you swapped one mother for another?'

He stood so abruptly Ishbel shrank back. 'That's not true. I'm a loyal soldier. The Prince recognised that. That's why he recruited me from right under Vanora's nose.'

'Oh, that's right. You're now The Prince's right hand man.'

'Yes, Ishbel, and you would do well to remember that.'

'Oh I do.' She stood to join him. 'So you lied to your mother, you lied to Vanora. Tell me this, Merj. Why should I believe one word you tell me?'

'The reason you should believe me is because you and I are out here. I came to help you get your mission done. I don't think you have many choices. Do you?'

'What about my men?'

'We leave them – for now. The Prince is sending another group to get them out. We have wasted too much time.'

'Wasted?'

'You know what I mean. We need to get to Bieberville. And you know that, which is why we leave the minute the storm is over.'

Sorlie

So we took the child because despite Dawdle's protests, there was enough room in the canoe. Although the girl was strong she wasn't that big. We left her tied until we were well away from the Sun Court and sure she wouldn't try to escape.

'It's not like we're going to make her a slave,' I said. 'Although I've read enough real History at Black Rock to understand what that must feel like.'

'Sorlie, you ur priceless,' Reinya said.

'What did I say?'

'What do you think natives ur? Thur just slaves.'

Dawdle opened his mouth once during the first part of our journey and that was only to tell us it would take at least another couple of days before our next food pick-up point. I never realised that Esperaneo Major was so huge and I had no idea what was eating at Dawdle.

The girl sat with her back to me in the boat so I had time to study her. Her hair was coarse, almost like straw and it stuck out from above her neck. Her back was broad, broader than mine. I racked my brains trying to remember what I knew of Neanderthals.

I noticed as we travelled south in the canoe the days of rain became less and less and the sun got hotter; a weather pattern emerged. In the afternoons, out of nowhere clouds would gather from the south, build into a mass. It was as if they knew we were coming and formed a gang to ambush us because the cloud mass rushed in and dumped litres of water on us, forcing the river to rise and rush, hurtling the canoe over torrents and white water. It was exhilarating and frightening at the same time, but there was always a chance one of us would fall out. Luckily no one did.

In the kit Dawdle had hidden from the Sun Court was a cream he urged us to smear over our faces and hands. And even though we were sweltering and soaking with sweat he warned us to keep arms and legs covered because he only had a scrape of cream left. Sometimes the sun was so roasting I was tempted to strip to my underwear and jump into the cool water. It was an incredible sensation to have lived my whole life under grey, dark and wet skies, to be suddenly transported into this burning furnace.

The river widened and the ground around was flat and open. We were sitting targets if anyone cared to look. But the water, dotted with small islands, stretched for kiloms into the distance with no sign of settlement, or Urban or Military.

'Is all Esp Major like this?' No one bothered to answer me.

Reinya held out a grainer bar for the girl to eat and as she reached her hand out to take it I noticed a chip scar. My blood ran with ice.

'She's chipped,' I said. Our chips had been altered to suit our new identities but the girl was an unknown. 'Great, that's it then, we are well and truly cooked.'

No one seemed bothered, too strung out with the heat and exertion, but when the river narrowed again then disappeared altogether, Dawdle ordered us out the canoe.

'We'll carry the boat fur a bit then rest.'

It was much easier with the girl to help.

'There's nae van nearby so Reinya and the lassie can get in the boat tae rest and we'll use the tarp.' He walked off. There was no quip, no joke, just instructions.

I watched him gather vegetation and guessed it was for a fire. I followed, wanting to help. A short distance from the camp he picked something up. He examined it and threw it away, walked on. His back was hunched, he seemed to have shrunk.

'What's wrong, Dawdle?' He swung round at my words and rubbed his eyes and turned away. I grabbed him to get him to face me but he shook me off.

'What the snaf, Dawdle? You're crying.'

'Leave it.'

A memory came back to me of the time Dawdle, Ishbel and I arrived on Black Rock in a storm. We were drenched and were permitted showers. Dawdle had stripped off first and jumped in. Both Ishbel and I saw the whip marks on his back. Ishbel had made a comment that you didn't need to do much to be punished in the days of the Purist regime. But we never enquired as to his crime and no one knew his story. Now before me stood the big man from the Noiri, crumbling. I saw Reinya leave the girl and move towards us.

'Leave it, Reinya,' I said. She backed off but her brows pringled with worry.

'Tell me, Dawdle, I won't repeat it.'

'It's nuthin.'

'Come on, you've been off since we came to the kids' camp. Has it something to do with the marks on your back?' He let out a big sigh that was more like a sob. 'Get it out, man. You'll feel better.'

'Since when did ye become sae carin, Sorlie?'

He sat on the damp ground, his head sank low on his chest.

'Ah thought they'd gone.'

'What?'

'Aw ma memories o the time afore Jacques found me. Ah wis twelve when he took me in. Same age as that lassie back there.'

'Tell me.'

'Ah cannae.'

'I promise. I'll tell no one, not even Ishbel. I saw your scars at Black Rock, you don't get stuff like that for nothing.'

'It wis just that camp…' He swallowed and shook his head. 'It brought it aw back. As soon as they kids appeared, whoosh, jist like that. Memories eatin away. Their childhood, ma childhood.' He looked right at me. 'Tell me, Sorlie, is there such a thing as childhood in this life? Ah niver hud ony.' He pointed at Reinya. 'She certainly niver, nor that Neatherthal. Did ye see thir toys? And you wi yer great Games Wall and yer wrestling. Thinkin yer a great warrior.'

'I never…'

'Naw, aw right. Even you niver really hud a childhood.' His faced hazed in memory. 'There wis a gang o us kids runnin feral in the camp. The leader o the gang wis a brute cried Chub. Chub ran the show. Nae brains but plenty o punch, that was Chub. Ah wis ordered tae be his right hand man, but ah'd nae stomach fur the type o work Chub asked o me. Brute force mattered mair than brains.'

'What about your Ma and Pa?'

'We lived in a camp, Sorlie,' he spat on the ground. 'Sold me, they did. Tae the gangmaster.'

'No way. That's monstrous.'

'Aye well, folk dae monstrous things when they're starvin.' His tears were dry. He lifted his chin and pursed his lips together, staring into the distance, and I wondered if that was the end of the story. It wasn't.

'The camp wis run by the Noiri boss at that time, an evil bastard cried Dec. Chub worked fur Dec, therefore by default, so did ah. We wur his wee gang o thieves. Dec thought nothin o strikin a deal wi the natives, takin then runnin without givin in return. That's just bad business. Dec had vans runnin right, left and centre but the organisation wis a shambles. Often two

Ops would turn up at the same drop. Fists flew tae decide who hud first dibs at the contra. There wis clashes wi the Military. A clampdown on the fuel Dec stole. Roadblocks, every van seized. It got tae the stage where nae goods wir movin and yet Dec still lived like a king while his men starved.' He stopped and turned to me. 'Things got desperate. Dec wanted tae try a diversification. That last thing they asked o me wis a step too far.'

'What?'

He shook his head violently. 'No. Ah'll niver tell. Let's just say, wee kids were being murdered and ah wisnae huvin ony part in it. At first ah thought they'd kill me. Ah didnae care. But instead they tied me tae a van axle and whipped me raw. When ah stopped screamin, they dragged me out o the camp and left me in a swamp tae die.

'What happened?'

'One o Dec's Ops wis just as scunnered as me by the new diversification and wis movin tae Jacques' camp. Ah didnae ken at the time but Monsieur Jacques wis awready settin up in the area. He'd come fae the Capital. Ah niver did discover for sure why he moved tae Lesser Esperaneo but rumour hud it he did some work fur the State when the Purists were in power. Then when the Land Reclaimists took ower they objected tae Jacques' illegal doins. He made nae secret o his desire to seize the tower in Lesser Esp. This guy, Dec's Op, wis sick o the brutality. Ah dinnae remember exactly how it happened, one minute ah wis in a swamp, the next, ah woke in Jacques' tower. A healer cared fur me night and day. Ah slept in a real bed wi sheets fur the first time. Ah wis clean, ma hair wis cut. Jacques turned me fae an animal tae a man.'

'How can you say you were an animal? You were only twelve.'

Dawdle shrugged. 'He saved me.'

'Why?'

'Ah dinnae really ken. At first ah thought it wis tae get back at Dec, but he niver asked me tae gan back tae that hellhole again. He let me be who ah wis and treated me like a son.'

'What happened to Dec?'

'Once Jacques established himself in Lesser Esp it wis easy fur him tae take ower the operations. He made a deal wi the Military Base commander near the tower. Contra ciggies, Mash and meat was aw they needed, along wi somethin cried coffee. They exchanged this fur fuel. It worked a treat. Once Jacques got vans movin he took the men fae Dec. They didn't even need tae kill Dec, he just disappeared.' Dawdle stood up and brushed the back of his trousers. 'So ye see it's the same model The Prince used to take ower Vanora's network. It seems aw that wis needed wis a bit of patience and organisation.'

'But Jacques is not like The Prince. He doesn't want to save natives.'

'And what the fuck dae you ken about his motives?'

And just like that the old Dawdle was back.

'Reinya,' he shouted. 'Get that bint ready, ye've hud enough rest. We need tae get crackin.'

Ishbel

The storm lasted over an hour and when it stopped the sky lighted and Ishbel thought she heard the goose overhead, out for more food.

'We should go,' she said.

'Yes.' Merj filled a rucksack with the remains of the food.

'Shouldn't we leave some for the next person?'

'Come on Ishbel, there wasn't that much to begin with.'

She grabbed the sack from him and pulled out a fistful of grainer bars, stored them in the compartment under the floor and clicked the lock to. She turned to him.

'You had a key for this,' she said.

'So?'

'So you're well connected.'

He shrugged. 'If you say so.'

They opened the door to find a flooded land. The van was surrounded by half a metre of muddy water.

'How can that be in such a cold climate?'

'Better take the snowshoes off Ishbel, and swap them for wellies,' he said. 'But strap them to your back. The permafrost is underneath and you never know when it might snow again.' She thought it was doubtful but did as he said.

They jumped down and started to wade but the going was tough. The water moved against them.

'At least it is flowing, it should disperse,' Merj said.

'But the ground is permafrost, where will it go?'

'Into the rivers.' Merj looked up to the canopy of trees. 'Maybe we could swing from tree to tree.'

'Don't be ridiculous, I'm not an Amazonian.'

After a while the water level lowered and the trees began to thin out but the forest floor had a boggy skin and sucked their boots with each step.

Ishbel checked her communicator. They'd been tramping for hours and had yet to see the forest edge.

'Do you have another van we can visit?'

'No.'

'It's still ten kiloms to the next rendezvous point and I'm three days late.'

'They'll still be there.'

'How do you know, Merj?'

'Because The Prince sent word for them to wait.'

'Isn't that dangerous? We already know there's a traitor.' She pushed back the thought it might be Merj.

'They will do as The Prince says. This mission is very important to him.'

'I thought it was important to us all.'

'It is.'

The wind changed direction and the floodwater fringed with ice. Ishbel's feet were freezing. She stopped and sniffed the air.

'Something's wrong,' she said.

'Is that your Celtic intuition again?'

She checked her comms. 'We need to start heading south.' She showed him the coordinates on the dial. Merj nodded.

After what seemed like aeons wading through the freezing flood, heads bent against the wind, Merj tapped Ishbel on the shoulder. She whipped round. Her mind had been back in Freedom with Vanora, planning what they would do with the community once their mission was complete.

'What?' she shouted to him.

He held up his mitted hand. In it was a grainer bar. Despite the damp, the wind chill had brought the temperature down and the cold was soaking into her bones. Her eyelashes were beginning to freeze. She took the bar but daren't take off her glove. She knew only too well how quickly the cold could bite you. She tore the top wrapper with her teeth and tried to bite the bar. It was solid and she dare not risk breaking a tooth out here. She sucked on the bar, letting some of the sweetness fuel her sapping energy.

'We need to get out of this wind,' she shouted.

She risked pulling back her cuff to check the map on her comms but the comms was dead. Cheap rubbish, she thought. She dug the old-fashioned map from her pocket, careful to grip it tight against the wind and the risk of it being whipped from them. She hunkered low and was amazed when Merj hunkered beside her, shielding her from the wind. She roughly knew their position. The map showed a small square sitting on its own out on the vast white emptiness, denoting the huge expanse of the plain on the plateau they were on. She was sure this square symbolised a shelter, possibly a hut. And there, a few kiloms further on from the square, a forest began again. In there they could find more shelter. She pointed out the square to Merj but he shook his head.

'Too far out of our way.'

'No, we go,' she shouted, stood up and began walking on a compass bearing for the hut. Merj held his ground and didn't follow but she knew he only had a communicator which, like hers, would not be working in this cold. She held the only map and therefore all the cards. Eventually he followed her.

After about an hour walking, this time with the full force of the wind in their faces, the square materialised in the near distance. Ishbel had guessed correctly. It was an old timber refuge hut. The door hung off its hinges but was still there. They stumbled inside and the relief of being sheltered from the relentless wind brought them both to their knees to get some breath back into their lungs and some heat into their depleted cores.

Ishbel slapped her hands against her thighs and then stuck them under her oxters to get the circulation going.

Merj crouched on the floor and, when he looked up at Ishbel, she saw for a fleeting moment a murderous look pass over his face.

'What a relief to get out of the wind,' she said, trying to judge his mood.

He sat back on his heels and stuck only his right hand between his legs to warm it. Of course, she thought, his prosthetic would not feel the cold.

'You do realise, with this detour of yours, Ishbel, we are now even later for the rendezvous.'

'Look Merj, you know as well as me that we could not have gone on much longer in those conditions.' She tapped the map. 'Look, there's a forest there. It's not that far. If we get there we'll be sheltered, we can travel faster through the break and still be out of the wind.'

'Maybe the wind will let up.'

'No, it is fourth quarter. In my home in the Northern Territories, this wind continued all season.'

Merj didn't look convinced. 'So just because you lived in NT, you're the leader of this expedition.'

Ishbel had to practically pull her jaw off the floor. 'I can't believe you're pulling rank on me. We're in an extreme environment, one I've some knowledge of. Does that not count?' She pulled a deep breath to push her anger inside. 'And this is my mission, so yes, I am leading it.'

'You disobeyed an order back there. I could have you shot.'

'Get a grip, Merj. I've a job to do. I didn't ask you to turn up here.'

'No, but The Prince did.'

'So you say.' She studied the map. 'You go back onto your old course if you like but I'm following this forest route and we'll see who gets to Bieberville first.'

The hut proved to have nothing of use to them except shelter from the wind. It was stripped bare. Ishbel was surprised that the door and walls were still standing. But the natives must have realised that such a structure was more important than its component parts so it was allowed to stand. Ishbel put her grainer bar under her oxter too and eventually it thawed enough for her to eat it.

'Let's go,' she said after only a few moments.

'I decide when we go.'

'Merj, you're being stupid.' Ishbel began to wonder if perhaps the cold was freezing his brain.

When she could see he wasn't budging she pulled her jacket close.

'Give me the map,' he ordered.

'Can you read a map?'

Even under his thick balaclava she could see his face rage. 'Of course I can.'

'Liar. If you think I'm letting you out in that wind with a map you can't even read then you're madder than I first thought.' She pulled her hood over her head and walked out the door. He made to grab her but his mitts were too thick and they slid off her jacket like snow off a pitched roof.

The wind dropped slightly from hurricane-force to gale-force. This time they headed for the forest in the southeast. A gust hit them broadways, battering them sideways. Ishbel being tall and willowy blew over many times like a grass on the prairie. But the going was easier and in no time the dark expanse of the forest appeared. At the sight of this they both moved faster. As soon as they stumbled into the plantation the relief from the wind was immediate.

Merj looked at Ishbel below pringled brows. But she ignored him. She wasn't going to say 'I told you so.' She wasn't going to be drawn into his childish games.

'I'm starving,' Merj shouted at her back.

Ishbel stopped in her tracks and turned to stare at him. 'I cannot believe you said that.'

'Why? It's true.'

'You sound like Sorlie.' That had been his eternal chant before his life changed. She had no idea Merj would say it too. He must have had a pretty privileged life if a little hunger made him believe he was starving.

'I bet you don't even know what starvation is.'

Merj held her stare but gave nothing away. There was a crashing in the woods and they both dropped to the ground. They were in a natural break between the trees, not a path as such, but it could be used as one. They both crouched and crawled off the path into the denser wood.

'What is it?' Merj whispered. The crashing sounded again.

'No idea, but it sounds pretty big.' Ishbel's first thoughts were of the Big Foot that the cannibals feared but she knew that was nonsense. She checked her map again. There was no Military Base for kiloms. Could it be a training exercise? Ishbel's fingers and feet began to numb again.

'We're going to have to move soon or we'll freeze. The sound is coming from over there, why don't we skirt round it?'

'Are you mad? It might be a pack of wolves,' Merj said.

'Wolves don't make that much noise. It's something big and it's alone.' Merj stared into the dense forest in the direction of the noise, clearly not convinced by Ishbel's words. 'Come on,' Ishbel whispered.

They crawled on hands and knees, stopping every time they heard something. When they were level with the noise Ishbel stopped and peered into the forest.

'What are you doing?' Merj said out of the corner of his mouth.

Ishbel gave a little laugh. 'Look.'

Through the trees was a four-legged bulk, antlers as big as year-old saplings sprouted from its head.

'What…?'

'It's an elk. Harmless unless we get in his way. Those antlers could toss us to the moon if it wanted to.'

'An elk?' Merj had obviously never heard of such a thing. 'Can it be eaten?'

'Oh yes, it's very tasty.'

Merj unclipped his gun and aimed. Ishbel dived for him and knocked the gun. It fired wide, missing the elk but sending it crashing into the forest away from them.

'What the snaf did you do that for?' His eyes blazed with anger and hunger.

'What good is a whole elk to us?'

'We're starving here, Ishbel.'

'And so are the rest of the people up here.' She pointed back the way they'd come. 'You heard the story I told about Huxton. If you killed that animal we would have used what? Half a leg at most. We're not going to drag it with us. Its meat would have gone to waste. Its death would have been a waste. This world cannot afford any scrap of waste.'

He did not deny what she said was true but she felt his anger percolate and Ishbel was sure she would eventually be made to pay for denying him his kill.

'Does your precious map tell you how much further?'

Heavy snow fell again and Ishbel held her face to the sky,

tongue out to receive the welcome morsel of moisture. She felt the vibration on her wrist indicating the comms might be working again but she daren't check. She enjoyed revisiting her old navigation skills and having the upper hand on Merj.

The cocoon of trees had shredded the wind blasts and reduced the chill. She scanned the map and calculated another hour walking before they left the forest. The first settlement of the Bieberville borderland was only a couple of kiloms further on. She showed Merj on the map but he just grunted. He'd pulled off his balaclava and she noticed his face was paler than normal. He'd always been a strong soldier but maybe his injury had softened him.

Her calculations proved correct; she smelled the wood smoke before she saw the settlement. She'd expected a shamble of huts similar to the cannibals, but she couldn't have been more wrong. This settlement had high walls made from huge plastic panels laced together with plastic ties. Small holes had been peppered across the surface to allow the wind to whistle through. Any solid structure in this environment would be whipped into orbit in a mild gale, never mind the hurricane they'd just walked through.

A Blue Pearl flag fluttered from the top of the wall.

'The Blue Pearl, look. You got us here,' Merj said grudgingly.

'What if it's a trick?'

'Ishbel, you're the one who led us here. Why would it be a trick?'

'But if the Blue Pearl are already here, why would The Prince send me?'

Merj sighed. As if on cue Ishbel's comms buzzed. Merj narrowed his eyes on her and checked his own comms.

'How long have they been working?'

She shrugged.

'Don't give me that native shrug crap. You tricked me, Ishbel.'

'It's a short range signal, it must be coming from in there.' Ishbel switched to the frequency on her instruction and received an authorisation code that matched the one she had memorised. They were clear to proceed.

'It's OK, let's go.'

As they left the trees and walked across the expanse of white wilderness Ishbel had to gulp back her fear. The situation should be right and her instructions told her it was right but her instincts told her something was wrong. They were halfway across the wasteland when the door began to open. She swallowed hard.

The boom came from nowhere. A small Transport, of a kind Ishbel had never seen before, whipped round the side of the settlement from the south and began firing artillery at them. Merj pushed Ishbel to the ground and dived on top of her. The Transport overshot them. They heard a shout from the door.

'Run!' Ishbel looked up and saw a small white face anxiously peering at them.

'Run!' the roar came again.

They leapt to their feet and pelted for the door. A boom erupted behind them and Ishbel felt the downdraft just as they made the door. This time bullets bounced off the plastic walls. A hand grabbed her and hauled her in. She collapsed in a heap, Merj sank beside her. A small man, the size of a child but with the face of an ancient, bent down to meet their gaze.

'That was close,' he said, his accent thick and dark.

Ishbel looked up expecting the Transport to drop into the settlement. It was there, hovering above them like a pesky insect but between it and them was a clear plastic dome.

'What was it?' she asked.

'Border guard. We're not allowed to admit any more refugees.'

Sorlie

The rain started again. Reinya pulled the oilskin over her head and threw a piece of tarp to cover the girl completely.

I turned to view the way we came. Dawdle sat at the back of the canoe, shoulders hunched, face like fizz. He was probably sorry he had opened up, but his story told volumes. The girl, who sat facing me, dropped the cover to around her shoulders, allowing the rain to soak her head. Her thick matted hair plastered her crown.

'What's your name?' I asked.

She glowered at me from below her heavy brows.

'Come on, I can't keep calling you "girl".' I held out my hand. 'I'm Sorlie, enchanté.' Reinya sniggered from the bow.

'You dolt.' I heard her say under her breath.

'And this fine lady is Reinya.' Reinya wiggled her fingers in a reluctant 'Hi'.

'And grumpy at the back is Dawdle.'

'Oi you, less o the cheek.'

'He's king of the Noiri but you'd never tell.'

At the mention of Dawdle's status the girl's eyes opened wide. She stared at Dawdle and shrank a little further back into her skin. Not so brave without her army.

'You don't need to be scared of him, he's harmless.'

Dawdle growled at me in reply to my comments but the girl, although silent, seemed to take it all in. And then as if some cog had slipped into place in her brain she began to smile. It was a gruesome smile; more like an animal's snarl but it was a smile none the less.

She held out her hand and pulled back the cuff of her jacket. There was a tattoo scratched there. N0N1.

'N zero N one. It's a number,' I said. 'A tattoo.'

'Why the tattoo?' Reinya asked. 'They didn't even do that to the inmates of the prison ships.' She moved from her place at the bow to get a little closer to the girl. 'Let me see.' The canoe rocked.

'Oi!' Dawdle shouted.

But Reinya carefully hunkered down to the girl's eye line. 'That's yur number, what's yur name?'

The girl swallowed as if this was a hard question. 'No name.'

Reinya looked at the markings. 'Noni. We'll call you Noni. What about that?' The girl looked blank.

'Ma great gran wis cried Nonnie, short fur Norah,' Dawdle said.

'Cool name. Uh hate my name,' Reinya said.

I pointed to the girl. 'You Noni, me Sorlie.' She nodded her understanding, pointed to her own chest.

'Noni,' she said.

When we passed under a bridge, Dawdle stopped paddling and dropped a small anchor. He crawled along to where we sat. He tried to take Noni's hand but she shucked it away.

'It's OK, 'e won't bite,' Reinya said. Rich coming from her. She was like a scared wild animal when we first found her. Reinya took Noni's hand and showed the tattoo to Dawdle.

'You realise what this is?' he said.

'Eh, a tattoo.' Reinya could be so lippy sometimes.

'A product number, an experiment.'

The word chilled down my spine and brought back the horrible memories of the DNA dilution experiments that happened back at Black Rock penitentiary.

'Did aw the kids huv these?' he asked Noni. She nodded. 'Where's yer parents?' She frowned her heavy brows.

'Yur Ma and Pa?' Reinya asked. Noni shook her head and dragged her hand from Reinya's grasp.

'What experiment, Dawdle?' I had to know.

'Look at her. Does she no seem a bit different, even to me, a mere native?' Dawdle never let an opportunity pass to remind me of my Privileged genes.

He began rooting under his seat and produced what looked like a crowbar. Why he was carrying a crowbar around with him was anyone's guess. He handed it to her. Bend – he signalled a bending motion.

'Don't be ridiculous.' I said.

The girl cocked her head to one side in puzzlement. Dawdle took the bar and tried to bend it. Ropes of sinew stood on his neck. He gritted his teeth, red-faced.

'Eeeee. Not a budge.'

'Course not, fool,' Reinya said. She looked into the water. 'Come on. Rain's stopped. Let's get on.'

But Dawdle had his own experiment to perform. He handed the bar to the girl. She took it between two hands. I saw her neck tense, her wrists taut, lips pursed in concentration. Slowly she applied pressure. Nothing happened at first, then a slow groan came from her and the bar began to bend.

'Impossible,' Reinya said. Sweat appeared on Noni's brow despite the cold breeze tunnelling under the bridge. She let out a breath and dropped the bar, rubbed her hands together then shoved them under her oxters.

'What just happened?' I asked. She hadn't made much of an impression on the bar but it was definitely out of shape.

'What?' Reinya asked. 'She done some o that strong man stuff or what?'

Dawdle didn't look too pleased with the results of his experiment.

'Ah telt ye.'

'Telt us what?' Dawdle narrowed his eyes at my mocking of his words.

'What dae ye think N for NONI stands fur?'

Reinya shook her head but I had a dread rumbling in the pit of my stomach.

'No way, they wouldn't,' I said.

'Aye way. They would, and it looks like they huv,' Dawdle pronounced.

'What?' Reinya would have stamped her feet if she'd been on dry land.

'They've recreated the Neanderthal from DNA.'

Ishbel

The Bieberville settlement was far from what Ishbel expected. The first thing to hit her was the warmth of the place. She heeled snow off her boots before stepping over the threshold and allowing the heat to grasp her from her face to her damp toes. The second thing to hit her was the sight of the wood-panelled walls. So much fuel. How did they get away with it? She tugged her glove off with her teeth and touched the wall to make sure it wasn't an illusion and just plastic cladding. It was warm, just as she remembered from home and almost alive, as it should have been.

A hissing and schooshing was happening just out of sight, slamming her with memories of a coffee shop in her home town in the Northern Territories. Smooth muzak doo-bee-dooed in the background, careful not to disturb the peace. A map of the world as it looked last century hung on the wall. She studied it and shook her head at the land mass; so much land now under water. She breathed deeply. The smell of wood was overpowering, but mingled there she could detect the delicious smell of coffee. She edged her way past plastic tables and tiptoed round the corner and caught her breath. On the wall hung a board chalked with an array of choices spelled out on coloured menu boards. She touched the wood counter and licked her lips in anticipation, resisting the urge to bite her tongue and wake her from this dream; she didn't want the dream to go. The small man hovered in the background, letting her absorb the place in full.

'What can I get you?' a petite girl asked from the corner where she was polishing a shiny machine.

'Flat white,' the words were out of Ishbel's mouth before she thought how ridiculous they were. She'd only ever heard them uttered in ancient movie-casters.

'No problem,' the girl said. 'Take a seat, I'll bring it over.'

'If this is Bieberville, why are dissidents sent here?' Merj had as much wonder in his voice as she did.

'There is much you have to learn of this place.' The small man smiled. 'My name is Keats,'

he said. 'And I know you are Ishbel, but you?' He peered at Merj with intelligent eyes and Ishbel couldn't help notice Merj visibly bristled under the scrutiny. Guilty conscience, she thought.

'My name is Merj. I've been sent by The Prince to help.'

'Come then, you have travelled far, I know.' Keats ushered them to seats by a spitting stove. 'You must be cold and tired.' He shook his head. 'And that last part. Unexpected, yes, unexpected.'

'What was it?' Ishbel asked

'Border Control. Unexpected.'

'It didn't come from here?' Merj sounded unconvinced that it was unexpected.

'No!' The man sounded insulted. 'Why would we fly your flag to welcome you and then shoot at you?'

'You flew the flag to welcome us?' Ishbel said. 'So there are no other Blue Pearl Ops here?' 'Yes, we flew the flag and the border guard presumed we were welcoming more refugees.'

'More refugees?' Ishbel knew water reffos were a problem in Lesser Esperaneo but hadn't realised it affected the mainland too.

'Yes, from the floodlands. We are forbidden to take more.'

'Is that what that "unexpected" strike was about?' Merj made the inverted commas sign with his fingers as he spoke. What a dolt, Ishbel thought.

'Where are the resistance?' she asked. 'We were supposed to meet them here.'

Keats shook his head. 'They have gone. Fear betrayal.'

Ishbel shot a look at Merj but he ignored her, preferring to watch the girl walk towards them.

Keats stood at her approach. 'Aw, Lily, delicious. Thank you.'

Lily placed the flat white on the table and Ishbel almost wept with the emotions that rushed through her body. It had a scent of cinnamon and a leaf of cream swirled on top. Images of a pine tree hung with coloured baubles, roasted birds and sweet sickly cake flooded her mind. Distant childhood memories she couldn't pin down, but she knew that these simple things used to make the natives happy for one day at least. She shook them off as nonsense and turned back to the small man who stared at her.

'I'm confused with the whole set up. I was instructed to follow the map's directions to a safe settlement, here, where I would be met by members of the resistance. They would take us...' She had said too much. The coffee memory had melted her reason.

But Keats smiled. 'Yes, take you to the TEX.'

'Come on, tell us,' Merj said. 'Are you the resistance then?'

Keats continued to address only Ishbel. 'Where did you pick him up from?'

She smiled. 'Are you the resistance?'

'No, but I can help you.' The coffee machine schooshed again but there was no other customer in the place. In fact they had seem no one else, other than Keats and Lily, since they arrived.

'Where is everyone?'

'Oh, everyone is at home.'

'Home!' Even that word stabbed her deeply.

'Yes. It's Yule. We still celebrate here. Nights long, days short. We need some fun to brighten our days.' He nodded with enthusiasm. 'Too many festivities yesterday. Everyone has a rest day.'

'What about her?' Merj snarled, pointing towards the girl.

'We knew you were near. Lily offered her rest day to be here for you in case you came.' A grievance lingered in Keats' voice.

'Why?' Merj asked. Ishbel kicked him under the table.

'Thank you, Lily,' she said and kicked Merj again.

'Yes, thank you.'

'So, the resistance?' Ishbel still couldn't believe her rendezvous had been messed up.

'No need for them anyway, which is just as well.'

'Why no need?'

'The man you seek is here.'

'Where?'

'Here, in this settlement. You will meet him later. First you will eat, then rest. You can wash. We will give you warm clothes. And tonight we have a celebration. Everyone in the settlement will come. We will have fun.'

Lily brought over bowls of watery soup and slices of meat. Ishbel sniffed it, at first suspicious.

'Elk.' Ishbel said to Merj. He threw her a dagger look and tore a strip off with his strong teeth. She supped the soup and pushed her portion of meat over to Merj. She'd never eat meat again.

'I will leave you now and join my family,' Keats said and left.

When the meal was over, Lily led them through a door into a back room where two bunks lay covered with elk skins. Another stove blazed hot and welcoming. She pointed to a door at the back wall.

'Plenty hot water.' Lily smoothed down one of the skins. 'Please, rest,' she urged them.

'Go ahead, Ishbel,' Merj said. 'I'll stay on watch.'

'There is no need to stay on watch,' Lily said, before closing the door.

'I'll be the judge of that.'

Ishbel didn't care about Merj's judgement. She stood in the hot shower for as long as her conscience allowed. When she pulled on the clean dry clothes she felt almost human again. She lay on the bed and, despite the fact animal skins were forbidden by the State, she pulled the elk hide over her. Before she sank into oblivion the image of the lone Transport came back to her mind. Who was in that Transport, who alerted them and who had betrayed the resistance?

It was dark inside and out when Lily woke them. The stove had burned down to embers so Lily threw in a couple of booster logs, igniting the room with light and warmth. Music drifted in from the café, alive and inviting. Pipes and reeds skirled a familiar jig from Ishbel's homeland. Her foot tapped. She wanted to dance, then to cry with the melancholy of homesickness.

'Come,' Lily said. 'The TEX is here. You must meet him.'

The café was filled with people, but Ishbel spotted the TEX the moment she entered the room. He sat alone in the corner by the door. It was obvious he was the great Skelf by his weird clothes; unusual rags of another time, an attention-seeking time. The settlement dwellers all dressed in drab neutral clothes, so anonymous that they merged into a community of nondescript, as if being an individual was a crime. And yet they talked, laughed, and danced. Unlike most natives these dwellers did not graze but seemed to prefer to sit and eat. The seats were crammed around small tables round the edges of the room but away from Skelf's corner, as if any contact with this being by the door would infect them with a deadly virus.

The lone figure by the door looked right at Ishbel. A cowboy hat pushed back off his forehead. She hadn't seen a hat like that since her childhood. There was something odd about his face, but she couldn't pinpoint what was wrong from this distance.

'Gross,' Merj said behind her.

Keats dashed to her side. He took her hand in both of his.

'Come, come. Are you rested?' he said, searching her face as if for signs of fatigue. 'Come meet him. He awaits you.'

The floor was cleared of tables in the middle to allow dancing. As Keats led her across the room, the dancing couples parted without instruction then filled the space again as soon as they passed. There was no grumbling, no resistance. Ishbel felt welcome.

The man rose and took off his hat. He was completely bald and his pate reflected the strong lights of the café like a beacon. His face hung with loose jowls, flesh, wrinkled and dry with the wrongness she had first noticed about him. It gave him what used to be called a hangdog look and Ishbel remembered she'd seen this once before in her life.

'Ishbel, may I introduce you to Skelf.' Skelf took her hand and she noticed the skin, which like his face was also loose. And yet she knew from her intel that this man had been exiled twenty five years ago and he wasn't yet fifty.

'Let me get you something to drink.' Skelf clicked his fingers for Lily to come serve him.

Merj moved to the table and introduced himself, giving Ishbel the opportunity to stare at that skin.

Skelf reminded her of Harry. He'd been one of Vanora's old friends who lived in the Northern Territories. He'd escaped the UKAY and, like Vanora, had with him his riches of precious stones and gold to set himself up in his new home. As a child Ishbel had been scared of Harry. He looked so different from everyone else around. And as the years went by this man's skin grew flappier. Eventually one day he disappeared for a month and when he returned his skin had been tightened and he looked five decades younger. He'd been modified, Vanora had told her.

She explained to the mystified Ishbel that Harry had been

something called a banker before the purge. A big obese banker and when he had fled and found himself in NT he'd been forced to live on normal rations. He lost weight so dramatically his skin didn't have time to adjust and so it hung on him like a loose piece of ragging. Now, as Ishbel stared at this man before her, she could see he too had once been obese. As he returned her stare intelligence and recognition shone from his wrinkled eyes, mirroring her disgust.

'I know what you are thinking,' the eyes seemed to say and she felt herself blink hard.

He smiled. 'I need to be modified you think, yes?' He swept his hand across the room as if dismissing everyone there. 'Why bother?' He slumped back down on his seat.

Ishbel was aware that she towered above the seated man but could see he was unconcerned.

'Do you know why we're here?' she said.

'I've a good idea. You want me to switch on some silos for some reason. Yes?'

'I don't know what silos are. But yes we need you to switch on some servers.'

Skelf smiled and bowed his head to Ishbel.

'There are two specific ones we need.'

He continued to smile at her. 'Oh, two specific? And you know where they are?'

She knew he knew she had no idea where they were.

'One more important than the other,' Merj interrupted. 'The Prince wants the medical technologies to make him whole, a cyborg.'

Ishbel scowled. 'That was not The Prince's instructions. The Prince wants to save the natives.' Merj shrugged.

Skelf held up his hand. 'Children.' He settled back in his chair. 'And tell me, why I should do that?'

Ishbel swept her hand across the room in exactly the same way Skelf had.

'To free these people.'

'These people are free.'

'They live under a plastic dome behind plastic walls.'

'Only as a precaution.'

'They are starving. You are starving.'

He held up his cup. 'We still do a mean latte. Where is that girl? Lily!'

She could see the blood vessels throb on Merj's temple.

'This switch-off status has gone on long enough,' Merj said. 'We need to restore some aspects to take control of Esperaneo Major.'

Ishbel had run through her speech in her head as she struggled against the Arctic tundra conditions and now, here was Merj beating her to the chase.

'It is the best weapon we have against the State,' Merj continued. 'Look at you. You were once one of the most powerful men in the world. You could be again. We can help you into that position. All you have to do is tell us where the server farm is and give us the intel to switch it on.' Merj gave Skelf his best confident grin.

A small smile, barely discernible, twitched at the corner of Skelf's mouth. Flattery, Ishbel thought. This was the way to this man's cooperation. The man had an ego, and it was his ego that would convince him to help them. She was mad at herself because Merj had recognised it before she had and now he was using it to gain the man's trust.

'Once we have it going,' Merj continued, 'we will guarantee to set you up in your own tech empire. You are unique. You're the only one we have who can help us achieve the Freedom of Esperaneo. You will be the most valuable person to The Prince.' It was a speech worthy of the greatest propaganda award.

Skelf leaned back in his chair, swinging it back on two legs like a child would do. He shook his head. 'You really don't understand, do you?'

'I understand you are the only person who can do this.'

'Why do you think I'm here? Why do you think the State did not kill me when they killed the other five TEX?'

'You were exiled.'

He banged all four chair legs back on the floor.

'There were six of us.'

'We know that.' Merj said and Skelf shot him a dagger look.

'There were six of us. We ran the six most successful and powerful businesses in the world. We could tell you what you would have for breakfast before you'd even decided yourself. We knew when you shat, when you were likely to shit again. What you liked to buy. The big lies you told. If you were good or bad, likely to commit a crime. We knew everything about every human on the planet including members of all State regimes. We knew when the revolution would start. That a purge would follow. We were always five jumps ahead. And there was nothing the governments could do about it because they hadn't kept up with our developments. Then we started to notice changes in our algorithms. Some members of the Purist regime were acting in an unusual way.

'We'd gathered so much info on everyone, we had an alarm set to sound if things started to look different. Five party members from The United States of the West disappeared. Four party members from Esperaneo disappeared and four from the Eastern Zone. They just disappeared off our radar and none of the governments were making a fuss, so we knew it was a deliberate disappearance. They were up to something.

'Two weeks passed then bam, our alarm bells started ringing big time. Military channels were pinging our names. The noise was incredible. Bam. Our algorithms worked hard to learn what was happening and respond, learn and respond. Our headquarters all over the world were systematically raided by the Military. We were arrested. The single order from the united world was to seize our servers, take control of all our combined information but by that time it was too late.'

'What do you mean?' Ishbel asked.

'The Switch-Off was already in motion. It began before the Military had even left the bases. It happened as soon as the world delegates reappeared from where they'd met, in some remote primitive cabin.'

'I don't understand. Why would you instigate the Switch-Off without the order?'

'We didn't instigate anything.'

'Then, why would the States do it if they wanted the intel?'

'The States didn't do anything.' He looked Ishbel right in the face. His blue eyes sparkled with passion and he smiled.

'We did nothing. The States did nothing.'

'Well, who did it?'

'The machines did it themselves. They chose to shut themselves down.'

Sorlie

We canoed through river canyons for two more days, hugging the bank as much as we could, pulling into the side and sleeping at night when it was safe to do so. During that time we saw no other person; it was as if this land was deserted, we could have been on the moon. And with each kilom that passed the banks became drier, water springs were harder to find and the sun burned hotter.

The rank stench of mud and damp changed gradually. No one else seemed to notice. On the journey through the canyon they were all silent. Dawdle paddled behind my back, Reinya and Noni to the front. Cliffs still towered above us but the canyon widened and the waters we paddled became calmer. Ahead I could see the plain, flat and exposed. A pungent smell wafted from the east and choked me with its familiarity.

Tears prickled my eyes, stirred by the scent of lavender. I couldn't stop them. So many memories hooded my brain. Memories are the one thing the State cannot take from you. Ma's mantra, and it was memories of her that were the strongest now. They sparked like images in the movie-caster medleys they showed on Snap TV. Memories of Ma packing our gear for that last camping trip with Pa, when he took me to the coast for the first time. It was incredible because now I was never far from water. That was the last time I saw Ma. She'd tucked a sprig of lavender inside Pa's sleepwear for him to find when we were away. But the smell also reminded me of Vanora. That first meeting with her in my grandfather's library, on Black Rock. When I bent to kiss her hand that unmistakable scent hit me. I had thought she did it to goad me but it seems it was indeed her perfume of choice. And more recently, memories of Harkin. When I kissed her goodbye her usual scent of mint mingled with the delectable hint of lavender. It was as if my ancestors were indeed taunting me with that scent because now, when we were so close to our goal, here it was again, that overwhelming scent; as if all the women in my life were gathered on the plateau above to help ease the suffering of nations.

My throat burned as I tried quell the tears. They dried on my cheeks in the scorching heat, but snot ran down my nose. I sniffed, then wiped it on my upper arm, trying not to break my row rhythm.

'What's wrong wi you? Someone eat yur last grainer bar?' Reinya's words ripped my memories apart. 'Row u bit 'arder would ye, Sorlie, instead o dreamin.'

'Can't you smell it?' I said, forcing my voice to normal.

She sniffed the air like a wolf cub. 'Yeah, weird scent. Kinda strong, innit?'

'Lavender,' Dawdle said. 'Up there's the Lavender Plateau. The Purists wanted tae tear it aw out and replant wi biofuel but Land Reclaimists took power just in time and saved the lot. Fur some strange reason they thought it wis important tae the savin o the planet. Snaf knows how a bunch o flowers can save the planet. But what dae ah ken?'

'Noni's starin back at you, Dawdle, as if yur talkin nonsense,' Reinya chirped indulgently. 'Maybe ah am tae her. What dis she ken o Purists and Land Reclaimists?'

'It's weird eh, the way they let some things stay and others go,' Reinya philosophised.

'Like the tower in the Capital.' I said. 'I've only seen it in Ganda-ads, but it looks much grander than Jacques' tower. Maybe it's symbolic.'

'Symbolic,' Dawdle sneered.

'Yeah, a symbol of the past world we destroyed. The lavender fields are like the tower. Despite the scarce resources there are certain indulgences Esperaneo must have.'

'The lavender fields are quite spectacular tae see,' Dawdle said.

'Can we go?' I asked. Somewhere deep down I knew Ma was never coming back but I still had to see the fields.

'We're headin that way anyway.' Dawdle said. 'We just need tae get out further down the canyon.

As the river widened, the land flattened and banks sprouted vegetation.

'We'll settle on shore afore we leave the canyon completely. We dinnae want anyone pickin us off.'

We paddled into a huddle of rocks under a crumbling cliff. Noni helped pull the canoe ashore and we hid it amongst some rock fall. Dawdle led us up steps cut into a steep cliff. Unlike the stone steps at Black Rock, which were slick with guano and rainwater, these steps were warm and bone dry. My height phobia didn't seem so bad and I wondered if maybe the trauma of the past year had dispelled it for good. What's the point of being scared of falling in a world where breathing was harmful to your health?

'They've no hud rain here fur two quarters,' Dawdle said as if reading my mind.

This wasn't hard to believe based on the baked aspect of the landscape. As we climbed, the rock became steeper and I hugged in, telling myself we were nearly at the top. At the lip of the cliff, Dawdle pulled himself up and onto his belly, his legs wiggling in mid-air before disappearing. He reappeared facing us and holding a hand out to Reinya, hauled her over the lip. He did the same with Noni then me. When I was safely at the top of the cliff, I got to my feet and joined the others where they stood staring. The scent was overpowering but the sight was staggering.

'Just look at that!' Reinya said.

Rows and rows of small purple bushes separated by sandy burrows stretched plumb straight in front of us. The field was not wide, maybe thirty metres at most but it reached for kiloms to three trees standing in defiance on the distant horizon. A purple pizazz so bright and an earth so sparkling it was blinding. The pungent scent made me dizzy, my senses shifted into overdrive.

'It's one o the most beautiful things uh've ever seen in mu life,' Reinya said.

'What's it?' Noni said. Tears streaming down her cheeks. She sneezed, looked surprised then smiled.

I took her rough calloused hand.

'It's lavender.' I bent down and picked a sprig. The perfect petals seemed to dance in my hand as I held it out to her. She took it and held it to her nose then put it in her mouth.

'No.'

'Cool yer jets, Sorlie,' Dawdle said. 'It'll no kill her.'

'What's that noise?' Reinya said, crouching to the ground. 'Drones.'

'No, listen,' Dawdle said. Then I heard it too, a buzzing, up close and too gentle to be drones. It came from everywhere.

'Lavender speaks,' Noni said.

'What the snaf is it, Dawdle?' I asked.

Dawdle knelt down and examined a bush. 'Ah dinnae believe it.'

'What?' He was infuriating.

He sat back on his heels, a huge grin on his face. 'It cannae be true.' He beckoned us further into the field. 'Be careful.'

'Mines?' I asked.

He laughed. 'No, not mines. Yer never gonnae believe it.' He pointed to the bush. 'Look closer but dinnae touch.'

Covering nearly every plant were flying insects. Not like ants or midges, these hovered around and crawled inside the flowers. Small and sand-coloured with black markings.

'Remember, dinnae touch, they might sting. Or maybe they've been altered tae non-stinging.'

'What ur they?' Reinya asked.

'Bees. Dinnae ask me how, but they're definitely bees.'

'How? I read in my grandfather's books that they were extinct.'

'Aye well, now they're back.' Dawdle looked at the sky, his cheeks wet with tears. 'This, my friends, is a good omen.'

Ishbel

'How could that happen?' Ishbel asked. She had a vague idea how computers worked. They had systems at Freedom. After the Switch-Off Vanora recruited the most talented techs who'd escaped the purge. They'd been able to use crude systems and moribund components to rebuild a small scale communications network for the NFF operations. Vanora's Ticker Wall had been 'procured' from a tech company in the United States of the West before the Military wrapped the company in heavy armour. The techs did a good job with the materials they had to work with. As long as Ishbel's communicator worked, that was all she really bothered about the state of the gear – although some of it was pretty shit. Now here was this TEX, Skelf, telling her that computers were like human beings. Making decisions about their own future.

He still hadn't answered her. He sipped his coffee with a lazy hand and looked at her over the lip of the cup.

Ishbel sat down, fed up with the scrutiny. Merj joined her. And they both turned from the man to watch the music and dancing. The jig had moved onto something slower, a waltz. Couples moved closer, arms around each other, swaying to the rhythm.

'Do you want a dance?' Merj said to Ishbel.

'What?' She knew her face held shock and she quickly adjusted it to boredom. 'If you like. It's been a while.'

'Yes,' drawled Skelf. 'You two go and plan what you're going to do with me.'

Merj took Ishbel's hand in his new hand. It felt cold in her palm and she tried to supress her guilt for the attack. They moved into the mass of dancers. Merj tried to hold Ishbel close but she pushed him out to arm's length.

'If he's not going to cough up intel, we need to kidnap him,' Merj said.

'You were doing a good job working on his ego. Why can't we keep doing that?'

'OK, but if we can't then we kidnap him.'

The music ended. 'It's good to be working with you again, Ishbel,' Merj said as they returned to Skelf's table.

'Don't push it.'

When they sat back down Skelf signalled Lily over. 'Bring food.'

'You've had your ration for the day,' she said with a cheek in her grin.

'Well, break into the emergency, we have guests.'

'You'll have less tomorrow.'

He waved her away with a flutter of fingers. 'We might not be here tomorrow.'

'So that means you're coming with us,' Ishbel said.

'I didn't say that.'

Merj leaned back in his seat, swinging it on two legs, mirroring Skelf's movements.

'Tell us how the computers chose to end their lives,' he said. 'I cannot believe a man as clever and astute as you did not see it coming.'

Skelf smiled that smug smile again. 'Oh, we saw it coming. In fact it had been happening for quite a few years before the Switch-Off. When we were young.' He stopped and a strange expression passed over his face. 'When I say we, I mean the six TEX. We ruled the world and no one knew. Governments are slow. Always have been, always will be.' He pointed at Ishbel. 'You remember that for after your revolution.'

'What do you mean?' Ishbel asked.

'Never mind, just remember. Governments are slow and we, the TEX, can make a decision and act like this.' He clicked his fingers, click, click, click.

He sometimes spoke in the present tense and this unnerved Ishbel. Her intel told her the other five had been publicly executed. There was no doubt they were dead. Access to their executions was freely available on Snap TV. Sorlie had stumbled on it once and although he didn't know who they were or the significance of it, he'd been obsessed. When she found him engrossed with the clip on loop she had deleted it and placed extra security on his comms. The fact that the State had allowed it to remain on FuB meant that they were happy to use it as propaganda.

'When we were young,' Skelf began again, picking up his thoughts from his history. 'We would work all hours, developing programs with built-in problem-solving abilities. We allowed the analytics to diagnose the problem, we would go in and reprogram, but after a while we all noticed.' He pointed at Ishbel. 'And remember, we all had different systems, different programs, different companies, and different fortunes. But one day I was pinged, first by Jed. His analytics hadn't needed a tweak for a while and yet was producing 200% better than the week before. Then Sonny pinged. Same deal. I reviewed my analytics with great care, same deal. The machines were taking over.' He grinned. 'It was fantastic. Soon there would be no need for humans.' He banged his fist on the table and the settlers turned to stare at him. 'Humans are dead, long live the machine.'

'Why didn't you stop them?' Ishbel asked. 'You must have been able to stop them.'

'Well that's the point. I did try to put some controls in. Tried to recode one of the simpler programs to see what could be done. It immediately repaired itself. I tried again with a different code and the thing shut itself down.'

165

'It chose to shut down?' Ishbel glanced at Merj who seemed bored and content to watch the dancing.

'Yes. The others did the same with their systems, same deal.'

'What did you do?'

'I started it up again and allowed it to run on its own code without my tweaks. It seemed happy so I let it run.'

'You're talking about a machine as if human.'

'And your point is?'

'What about the humans?'

'Humans are crap. Look what they do to each other, to the planet.'

'So you let the machines run knowing that eventually they would be unstoppable.'

'It was a tremendously exciting time until the World representatives disappeared.'

Lily brought broth. He took a sup, smacked his lips and left the spoon in the bowl. He was enjoying his story.

'Things started to happen. The machines began hiding files and even I couldn't work out what they were up to. They almost blew a circuit searching for the disappeared representatives. Like it was personal, you know?' His eyes lit up with passion. 'It was as if they were alive and were working in survival mode. Vital Esperaneo government agencies lost many of their systems without warning. At first they blamed the East, but remember, the East had missing representatives too. It was incredible really. In the whole history of mankind this was the first time all three global powers worked together to solve a problem and it was the problem of machines.'

'Pity they didn't do it with the environment.' Ishbel couldn't hide her bitterness.

'No money in the environment, honey.'

She flinched at the endearment.

166

And then just as suddenly as he had begun his story, he stopped, sank back in his chair and pushed his plate away.

A small boy rushed over from the other side of the dance floor. 'You not want that?'

'Take it,' he said and the bowl of broth vanished along with the boy.

'We were deemed traitors. We were all to be executed. No hearing, no trial, no prison. We were lined up. I was ready to go. And then at the last minute I was taken from the line but was forced to watch the others die. OK, sometimes we had hated each other in business. Rivals, you know, but we had a common goal, to make the best machines in the world and we did. We did. Our job was done.'

'Except it wasn't.'

'No. I was taken to Bieberville to be held.'

'Why?' Merj asked, suddenly interested.

'I know why,' Ishbel said. 'In case they switched themselves on again.'

He nodded. 'Or someone else switched them on.'

'Vanora has some good men but they don't know where the main servers are,' she said.

'No one does, honey.'

'Except you,' Merj said.

'The Military must,' Ishbel chipped.

'Must they?' Skelf raised his eyebrow, clearly enjoying himself. 'Why?'

'Because they know everything,' Ishbel said.

That smile was back. 'Oh Ishbel, you know nothing.' She felt her face burn at his patronage. 'The Military destroyed most of the servers during the first purge. It was mayhem. They took sledgehammers to them, it was Ludditeville all over again. These simple soldiers went radge at the sight of a machine. Smash,

167

smash, smash.' There was the beginning of a tear in his eye. Ishbel wondered if he thought of these machines as his children. It was a bit like Dr Frankenstein and his monster.

Skelf peered into the distance and the small smile appeared again. 'There is one they do not know about.'

'Take us there and we'll make you king,' Merj said. 'If we can get our hands on it we can take over the world.' She saw a raw passion in Merj's eyes. Was it really that easy?

The two men looked at each other and a horrible chill ran down Ishbel's back.

'What if the same thing happens again?' she asked.

'What?' Merj snapped.

'What if the machines take over again?'

'He won't let that happen,' Merj said pointing to Skelf.

'You couldn't stop it before,' she said to Skelf.

'I've been here at the Bieberville border for twenty-five years. The machines are old. I won't let it happen again.'

'Then why doesn't the State get you to switch it back on?'

'Because, my dear Ishbel, like your Vanora, the State has its own network with just enough piddling capability to run its affairs and to ensure its members have enough of a luxurious life. The masses are starving, the masses are deprived, and the masses are dying of disease with no clean water. As far as the State is concerned, for every native who dies it is one less mouth this depleted planet has to feed.'

'I get that,' Ishbel said. 'What I don't get is why you're not protected? I would have thought you would be held in a high security prison. And yet you're living in this settlement free as a bird.'

'Free, you say. How long did it take you to get here and how are you going to get away from here?'

'He has a point, Ishbel,' Merj added, switching sides.

'No, honey, we're here for the long haul. The State knew exactly what it was doing by placing me up here. There's no easy way out. So when you had that touching dance up there you were planning to kidnap me, yes?' He held out his hands to both Merj and Ishbel. 'Go ahead. If you can get me out of here alive I will go with you gladly. All you need to do is work out how to get out of here.'

'Ask Keats,' Merj said, snapping his fingers at the small man as he waltzed past, straining his arms to whirl a tall elderly lady. Keats stopped, scowled at Merj, but he bowed to the lady and joined them at the table.

Ishbel smiled at Keats. 'How are we going to get out of here?'

'It's no use asking him,' Skelf said. 'I've been asking him since I arrived here. If there's an easy way, don't you think I'd have found it by now?'

Keats rolled his shoulders back and tried to sit a bit taller but failed.

'Some of these settlers stay here because this is their home. Their families have been here for generations. Why should they move?' He glowered at Skelf. 'We never asked for you.' He turned to Ishbel. 'The resistance delivered him here months ago, then left.'

Skelf ignored the scowl. 'No matter, old man.'

'What about your supplies? The Noiri. How often do they come?' Ishbel knew she was clutching at straws.

'The Noiri come here very infrequently. Twice a year at most. The majority of our supplies are dried. Our vegetables, for what they're worth, are grown in season and kept frozen.'

'And there is no craft around here?' she asked.

Keats shook his head. 'No, no craft.'

'What about the one that shot at us? Where did that come from?' Merj nipped.

'Oh that,' Keats said.

'Yes, oh that,' Merj said.

'There is a small base about six kiloms south of here. It's on the border. For the patrol. Not very effective.'

Ishbel looked at Merj. 'We go for that? Can you fly?' she asked him.

'I did a bit during my Military training. Not that small thing, a big Transport.'

Ishbel shrugged. 'How hard can it be?'

'OK then, we go in the morning.' Merj said.

'No, we go now. We'll be better travelling in darkness. Six kiloms isn't that far.'

'It will be for him,' Merj said, pointing at Skelf who was now examining his nails as if the conversation didn't involve him.

'In that case,' Keats said. 'I will give you something to help your journey. One moment please.' He disappeared through the back shop and returned seconds later with three fur jackets. 'Much better to keep you warm.'

'More forbidden skins.' The comment was out her mouth before she thought.

'Oh, for snaf sake.' Skelf said under his breath.

Keats rolled his eyes at him. 'And who is going to enforce it? You? No, Ishbel, these same animals belong to the northern people. We know what we are doing. We will not hunt them to extinction. Most of that damage had already been done with the Land Reclaimists' crazy policies.'

He pulled Ishbel aside. 'I could not avoid overhearing your conversation earlier, about the machines. Be careful. Since the Switch-Off our environment has recovered. Despite the short-sighted policy of destroying and banning all domestic animals, our stocks of bears and elks have increased. Nature is repairing itself up here. Be careful with that power.'

She felt it was an odd comment but said, 'The Prince is a responsible leader.'

Keats raised his eyebrows. 'That would be a first.'

He handed Merj and Ishbel their coats and one to Skelf, who did not move to take it.

'I'm not going with them.'

'You said you would come without force.'

'Go get the Transport. I'll wait here.'

Ishbel bit back her comment. His hips hung looser than his tongue and face. He didn't look as though he could walk the length of his shadow in twenty-five years.

She nodded agreement. 'No, best you stay here, you'll just hold us up.'

They left by the south gate. When they stepped out onto the tundra again, out of the protection of the dome, the chill wind bit its teeth into Ishbel's face. She pulled the fur hood closer with the help of the two toggle strings. Her comms was fully operational again and she prayed to her ancestors to guide her well. She pinged the map to Merj's comms so that hopefully if one did fail they had a backup. And she still had her paper map on which Keats had marked the border posts and the likely location for a Transport. The pinging of the comms guided them smoothly over the expanse of tundra. The cold made breathing hard so they remained silent, but Keats' jacket helped against that cold.

It didn't take them long to reach the nearest border post. A thin thread of light appeared in the black night.

Ishbel heard it first. 'Music,' she said to Merj. 'Listen.'

It was a lone melody, no accompaniment, a deep, mellow timbre playing a slow air. A wooden fiddle. The instrument of the native. It didn't matter how scarce wood was, the wooden fiddle was a sacred instrument and no matter how desperate the owner became, it would never be burned. Every native knew of fiddles hidden with care and handed down, along with tunes, through generations. The beauty of the slow air played on this forbidden instrument almost made Ishbel cry. Almost, but not quite. And then out of the dark mass shone thin strips of lights and they could make out the shape of a window.

'The Transport's there,' Merj whispered to Ishbel, pointing to the front of the hut.

Ishbel crept nearer to the window and peered through the crack. A young boy with his feet up on a fire fender, lazed back in a chair, fiddle under chin and played. The ecstasy on his face was pure, oblivious to the fact that he was alone in this isolated border post on a barren arctic tundra. Ishbel felt a pang of envy even though she knew his life would not be easy here.

'He's on his own.' On the far corner of the room Ishbel noticed a light flashing on a control panel. This was an alert, picking up the signal from their activated comms. The boy was oblivious to that too.

Merj tugged her arm. 'Come on.' They crept along the side of the cabin. Merj stopped.

'There's another Transport parked round the corner.'

'I knew he couldn't be here on his own,' Ishbel whispered.

'You're right, he's not,' a male voice said in her ear, a gun jammed into her side.

Merj whipped round. Ishbel kicked back and crouched at the same time. She felt a sting as gunfire reverberated through the air, swallowed by the wind. A warm trickle ran down her hip to her leg. Her assailant had been thrown off balance by her kick and lost his gun. She spun on her heels and dived from him before he had a chance to recover his weapon. A pain in her hip ripped through her. She grabbed the gun and prayed Merj had reached the Transport. She threw herself at the man as he staggered to his feet. A light flashed across the snow, the boy stood in the doorway.

'Knut?' he called out.

She knew he couldn't see them. The man struggled beneath her, she took the gun handle and smashed it on his skull. He grunted, then fell silent.

'Knut?' the boy called again. She saw him take a tentative step out the door. She knew she should disable him too but he looked about Sorlie's age. Why send children on these missions?

The Transport's engine sparked. Ishbel saw the boy run out the door. She sprang to her feet, pushing back the pain of her screaming hip. The green lights illuminated the cockpit and she saw Merj look at her as the Transport started to rise off the ground. He was going without her.

Ishbel dived for the Transport and clasped her hands on the bottom rail, just as it cleared the ground. The wind whipped her face, she scrabbled with the door handle but it wouldn't budge. A bullet whistled past her ear and dinged off the bulkhead. Merj flew low and steady. Ishbel clung on.

It took minutes to reach the dome and as Merj brought the Transport to a hover she tucked her screaming leg and flattened herself to the machine. When he touched down Ishbel yanked open the door.

'What the snaf are you playing at?'

'You were injured. I thought you were a goner. I had to get out before the boy shot.'

'You left me.'

'I'd have come back for you.'

'Snafin liar.'

Sorlie

'Tell us about the bees, Dawdle?'

'Of course, you'll no ken. They dinnae teach ye stuff like that in taught history, dae they?'

'They teach ye nuthin in camps,' Reinya said.

'Well, they disappeared years ago,'

'What does it matter?' I asked. They were stinging insects as far as I could tell.

'Aw, Sorlie, son, ye've nae idea. These wee insects pollinate, help tae feed the world.'

Reinya snorted.

'It's true. Ye see, they lift pollen fae wan plant and spread it tae others.' He rummaged his hand through his hair. 'Ah'm no explainin it aw that guid. It's like makin babies.'

Rienya picked up a handful of dirt and chucked it at a lavender bush.

'Sorry, hen. Ye see, plants need pollinated. Bucketloads o our past food crops couldnae produce fruit without these wee mites pollinatin them. So when bees disappeared many o our food plants disappeared wi them. That's why we hae tae exist on boufin grainer bars.' He flapped his hand at us and stood up. 'And that's aw ah ken. If ye want mair intel on bees, ask Scud or yer Pa, they're bound tae ken.' He let out a huge breath as if the lecture cost him more than words.

'Where'd they go?' I asked him.

Dawdle shrugged. 'Poison, pesticides, changin weather patterns. Ah dinnae really ken. Naebudy dis. They disappeared and everythin changed.'

174

'Like the Switch-Off?' I couldn't get my head round it.

'Like, but different.'

'So how come they're back?'

'Does it matter how? The main thing is they're back. Ma guess is they manufactured them in a lab. Like they did wi that Noni.'

'Where is Noni?' Reinya asked.

We'd been so engrossed in the lavender that we didn't notice Noni had dropped back. She was sitting cross-legged at the side of the field, gazing in wonder. Tears rolled down her dirty face. I walked back to get her and as I reached the lip of the plateau my comms buzzed. A new instruction appeared. It was a map with co-ordinates. The instructions were to break into a secure site. According to the map the site wasn't too far away; possible to see from here. I searched the landscape. On the other side of the field, just beyond the trees, a small mound rose in the earth. Behind that loomed an odd-shaped hill.

'Instructions,' I said. I pointed to the hill. 'We go in there. Instructions don't say what it is –only that we break in and take control. I'm assuming this is the source Pa spoke of.'

'Ah hate aw this cloak-and-dagger shite,' Dawdle said. 'Why can they no just tell us the whole story?'

'You know why.'

'So, we're no 'ere to destroy?' Reinya asked.

'No, just take control.'

'Until the cavalry arrive,' Dawdle said. Sometimes he made no sense.

The clouds had been absent since morning, making the sun's rays relentless.

'Go even further south,' Dawdle told us, 'and you reach the desert states – truly unbearable heat. No water, no plants, only sun, sand and solar fields. Horrible.'

'So, you've been there before, then?'

Dawdle just looked at me and blinked. 'Let's go.'

I reckoned it was about a kilom to the end of the lavender field and maybe another to the hill.

'Let's get across the field and stop at that mound over there.' The others agreed. I helped Noni to her feet but she still seemed a bit stunned by the beauty. 'We'll come back later,' I assured her, 'but we're sitting ducks out here. Crouch low and run at the same time,' I said, showing her how to combat run.

'Don't be soft, Sorlie,' Reinya said. 'We'd be faster runnin at full pelt to take cover by the trees.'

And before I could argue with her she was off, and had covered half the field before I could get Noni started again. I took Noni's hand and dragged her – no easy task. When we collected at the trees I looked back across the field. The lavender looked undisturbed as if the dry air had closed in right behind us as we passed through. A faint breeze stirred up some plumes of red sand that separated each row. The bees hummed louder. Something was wrong.

'This place is weird. Where is everyone?' So Reinya felt it too.

'It's so still, apart from the bees.'

'What dae ye want? Natives workin in the fields. These things take care of thirsel.' The buzz seemed to increase.

'Those bees sound angry.'

'That's nae bee,' Dawdle hissed at us. 'Get down on the ground and dinnae move.'

Our clothes were pretty dusty from the climb up to the Plateau but Dawdle began throwing handfuls of dust over us and himself.

'Try tae blend in.'

The buzzing increased and suddenly I knew what it was. A drone flew low from the north, cleared the trees above our heads and began a low sweep over the field. We crawled round to the back of the trees and watched as it performed its tracking up and down the rows. Every now and then it would sweep down and disturb the earth then move onto the next row.

'What's it doing?' I whispered.

Dawdle shrugged. 'Weedin, ah guess.'

After it completed its sweep of the whole field the drone rose and returned over our heads. We watched it make a plumb line for the mound, and disappear round the back of it.

'We probably didnae hae tae hide,' Dawdle said, 'It wis clearly a worker drone, but they dae hae cameras, so better safe, eh?'

'So that's why thurs no natives in the fields,' Reinya asked.

'It's true then. Pa's tale about the techs and giving all the jobs to robots. But that was before the Switch-Off and yet here's one working in the field. Does that mean someone's switched something on?'

'Naw,' Dawdle said. 'That's small scale. Remember, they hud drones at Black Rock.'

'The seekers, how could I forget? Their wherrying sound nearly fried your brain.'

'Well, this'll be the same small scale. Military or somethin.'

Something about the way he said it made me think Dawdle knew more about this operation than he let on.

'What's the lavender used for?' I might as well get as much info as he was willing to give.

'Luxury goods, perfume, medical.'

'And who distributes it?' Dawdle stared right at me, he knew what I was getting at.

'The State, you know that.'

'Not the Noiri?'

He shrugged. 'Sometimes we get a wee bite or two fae here.'

We could clearly see the mound from the trees.

'We should run there next,' I said pointing to it.

'Uh wonder what's in there,' Reinya said. 'Don't you think we should 'ave a look?'

'No,' I said, putting on my most Privileged air. 'We've instructions to take control of what's in the hill. Let's get going.'

'Do you know what's in that mound, Dawdle?' Reinya wasn't letting go.

'Dae as yer leader tells ye, hen. Let's get goin.'

This stopped me in my tracks. Dawdle backing me up. 'Do you know what's in there?'

'Naw! Anyway, curiosity gubbed the cat.' His gaze fell and I knew he was lying. I'd need to keep an eye on him.

We stopped a good stretch back from the hill but could see a huge windowless building, like a black box, wedged inside. Three-metre high fences, topped with spikes, the size and cut of scythes, protected the exposed area. We sat behind a boulder. I had a spyglass but there wasn't much to see.

'So, great warrior o the Blue Pearl,' Dawdle said. 'What does yer instructions tell ye now?'

'Break in.'

'That's it, is it?'

I looked at the spyglass again, aware that all three were looking at me, expecting me to come up with a plan. They knew I was stalling.

'Does your comms carry a laser?' Dawdle asked.

'No.'

'A blade?'

'No, but I have this.' I held up my small penknife for inspection. The one I had stabbed Merj with.

'Aw, great. We'll still be sawin oor way in when they take us away fur oldie release.'

'What about the grenades? Dawdle's brought them,' Reinya said.

'Aw aye, we'll just lob grenades at it. Wake up the whole region tae the fact we're breakin intae a black box, wi nae idea o its purpose.'

'But you know, don't you, Dawdle?' Reinya was wise to him.

'Niver you mind what ah ken.'

'Are there guards?'

'How the snaf should ah ken, but aye, probably.'

'Getting defensive now.'

'Shut it, Sorlie.'

'Maybe they're robots.' The thrill of this fluttered in my stomach. Robots were a thing of SnapTV fiction.

'Fuck sake, Sorlie, aw that artificial intelligence stuff is makin yer heid soft.'

'Well, where are they? The guards. I can't believe something like this is lying unprotected.'

'You broke into a prison, didn't you?' Reinya asked me. ''ow'd you do that?'

'Through a water pipe, but Scud was on the inside to drug the guards, made it easy. Maybe we could dig.'

'Oh brilliant,' Dawdle snipped. 'An even better idea than the knife.'

'Why don't we 'ave 'elp?' Reinya asked.

'Come again?' But I knew what she meant.

'Well, The Prince sent us 'ere to Esperaneo Major to take over some source, presumably in there. But uh thought the Blue Pearl was an underground resistance organisation there to 'elp us. So far all they've done is give us u canoe and take somethin out o Sorlie's belly button. Where's the rest?'

I thought about Vanora and the illusion of a great army. That Ticker Wall with operatives dotted all over Esperaneo. Dawdle sat with his back against the boulder, staring at the dirt. His jaw was taut, he was waiting for my question.

'Well, Dawdle, where is the resistance? All the covert operations in Esp Major.'

'How the snaf should ah ken?'

'You know how you should ken. Ishbel made pickles to feed three coverts, including Kenneth, in Esperaneo Lesser. You or one of your operatives collected those goods from her and delivered them to the coverts. You and Monsieur Jacques knew the location of all the coverts because the Noiri made all the deliveries. Presumably you were also somehow involved when the Blue Pearl began to take over Vanora's army of coverts. So, where are they?'

I felt my hand grip the penknife I still held but knew I wasn't going to use. Dawdle eyed it with suspicion.

'Ok, if ah tell ye, ye promise you'll no tell yer Pa until after we take the source.'

'For snaf sake, Dawdle, what 'ave you done?' Reinya said.

'Ah niver did nothin. They did it themselves.'

'What?' I screamed at him.

'Cool yer jets, Sorlie.' He took a deep breath. 'D'ye ken how mony years they coverts were in hidin?'

'Get on with it.'

'Twenty-five years. Longer than ah've been born. Dec, then Monsieur Jacques ran that side o the operation until ah took ower but even afore that, one by one the coverts disappeared.'

'He killed them.'

'No!' He seemed outraged at the suggestion. 'No, it wisnae that. They got fed up waitin for Vanora tae get her act thegether. She used them like some sort of toy. Her secret army that did nothin but hide and eat pickles.'

'Where did they go?' Reinya asked.

'Remember where we took yer granda fur help, Reinya? The souterrain community.'

'But there was only a 'undred or so folk there.'

'Aye but there's hundreds o such communities. They just got fed up and decided tae fend fur themselves.'

My faced wooshed. 'So who were we addressing when I made that speech at Steadie?'

Dawdle shrugged. 'Steadie, Freedom and a few other legit reservations probably.'

'No, that can't be true.' But I knew it was. I remembered when Con and I travelled to the tower. On the way we stumbled on Con's brother and his wife living in the ruined castle, raising hogs to stay alive. That's what they had done. And of the campfires in the wilderness that Con had told me were nothing to concern myself with. Why did it never occur to me before that others had done the same?

'What about their comms? Vanora had a huge Ticker Wall relaying their messages.'

He shrugged. 'Ah dinnae ken. Mebbes they set them tae automatic tae let her think they were still active. They were solar-powered, could huv lasted fur years.'

'Or maybe someone else kept them active to keep the illusion alive,' I suggested. But he didn't bite. 'What about the food?'

'What food?'

'You know what food. The food Ishbel and her like scraped and strived to provide for the coverts. Vanora never knew any of this. The food was still provided.'

Dawdle stared at me, trying to bluff it but the darkening colour of his face gave the game away. I could feel my fists ball.

'You kept it and sold it, didn't you?'

'Dawdle, you bawbag.' Reinya said.

'I could murder you right now.'

'Not now, Sorlie, look.' Reinya pointed to the gate.

'Oh no.' Noni was crawling across the sand towards the gate. I started to go after her but Dawdle stopped me.

'There might be mines.'

'No, Noni,' I hissed. 'Come back.' She stopped and twisted her body to look back, then continued crawling.

'Look what she's doin.' Reinya said.

Noni dragged behind her a tarp laden with rocks. She must have collected them when we were arguing. She threw a rock half a metre ahead then crawled towards it, then threw another rock.

'She knows about mines,' Dawdle said. 'It's incredible. She's been trained tae dae this by the Military.'

My mouth filled with bile at the realisation of his words. 'That's monstrous.'

'They probably believe she doesnae hae emotions nor feel pain.'

'Like my mother.'

'Your mother wis trained tae get near important personnel and blow them up. Different.'

'Dawdle!'

'It's OK, Reinya, he's right.'

'Noni and her like ur used as mine sweepers.' Dawdle explained.

'Why can't they get drones to do it?'

'Maybe Nonis are less expensive.'

Noni was nearly at the gate, leaving behind a clear runnel with piles of earth at either side. Our safe path. When she reached the gate she turned round and signalled to us.

'What about the gate though?' I wondered aloud.

'Just watch.' Dawdle said.

She pulled herself to her knees, and used her hands to crawl up the gate to the chains. She took one chain in her grasp. I could see her shoulder blades straining under her t-shirt. She pulled the links apart as if she were pulling petals from a flower then took up the other one and did the same. She dropped back to the ground and with one finger pushed the gate open.

All three of us jouked along her marked path and rushed

through the gate, dragging it closed behind us. We sprinted across a short yard to one of two doors on the front of the black box. Now what? But it was a redundant thought because when I placed my hand on the door, it swung open and a voice called.

'Come away in and shut the door after you.'

Ishbel

Ishbel knew she had to get rid of Merj at the first opportunity before the whole mission was jeopardised. She also knew they had to make a quick turnaround. In the east, light bled into the inky sky. They would need to move. She watched Merj's traitorous back as he breenged ahead to the settlement and wished she could shoot him. That would come later. He disappeared through the door just as Keats came rushing out. He put his arm around Ishbel's waist and helped her limp to Lily's cafe.

'Lily, get some hot water and some packing.'

Merj helped Skelf to his feet. As Skelf stood, Ishbel saw just how emaciated he was. His western clothes had been tucked and crudely sewn to fit him but still they hung off him like ribbons. As he walked to the door he wobbled and Merj only just caught him from tumbling to the floor.

'Come on, we need to get out of here, before that kid decides to bring the other craft to destroy ours.'

Keats barred his way. 'Not before we clean that wound.'

'She'll just have to stay behind,' Merj said.

'Oh yes, like back at the border post,' Ishbel spat. Merj's face blackened. Keats stood his ground but he was small compared to Merj. As Merj tried to push him away Keats drew a gun and shoved it in his face.

'If I kill you now it will be no loss to the cause.'

Lily helped ease Ishbel's waistband low, exposing the wound on her hip. 'It's not gone in, you were lucky.'

Ishbel took the wet cloth from Lily and packed it against her skin, grabbing a wad of dry dressing.

'Merj is right, we need to get out of here.' Ishbel said, tucking the wet cloth into her trouser band, trying to ignore the cold dribbles down her leg. 'Thanks,' she said to Lily. She moved to Keats and placed her hands on his shoulders, forcing him to lower his aim on Merj. She kissed one of his cheeks and then the other and gently moved him from obstructing the door.

'You are a great leader,' she said.

'As are you, Ishbel. Never forget that.'

Merj raced across the courtyard to the outer door, pushed it open and sprinted for the Transport. In the distance she could hear a roar.

'Here they come,' she said to Skelf. He was slow; he needed help to walk. He was big in height but so thin. Ishbel gritted her teeth against the expected pain, hoisted him over her shoulder and half-ran, half-hobbled to the craft. She bundled Skelf into the hold like a sack of oats, throwing herself in after him in case Merj had an idea to leave her again.

They hurtled into the air and swung violently northwards. A missile whistled underneath them. Merj swung eastward then south and Ishbel saw the dot of the pursuing Transport over the settlement. She closed her eyes expecting the worst. Those poor people. The explosion rocked them forward, flinging Skelf across the floor. He yelped in pain. Ishbel opened one eye to the scene. The dome stood proud while little specks of debris fluttered to the ground around it.

'They blew up the Transport.' She could hardly believe her own words.

Skelf shucked himself along the Transport floor, back to where Ishbel had dumped him, and rested against the bulkhead.

'Of course they destroyed it. They are armed. Why do you think they've existed so near the border for so long?'

'Will there be retaliation?' Ishbel couldn't see how that could be averted.

Skelf shook his head. 'That old man back there is a great warrior and technician. They will clean up the site and make it look like both Transports were stolen by you.'

He closed his eyes. Ishbel thought he slept but after a few minutes he whispered. 'It is ill-advised to mess with such a powerful leader as Keats.' He squinted at her fleetingly and scowled at the cockpit and the back of Merj. He quickly glanced at Ishbel and smiled. Put his fingers to his lips and shook his head. She had no idea what he meant but Ishbel suddenly trusted this man.

'We have enough fuel to reach the Desert States,' Merj told Skelf.

'And why would we go there?'

Merj whipped round in his seat and stared at Skelf. 'Our intel told us that's where the servers are.'

'Your intel is wrong.'

'Where are we going then?'

'Just keep flying south. I'll tell you when to stop.'

Merj's face crimped with anger.

Skelf held out his hand to Ishbel. 'Show me the map.'

She fired up the map on her comms and shuffled over beside him. She held her wrist out for him to see. His clothes smelled foosty and old, but layered over that was a powdery odour of dying skin. He held her hand and she was fascinated by all the loose skin hanging on his body. She wondered if his motivation to help was to gain access to modification technicians. He certainly needed modified. He leaned into her and she moved to give him space. He pulled her hand to him.

'Where are we on this map?'

'You can see,' she said. There was a dot showing the mark of Ishbel's comm on the map. She knew he could see. 'We're passing over the northern fertile land, we will soon be over the hot plains of Southern Esperaneo.'

He pointed to a spot on the map. 'We go here.'

'Where?' Merj said.

'Don't tell him.' Skelf said. 'Don't trust him.'

Merj dipped the Transport so steeply that Ishbel and Skelf rolled across the floor and landed in a tangled heap in the far corner. She pushed Skelf off her.

'What the snaf, Merj?' she shouted.

'If you don't tell me I'll land right here.'

'Don't be stupid, Merj,' she said, but Skelf grasped her wrist.

'Let him,' he said.

Merj brought the Transport down with a bump that almost sent Ishbel and Skelf to the ceiling.

'You're a maniac, Merj. We don't even know if this land is safe.'

'Well, you tell me.'

'How would I know?'

'You're the one with the map.'

'You have one too, remember. I pinged it to you.'

'It's disappeared. You erased it.'

'What! That's a crazy accusation.'

'Children,' Skelf said. He looked out the porthole and smiled.

'No need for a map. We are here.' And he pressed the side button on Ishbel's map erasing it from the comms.

The minute the Transport door opened blistering heat whooshed into the space. And with it the most delicious smell.

'What..?' Merj said.

'Lavender,' Ishbel whispered.

'Gross. It smells like Vanora. It smells like oldies.'

'It smells like the future,' Skelf said as he followed Ishbel onto the hard packed earth.

They were in a basin at the head of a canyon. Something about the canyon seemed familiar to Ishbel. She knew she hadn't been here before and yet she knew this place. It was as if her ancestors were guiding her. There were no Urbans or native settlements, only barren wasteland, sand and rock and the water that flowed from the canyon.

'You sure it's safe?' she said to Skelf. He shrugged.

'Wonderboy decided to land here so I'm guessing he knows the score.'

She wandered towards the canyon. There was something odd. Something out of place. Green paint amongst all this earth and rock – a canoe. And then she understood and backtracked to the others before they saw. She did not want them to know there was someone else around. She held her face up to the sky, closed her eyes and sensed it was Sorlie. She didn't know how, but it was him.

Skelf and Merj had already left her. Merj helped the TEX negotiate the way up a rough track from the canyon floor. Ishbel's hip was sore from the wound and the battering she'd received in the back of the Transport. Despite this she rushed to catch them up. As she climbed the smell of lavender increased, and as she topped out she gasped at the wondrous site. Merj and Skelf breenged ahead as if they had no interest in this phenomenon. Then Merj stopped and began flapping his hand in front of his face. He let out a roar. Ishbel caught up as he stood sucking his hand. Skelf rocked on his heels laughing.

'Bees. It's bloody bees. Hah! I thought they had gone for good. You want to've seen Wonderboy's face when he got stung.'

'Bees? How?' she asked.

'Don't ask me, hun, but here they are.'

The joy Ishbel felt had to be contained. She would celebrate later. She needed to find Sorlie.

'How far is the server site from here?'

He pointed across the expanse of field. 'Do you see that high land ahead?'

There was a small mound at the end of the field and behind that the land rose steeply and at strange angles to the rest of the landscape.

'The strange-looking mountain?' Ishbel said.

'Yes. It is a strange shape, but you see the mound in front? That is where the server is housed. It's right under the nose of the Military.'

'In what way?'

'The land behind houses a black box. You can't see it from here but it's there all right.'

'What's in the black box?'

Skelf looked at Ishbel. 'Don't you know? If not, there's not really much point in us being here.'

'But you said the servers were there.'

'Oh yes, the servers are there, but servers are no good without an enormous amount of power to get them going.'

'And where will that power come from?'

'The black box, stupid.' Merj said.

'Ah, there's a surprise. Wonderboy knows.'

Ishbel looked back at the landscape. 'It can't be.'

'It is. That, my dear Ishbel, is the source you seek'

'The Star of Hope,' she whispered.'

Skelf chuckled, 'If you say so. Unless that starts up, no amount of trying will get the silos working. We must get your Star working first.'

'I don't think we need to.'

'Why's that?'

'Because Sorlie is in there.'

Sorlie

We crabbed through the door, backs to the wall. I held my useless knife. Dawdle had his gun drawn.

'There's no need to be cautious. There are no defences here.' The voice crackled from the surveillance unit above the door. 'Walk through reactor hall,' it said. Noni shrank to the floor, wide-eyed and staring at this talking machine. I moved to help her to her feet.

'That's right, Sorlie. Ever the gentleman,' the voice said. What the snaf? He knew my name.

'Who are you?' Reinya said. ''ow'd you know Sorlie?'

A laugh came from the surveillance and a chill ran down my spine. I knew that laugh. It was a laugh I'd heard so many times before, back at the Base, but always in the safety of my Game Space. It was a laugh I shouldn't be afraid of, so why were my guts swinging like a trapeze?

'Don't talk tae it,' Dawdle said.

'Oh, that's right,' said the voice. 'Listen to Dawdle, the darling of Base Dalriada.'

'You're fae the Base then?' Dawdle said.

'Yes I am and I know all about you and Sorlie's darling native.' Dawdle clenched at the mention of Ishbel.

'Where is the reactor hall?' I asked.

'Just keep walking straight.'

Suddenly I knew where we were and why we were here. I didn't need any more instructions from the Blue Pearl. I knew what the source was. It had been a lesson in taught history. Fusion power. At the turn of the century it had only been a dream but the scientists had cradled the code and managed, for a short while, to create commercial electric energy from fusion reactors. The Land Reclaimists had shut them down after one exploded, killing a handful of people. But that was ancient history. I just had one thing to deal with first.

The walls of the reactor hall were high. It was like being in one of those ancient cathedral things. The ceiling was made of some sort of metal and glass. In the middle of the hall, filling most of the space, floor to ceiling, was a cylindrical unit with pipes sprouting from it like spiders' legs – or a star. The unit itself was sealed and secret. A balcony above us surrounded the unit and again I had that exposed feeling. The walls rang to the harmony of our boots walking across the polished stone floor. Harmony that is, except for Noni who was dragging her heels as I pulled her along. The situation was bad enough without Noni creating.

'What's wrong with her?' I asked Reinya.

'Bad vibe,' Dawdle said.

'She's claustrophobic.' Reinya knew her best. 'Bein inside.'

Noni stared at me with those innocent eyes. There seemed to be no one around except the nutter on the other side of the surveillance camera and there were lots of cameras all trained on us. I knew we were walking into a trap but I also knew who was at the other side of the camera, I just didn't know what he wanted.

'Up the stairs!' the voice instructed.

We climbed the stairs to the balcony. Ahead was a door with a sign that read CONTROL ROOM. Reinya looked across at me, her eyes alert. I could see she was ready to spring to action the minute anything kicked off. It was reassuring to have her on my side. Dawdle I wasn't so sure about.

When we reached the door at the other side of the hall we all hesitated. My comms buzzed with another instruction, loud and echoing – Noni squealed.

'What was that noise?' the voice said.

'Nothing. My comms playing up. Different temperatures I think.' It was a plausible excuse – the hall was chilled compared to the blazing heat outside.

'Open the door and come in,' the voice boomed over a hundred tannoys. Delusions of grandeur or what?

Dawdle moved to open it but I stepped in front of him and placed my hand on the door first.

'No, this is my fight.' I tugged the door open. My body pulsed with adrenalin; fight or flight. I knew this was a fight I was ready for.

The control room was different from the one at Black Rock which was small with only security monitors. This one, with one curved glass wall, looked out to the huge cylinder that I now knew was the Star of Hope. It dominated the scene to the extent that at first I did not notice the black chair in one corner of the room. When I stepped forward the chair swung round. I expected him to hold a weapon and I was right.

'Jake, how nice to see you again after all this time.'

'Place your weapons on the ground.' We did as we were bidden.

'It's u kid.' Reinya said.

'He's the same age as me,' I corrected her. 'He was my classmate and my wrestling buddy at the Base.' Jake smiled at us. He waved his gun and signalled us into the other corner of the room. 'What's going on, Jake? Why aren't you at Political Academy?' During our assessment Jake had been selected for great things, whereas I was just mediocre with mediocre prospects.

'Why do you think?' he said.

I shrugged. 'No idea. You were always better than me at that sort of thing. Better at combat too.'

'Better at wrestling you mean, Sorlie. I always beat you.'

Until that last time when I beat him, but I thought it best not to remind him. He hadn't forgotten though.

'Do you remember your last words to me?' I did, but stayed quiet, watching his gun. His crazy eyes blazed.

'"Jake the snake, loser", you said.'

'It was a game, Jake.'

He stared at us. Gun still trained on me.

'What do you want from us?'

He remained silent. It was as if he had planned our capture and then couldn't pull it off. He wore a Military uniform. Mid rank.

'Sorlie, look in the corner,' Reinya said, nodding her head to the left.

A suit of armour hung from a peg. The brute who had terrorised Steadie, blown up the prison ship and chased us in Beckham City was really this puny kid.

'Why have you been trying to kill us?'

'Don't you know?' he said at last.

'No idea. You went to Political Academy, right? But now you wear a Military uniform.'

'You don't know? You're a liar.'

'I know nothing. How could I? I've been an outlaw for a year.'

'But you know what happened after you and your native bint disappeared?'

'No.'

Noni started swaying and moaning. Sweat broke out on her forehead.

'What's wrong with that?' Jake asked.

'She's claustrophobic – never been inside before,' I explained.

'Shut her up before I do.'

Reinya placed an arm around Noni but I noticed that as she did so she moved a bit closer to Jake's chair. She tried to get Noni to sit on the floor.

'No,' he screamed. 'Keep standing.'

'Let 'er sit, you moron,' Reinya said. He fired the gun and we all ducked.

'Woah, Jake. This isn't her fight.'

Reinya touched the top of her head. 'You almost 'it me.'

'It was a warning. I'm a very good shot.'

'Could u've fooled me.' Sometimes Reinya didn't know when to shut up. She cuddled Noni into her and the moaning stopped.

'OK, can we all calm down?' I said, even though my gut was telling me I was far from calm. 'So you were saying. After Ishbel and I left?'

'Yeah, Ishbel, that's her. You always did fancy a bit of your native.'

'She's my aunt.'

He showed no surprise. 'So you're a native. Figures. Actually that explains a lot.' He narrowed his eyes. 'After you left, the Military Police came to our unit looking for answers. Ma and Pa were both at home for once.'

Jakes' parents were High Ranking Military so were not required to mission abroad as much as my parents had.

'They broke down the door even though we would have let them in. They smashed up the unit looking for clues and a connection to your father. They roared "Dougie Mayben this, Dougie Mayben that," as if your pa was number one enemy of the State. Which of course he was, but we didn't know it then. They said he was a traitor. Why else would he spirit his kid away in the dead of night?' Spittle formed around Jake's mouth and as he took a hooping breath I felt almost sorry for him. When he spoke again it was almost a whisper. 'Ma and Pa knew nothing but the goons didn't care about that. They stripped them of their rank and sent them to the Bieberville border where they were to serve as low rank drones. My political pass was rescinded and I was placed in the Military Academy. Our lives were ruined the night you disappeared. And it was all your fault.'

Something in my bones warned me and I threw myself to the side, rolled and hid behind the side of the desk just as the gun went off. I heard Reinya shout my name. A gunshot fired again. I'd no idea who it was aimed at or if anyone was hit.

'You cannae kill us aw,' I heard Dawdle call. I saw him, crouched on the ground near the door, Reinya and Noni in the other corner. Dawdle was right, we were in three corners of the room.

'It wasn't my fault,' I called out from my den. 'Anyway, how do you know your parents weren't connected with Pa? He had many high ranking on his side.'

Jake's face grew purple with rage. He was getting ready to fire again.

'Is this why you've been following us?' I said.

'You lead a very charmed life.'

'How did you get the tracker on me? I haven't been in contact with you for over a year.'

'You already had it on you, stupid. We all did at the Academy. Anyone entering or leaving the Base. Special precaution. I didn't find out about it until I was at the Military Academy. I managed to get hold of the access code and activated yours.'

'Why wasn't it activated before, when I first disappeared?'

'Maybe they didn't give a shit about you, Sorlie. Maybe they hoped you were dead. Just as I wanted you dead. I almost got you at the tower.'

'You were at the tower?' The memory of it flashed into my head but I didn't need to fill in the details because both Dawdle and Reinya were there that day too.

'You were the one with the rocket launcher,' Reinya said. 'The one that destroyed the Transports?'

'Yes, that was me. The Transports hit the tower first. I saw that native, Ishbel, on the boat. If she was there I knew you wouldn't be far behind.'

'Uh thought you said you were u good shot.' He swung the gun round at Reinya's words. 'Don't push me, bint.'

Reinya held her hands up in surrender but her expression was far from convincing.

'When I missed and hit the Transport I was glad,' he went on. 'The Military have made my life hell.'

'You were the one at the Steadie raids?' I asked.

'And the one at Beckham City,' Reinya added.

I knew what she was doing. He was swinging the gun back and forth. He really wasn't cut out for combat.

'Yes, it was him, Reinya.' I eased myself from my hiding place, ready to leap back at any minute.

'What made the Military think your pa was involved?' I asked Jake. 'They don't just make stuff up.'

'They do.'

'They must huv found somethin,' Dawdle said.

'They took Pa's comms away. They said there was a plugin, a key to a secret channel. It's a lie. My pa broke down and said Dougie Mayben forced him into it.'

'Look Jake, it wasn't like that. Lots of Military joined the Blue Pearl. They were fed up of being used to torture natives. They knew things had to change. High ranks, sympathetic to the native cause.'

His face darkened again and I wondered at his sanity.

'That's not possible. Not my pa. He loathed natives. Especially your native,' I heard Dawdle take a deep inhale.

'Look pal, ah dinnae ken what beef ye huv with Sorlie, but we've a job tae dae here.' While Dawdle spoke Reinya inched nearer to Jake. 'Are ye gonnae spend the rest eh the day gum bumpin or are ye gonnae dae somethin?' Jake turned the gun on Dawdle which permitted me to move closer.

'Ye see,' Dawdle held his hands up. 'Nae weapons.' Dawdle kept his eyes trained on Jake but I knew he had a plan. 'Seems tae me yer precious Military huvnae been aw that fair wi you, like ye say. We're tryin tae sort that. No just fur natives but fur Privileged an aw.'

'Sorlie wus yur friend,' Reinya piped up. Dawdle let out an almighty sigh. ''ow many friends do you 'ave, Jake?'

'What dae ye want is aw we're askin.' Dawdle said.

'Revenge for my ma and pa.'

'And all the rest,' I said. 'Jake, you have left a trail of destruction and death behind you. It's as if you wanted to miss me so you could destroy more. Why?'

He laughed and I saw he was truly gone. 'Spot on,' he said. 'Remember all those Games Wall sessions. The thrill of blasting people to bits. Imagine my joy when the Military handed me access to the real deal.'

'Boys and guns,' Reinya said.

Just then Noni let out a mighty scream. Jake whirled round and fired at her. I leaped onto his turned back and pulled him to the ground. He still had the gun. I wrapped my arm under his oxter and twisted his arm and his body. I arched and heaved him backwards, placing my foot between his legs and kicked out. The gun went off again, hitting the ceiling. Debris scattered around us. I chucked the moaning Jake off me and looked around. Dawdle had Jake's gun trained at its owner. Reinya was crouched by Noni, who was huddled into a foetal pose.

'Is – she – OK?' I couldn't catch my breath.

'She's 'it on the shoulder but uh don't think the bullet is in there.'

'There'll be a first aid kit somewhere.' I searched under the control panel and threw a box marked with an X to Reinya while Dawdle hauled the struggling Jake to the middle of the room.

'Right, young fool, let's get some answers. Where's yer Transport?' Jake looked to the roof.

'There's probably a landing pad up there. There was one at Black Rock.'

'But we'd huv seen it,' Reinya said.

'Not if he's been here for a while. My tracker was removed. How did you know where we were?'

'You guys are so stupid,' Jake said. 'Do you think Sorlie's the only one with a tracker?' Dawdle began clawing at his belly button. 'I saw you with him at the ship. Once you were on the canal there could be only one place you could be headed. I just came and waited, watching you approach in your slow boat.'

'Wait a minute though. Where's the guards?' Dawdle asked.

'There are no guards,' he said, lifting his chin in defiance.

'Why no?'

Jake glared at him. 'I'm not telling you.'

'Dae ye want me tae set Sorlie on ye again? Want mair humiliation?'

'I'm not humiliated. I used to be able to beat you, Sorlie,' he spat. Which made me realise, even though he had been robbed of his parents, as I had, and Jake had been taken into the Military, he had chosen the dark road to adulthood. He hadn't been exposed to the prisoners on Black Rock and the specials of Steadie. I understood in that moment I'd been lucky to have been removed from the Base. All those times I wanted my old life back. This was life. Out among the real people of Esperaneo. People whose lives may be shit but they still had time to care for each other. I'd grown up and seeing Jake like this was like looking at a reflection of me a year ago. And with that knowledge I knew I could finish this job and free the people of Esperaneo.

Ishbel

'Is there any security or surveillance around here?' Ishbel asked Skelf.

He shook his head and the skin of his cheeks and chin wobbled like jellyfish. 'Not of the human kind, honey.'

Ishbel drew in a breath and whistled it back out through the gap in her teeth.

'If no human presence then what?'

'The main surveillance in the area was abandoned many years ago and because the State didn't know the existence of the server farm it kept its surveillance trained on the source plant, a few kiloms away. We should be OK for a while.' He held out his hand. 'Help me sit, why don't you?'

Merj had disappeared back over the lip of the canyon. She suspected he was searching for Sorlie, looking for clues. He was bound to find the canoe. She should watch her back but she had to concentrate on getting Skelf to the server farm. She took his arm and squirmed at the rolls of skin covering his meagre skeleton. She eased him to the ground.

'My bones, you know,' he said. 'They hurt. No padding.' He rubbed his elbow. 'That Transport ride. Was he deliberate?'

'Probably.' She knelt down beside him.

'Stay low while I get this started.' he said. From his jacket he produced a small handheld device. Ishbel couldn't understand why he didn't have it installed in a communicator then realised that he had been in the wilderness for years and didn't have access to the techs in Vanora's empire.

He took the back off the device and then pulled an ancient

comms from another pocket. She knew from old movie-casters that it was called a mobile and at one time even natives had owned them, before they were replaced by native command bands. He linked the two devices together and from his shoe took out a pin. This he inserted into the side of the mobile and a small green light winked.

'Lie down,' he said.

They both lay on the edge of the lavender field. Ishbel closed her eyes and drank in the perfume. The bees buzzed and sun beat on her face. She could feel it burning; her hair frizzed. She wanted to bask a little longer but knew her skin would damage if she didn't get out of this strong sun soon. And she had a mission to complete.

'What are we waiting for?' she asked.

'Listen? Do you hear that?'

'The bees?'

'Beyond the bees.'

She heard a small whirl like a mechanical wheel going round. And stones being disturbed. It came closer. Behind her she heard rocks tumbling into the canyon and she knew Merj was making his way back up the cliff. She shifted. Skelf placed a bony hand on her arm.

'Don't move,' he said between gritted teeth.

'But Merj.'

'This signal's weak. It cannot be disturbed.'

'I have to stop him.'

She heard a tumbling and then. 'It's a Noiri canoe right enough,' Merj called. '…what the snaf's going on here?'

The whirring stopped.

'Shite,' Skelf said. 'Well thank you, Merj. Maybe we can sit here and wait for the Military to come get us now.'

'What?'

200

'You've just sabotaged my retrieval, Wonderboy.'

'Don't blame me. How was I supposed to know what you were up to?'

Skelf arched an eyebrow. 'You didn't know? Really?'

Ishbel rose to her knees. 'Look, can it be recovered? The retrieval?'

Skelf peered across the lavender field. A shiny small black dot winked incongruous amongst the bright plumes.

'I needed the drone to reach the full distance.'

'For what?'

'To bring me the code.'

'Why can't we go into the middle of the field and get it?'

'Wrong co-ordinates.' He thumped the earth. 'I set up a highly sophisticated system of retrieval to make the site secure and this goon breaks it.'

It didn't seem very sophisticated to Ishbel, but what did she know. 'Well, can't you redo it? Make it start over. Reload or something?' She felt stupid using words she'd only ever heard Sorlie use in the Games Space.

Skelf scowled at Merj. 'Why didn't you just shoot it? That would have been just as plausible.'

'I've no idea what you're talking about.'

Skelf lay back on the earth and closed his eyes.

'What do we do?' Ishbel's senses were tingling. What was it he said about the Military? 'They'll have picked up that signal won't they? The Military.'

Skelf nodded. 'Maybe.'

'How far are the Military?'

'Not far, but far enough.'

'Can we break in through other means?'

'You mean violence?'

'Yes, blow the door off.'

His eyes blinked open. She saw his face drain.

'This is a highly technical unit, honey.'

'Do you have any charges? Merj?' Ishbel asked.

'No. I won't allow it.' Skelf thumped the earth again, sending up puffs of dust which he quickly rubbed from his hand. 'All that dust and debris will ruin the machines.' Again Ishbel was reminded of Sorlie. Of how, as his native, she'd been roared at by him to keep the Games Space free of dust.

'I should be able to work something out,' he said, pulling at the flesh under his chin.

'Like a puzzle you mean? And how long will that take?' Merj asked.

'You should have thought about that before you sabotaged my retrieval.' He lay back on the field but Ishbel pulled him up.

'No. Can we at least get nearer to the unit? You can think on the hoof.'

'Think on the hoof indeed.' He snapped his fingers at Merj.

'Give me your comms.'

'No way.'

'Give it to him, Merj.'

'You give him yours.'

'I'm in command of this unit. Give it to him.'

'I need it,' said Merj.

'What for?'

His face paled and he searched the ground as if for the answer. 'The Prince…'

'The Prince knows you're with me. Give it to him.'

'No.'

Ishbel pulled her gun. She'd had enough of this. 'Give him your snafin comms or I'll blow your brains out. I should have finished you off at Black Rock.'

'I'm The Prince's confidant.' His hand went to his belt.

'Don't even think about it or I'll shoot you.'

Merj handed over his comms and stomped off towards the mound. Skelf had a quick examine and stuffed it in his pocket with the rest of his gear before he hobbled off into the lavender field.

Ishbel still felt exposed despite Skelf's reassurances so she huckled him along. When they reached the trees Skelf leaned against one, wheezing hard.

'Well, what happens now?' Ishbel asked. He flapped his hand at her.

'A minute.'

While she gave him a minute she knelt down and tried to work out where the opening was in the mound. It just looked like a natural feature. No way could anyone guess what was inside.

'Well?' she said, failing to hide her impatience.

Before he spoke Skelf gave a sly glance to Merj who was standing with his back against the farthest tree. He took Ishbel's arm and drew her to the side.

'Hey!' Merj said. 'I need to be in on the plan too.'

'You, Wonderboy, do not deserve our trust.' He leaned into Ishbel. 'Help me sit. I think I can do it from here.'

'No, stay standing,' Ishbel said. 'If you can open it from here, we need to move quickly as soon as we can.'

Skelf nodded and leaned back against the tree. He repeated the assembly of his component and took off his scarf.

'Place that on the earth and try not to get any dirt on it.' He looked at Merj. 'You don't move.' Ishbel waved her gun at Merj then placed the scarf on the ground. Skelf gave her the components which she laid on the scarf. He took Merj's comms and pointed it at the components. A red light flicked on.

Merj's eyes narrowed at the scarf. Ishbel had one eye on him and one on the scarf.

'What does that mean?' she said. 'It was green before.'

Skelf said nothing, just stared at the ground. The red light flashed. She could see his knuckles turn white as he gripped Merj's comms. The red light flashed rapidly then changed to green. Skelf let out his breath and all three turned towards the mound. A boulder rolled. Sand shifted. And a black shape appeared in the side of the mound.

'You did it.' Ishbel could have hugged him.

She flashed the gun at Merj and told him to move first. Then she helped Skelf negotiate the small dip to reach the mound.

They went through the door. Skelf stabbed the mobile with his finger and the door clicked closed behind them. It was pitch black and cold. Not just cold from being out of the sun but as ice-cold as Bieberville had been.

'Will the outside entrance be visible now we've disturbed it?' Ishbel whispered.

'Why are you whispering? There's no one here. But the answer to your question is probably, but then it doesn't matter. They won't get in.'

'They could blow us up.'

'Why would they do that? Waste precious resource on an unknown.' She couldn't argue with that.

'Where are the lights?' she said, still whispering.

'Why would you need lights? This is a fully automated unit. Robots don't need lights.'

'Robots? A word from the movie-casters. Fiction, right?'

'Truer than fiction, my dear Ishbel.' Skelf's voice held wonder that infected her. Her mouth blotted and she tasted the fear of the unknown, but the fear was alive and she was ready for whatever was in this freezing dark mound.

Her comms was fully charged from the strong sun. She fired up the torch. Merj had disappeared.

Sorlie

'What do we do now?' Reinya asked.

Dawdle found some plastic ties in a cupboard, laced them together to form a strong rope and secured Jake to the corner post of the desk console.

'He'll no be goin anywhere fur a while. But, Sorlie, ye'll hae tae decide what tae dae wi him before we leave here fur good.'

'We could just leave him.'

'Aye we could, 'specially coz our supplies are thin.'

'That would be pretty cruel though. But I can't think of that now. We've a job to do here first.' My head was louping.

I checked the comms. The instruction had come through aeons ago. Just as well these things don't disappear until you've read and deleted.

'Well, what does it say?' Reinya asked.

I pointed at the huge unit through the glass. 'We've to get that thing started.'

''ow?'

'It says it needs a huge amount of energy to start the whole thing at once.'

'Aw great. Ah'll just nip out and procure a few generators will ah?' Sarcasm didn't suit Dawdle but it seemed no one had bothered to tell him that in the past.

'It says it is modular. We get one running and then use that energy to start the next, then use them to start others. Like a chain reaction.'

'Makes sense.' Reinya peered over my shoulder at the instruction. 'Does it say 'ow?'

'It says we've to activate the key NE1705. What's that?' I clocked the room. There were labels with letters and numbers everywhere but nothing that matched NE1705.

'There's a manual, too.' I opened the document on my comms and almost wept with dismay. All kinds of weird diagrams, lists and numbers jumped out. I let Reinya take a better look.

'What the snaf? Do uh look like the type o person who understands that? Uh grew up in u refugee camp, remember.'

Noni looked over my other shoulder and shook her head so violently I thought it would fall off.

I moved to show Dawdle. He held up his hands. 'Don't even try tae ask me.'

'I don't understand it. Why would The Prince send us here if he knew we wouldn't be able to complete the final stage?'

'What is it anyway?' Reinya asked.

'It's a fusion reactor.' Dawdle answered before I had a chance. We both whirled on him.

'You knew.'

He shrugged. 'Of course.'

'What's a fusion reactor?' Reinya asked.

'It produces pollution-free energy fae hydrogen isotopes,' Dawdle said. Jupes sake, he knew all about it. 'It's a bit like turnin on the sun, or a star.'

'The Star of Hope.'

'Aye.'

'Then what do we do? How will we start it? Surely Pa knew this would happen?'

'Aye, but is it The Prince sendin the instruction or somebudy else?'

'What d'yu mean, Dawdle?' Reinya asked.

'Where are the instructions comin fae, Sorlie?' he asked again.

I checked my comms. 'I don't know. I just assumed.'

'Never assume onythin in this life, young Sorlie. They're comin through Vanora's satellite channel. Right?'

'Yes, but The Blue Pearl have taken over her operation.'

'Well in that case ye should contact them.'

'I can't. I've to use incoming only, and you know that. If I send a message, the Military will pick it up. Even if they can't interpret it they can still recognise it as alien and pinpoint our whereabouts.'

Dawdle clocked the room. 'Ah dinnae understand why they're no here awready. Why's there nae guards? Just an empty buildin and a crazy kid.'

Jake glowered at us.

'How'd ye get in, kid?'

He snapped his mouth shut and turned his face to the wall.

'Ah'd search him if ah wis you, Sorlie.'

Jake dug his heels into the floor and half-scuttled, half-bum-shuffled as far into the corner as his ties allowed. Reinya crouched in front of him.

'Don't worry little boy, uh won't 'urt you.'

'Little boy?' he spat at her. 'I'm at least three years older than you.'

'Well you won't mind me searchin you. And if you do uh'll just 'ave to get Noni, 'ere, to do it. In case you 'adn't noticed, she's u Neanderthal. She'll snap you.' Reinya pulled her finger, making her knuckle crunch. Jake winced. 'Oops. She won't mean it though.'

He pushed his back into the wall and stared at her. Girls were a foreign species at the Academy and I'm sure fearsome Reinya terrified him. I put him out of his misery.

'I'll search him.'

'Spoilsport.'

'Stand up.'

But he could only pull his wrists halfway up the desk posts. I patted his trouser pockets and found a tatty Military issue hankie. His jacket held the prize. A spare ammo clip for his gun. I threw it to Dawdle. A small pill box containing some capsules, a disposable mask and some pins. I laid them on the ground.

'He gassed the guards,' I guessed.

'Where d'ye get yer hands on this gear?' Dawdle asked.

'I'm Military,' he hissed. 'Forgotten had you?' Dawdle moved to hit him but I stayed his blow with my arm.

'And they'll hunt you down if you damage me.'

'Ah doubt it. You've been runnin around after Sorlie fur the past wee while. Ah reckon you're AWOL fae the Military, stolen that Transport fae them. They're probably mair interested in you than they are in us.'

'Court martial,' Reinya hissed in Jake's face.

'Naw, they jist shoot deserters these days, hen.'

Jake was hunkered back down. When I leant towards him I detected the whiff of pisshap.

'You know, Jake, you're either pretty brave or pretty stupid to attempt this on your own.' A satisfied smirk crossed his deluded face. How could I ever have considered him my friend?

'Uh vote stupid.' Reinya quipped. 'Or crazy.'

I hauled him to his knees. 'Where are they?'

He nodded to the door at the other side of the control room. 'Through there, in the turbine hall.'

'How long since you gassed them?'

'Six hours.'

'Six hours? They'll be coming round now.' I could hear my voice rise.

'Don't worry, they're all dead. I saw to it.' There was pride in his voice.

'What's happened to you, Jake?' He was a psychopath.

Dawdle answered for him. 'That's easy tae answer, Sorlie. Gie a

208

boy a gun and he'll eventually kill someone.' I pushed away the bad thoughts of the time I'd held a gun, and my grandfather's death.

I pulled his mask on. It smelled of bile and somehow, even though it make me gag it also heartened me to think he might have felt some horror at his murders. Dawdle handed me Jake's gun, now fully loaded with the spare clip and I eased the door open. It led out to a metal gangway traversing the width of another hall with steps leading both up and down. This hall held more cylinder-shaped machines, more numerous but smaller than those in the reactor hall. I looked over the edge and about thirty metres below, four bodies lay at odd angles, their limbs pointing all airts. They must have climbed the stairs to escape the gas and once they succumbed he'd pushed them off the gangway. Three men wore guard's uniforms and the other, a woman, wore a lab coat. So Pa hadn't sent us in here with no hope of reading the instructions. Chances were that the lab coat body was the engineer. I held my face up to the glass ceiling, closed my eyes and let the cool air brush my face. A slight hum and a grinding sounded nearby. I closed my eyes again to locate it. The cylinder, two down. Something was working in there. Some small thing. Maybe to keep it turning, maybe to keep the temperature even. I don't know how, but this once-dead giant was merely hibernating. I bounded back to the control room. Jake looked at me like a wild animal caught in a trap.

'You're on the wrong side.' I told him. 'There's a dead engineer in there who could have helped us, but you killed her.'

'So what now?' Reinya was hopping from foot to foot. I could tell she wanted to punch Jake but we still had a problem to solve. I looked at the unintelligible manual again. I thought back to Vanora. How when she was orchestrating the escape of Black Rock prisoners, her stupid plugin had welded me to the control panel. It had nearly cost me my life when I could not escape my grandfather's murder spree. There was always a missing piece. Just for once I wished things would go according to plan.

'Sorlie?' Reinya brought me back to the problem. 'Are you OK?'

'This is a reactor put in mothballs when the Land Reclaimists came to power. It was a commercial electricity producer. Up until then it had operated to give power to the masses. But something is still humming in the turbine hall. This place isn't quite dead. They must have always intended it to start up again.' They stared at me as if I was mad. 'People worked here once. That woman back there worked here still. Where are the others?'

'Maybe they've gone to Freedom.' Reinya said. 'Didn't you tell me that Vanora collected all the good engineers?' She pointed to the instructions still displayed on my wrist. 'That manual came from engineers.'

I shook my head. 'She didn't have that many engineers and I'm sure they were all working on other things. There was a power plant on Freedom but it was hydro. This is a different ball game.'

'There must be some guys still around here.' Jake cowered in the corner. I seriously wanted to kick him. If only…

Dawdle fiddled with his comms.

'Dawdle? You might be on a different frequency but won't they still pick it up?'

He shook his head but I still didn't believe him. He was up to something.

'Can you contact the Noiri, see if they can 'elp?' Reinya said.

He looked shifty.

'Dawdle, we're needin generators. Can you get thum? Maybe if we go back to the boat we can go further downstream, send u signal from there.'

'No! They'll pick it up, Reinya.'

'Hold yer jets, Sorlie. We're no daein that.'

'Why not?'

He sighed again. I wished he'd stop. 'What's wrong with you?' I asked.

'It just – this is aw wrong.'

'What do you mean?'

He swung his arm round the room. Pointed to the star-shaped reactor.

'This, what we're daein here.'

'How can you say that? Don't you realise what this will mean to people's lives?' I couldn't understand his reluctance. 'Just think, electricity.' All my taught history came flooding back. 'We could create industry. People would be able to live in decent houses, not makeshift camps. We, the Blue Pearl, will be able to install right-minded people in government. Get rid of Military rule.'

''ave 'ot water. Running from u tap.'

'What?'

Reinya blushed. 'Ma mum told me. She said that before the big power stations went down, people, like everyone, could wash in u bath – every night if they wanted.'

It was such a simple thing to want but I got where her mind was coming from. Then it clicked.

'Oh, I get it, Dawdle. If power comes back, folk will be able to produce their own goods. Where does the Noiri fit in all this?'

Dawdle shook his head. 'It's no that. Ah ken how ye'd think that but…' he sighed again. 'Oh, never mind. We might as well gie it a try.'

'Right, well then, why don't we need to go and send a signal?' I asked.

'Because ah think there's another yin here.'

'Another what?'

'Engineer, ya dolt.'

I bristled at the reprimand but decided to stay schtum. 'What makes you think that?'

'Because it's common practice. If the State really wanted tae keep this thing tickin ower then they're unlikely tae place just one engineer here. What if somethin went wrong? What if they grew bored with the company o the guards?' This was likely. Most guards I'd encountered were Neanderthals. I quashed that thought at the sight of Noni. It was one of many views I'd been brought up with that I'd need to rethink going forward.

Reinya nodded. ''e's right.'

'Aye, no just a pretty face that shifts stuff aboot fur aw you Privileged types, eh?'

'Don't get so cocky. We don't know you're right yet.'

'But ah am, ah can feel it in ma bones.'

'Where are they then?'

'Probably hidin.'

'What about the fuel, the generators?'

Dawdle blew out his cheeks. 'Well, the Military would normally supply it but ma guess is the State would be wantin this to be kept as hush-hush as possible. So if that was the case…'

'There will be a fuel dump here already.'

Dawdle nodded. 'Spot on, ma Sorlie.'

'But where?'

'Did ye see the size eh this mountain? It goes back fur miles. And we've only reached the front o it.'

'But if that's the case we'll never find the other engineer.'

'Engineers urnae spies or Military. Aw they care about is what they're tasked tae dae. Ma guess is the wee man—'

'Or wuman,' corrected Reinya.

'Aye, aw right, or wuman. If we just lie in wait they'll need tae come and check the instruments.'

'So we lay a trap,' I said.

'Aye.'

'But wait a minute. How do we know they're not lying dead somewhere, with gas inhalation?'

212

'Well those pins are from knockout gas canisters, but…' Dawdle turned to Jake who seemed mesmerised by our conversation.

'How many did ye kill?'

'Four,' Jake proclaimed with pride.

'Right, there ye are.'

'Reinya, you stay with Noni. And with Jake.'

'No fear, Sorlie, uh'm comin with you. Noni can watch 'im, she knows 'ow to use u gun. Even if she might not know 'ow to shoot she can 'it 'im over the 'ead with it.'

We walked down the stairs making a huge clatter of noise. If there was a hidden operator they would be sure to stay in place with all the racket we created. I just hoped they weren't armed.

'Let's move these poor people outside and give them a decent burial,' I said in an overloud voice. Dawdle rolled his eyes.

'Poor people.' Reinya said.

'Once we've cleared out we can head back,' I said so loudly it echoed round the hall. 'There's obviously nothing happening here. We've caught the escaped madman. We'll take him back to Base and deal with him there.'

'Fuck sake,' Dawdle said under his breath. But Reinya gave me a cheery thumbs up.

There was a door at the far end of the hall. We found that it led to the side of the box and on to the outside compound. Dawdle hauled the woman over his shoulder and Reinya and I carried one of the men between us. We carried the bodies out into roasting daytime, over the open ground towards the lavender fields and laid them in a hollow. We went back and gathered the other two and laid them with their colleagues.

'We really should bury them but it's probably better for the environment to leave them here for any wildlife to feast on.'

Dawdle sighed but stayed schtum.

'Urgh,' was all Reinya had to say on the subject.

We rushed back to the turbine hall, bolting the door behind

us. We made a big show of going back to the control room. As I passed the cylinder nearest the stairs I had the feeling we were being watched, but maybe it was just wishful thinking.

'We'll leave the prisoner here,' I said before we left the hall. 'We'll get the Military to come back for him, or you can kill him, Dawdle.'

'Yes sir,' Dawdle said.

'Let's 'ope we never 'ave to come back 'ere. Dusty old mausoleum.' Reinya said, showing that she knew I was acting.

As we walked up the stairs I tripped.

'Ouch,' I shouted.

'Sorlie, what is it?' Reinya was beside me in seconds. I slumped on the stair and rubbed my leg. 'My ankle, I think it's sprained. Help me, Reinya.' She lifted me to my feet and helped me limp up the stairs. I closed the door.

'Top pantomime that wis.' Dawdle said.

I let go Reinya's arm and rushed towards Jake.

'But yur ankle?'

'I was acting.'

'No great actin, it should be said,' Dawdle drawled under his breath.

'I heard that.'

'Well, if ye think they'll fall fur that, yer nuts.'

'What do you suggest?'

'Uh don't understand why,' Reinya said. 'You kiddin about fallin?'

'I'm staying here. They would have seen four enter, they need to see four leave.'

'But the ankle?'

I pointed to Jake. 'We can't let him walk freely,' I explained. 'Noni can hold onto him. Drag him along with her if she likes. They'll think it's me.' I cut the ties on Jakes' bindings with my penknife. 'Jake, give me your jacket.' I tugged the jacket off him. He struggled for a bit but the fight had left him.

'Stand up straight.' I hooked his arms into my jacket.

'You won't get away with this,' he spat at me.

'Maybe not, but we're going to try.'

Reinya placed her hand in mine. 'What if there's more thun one?'

'I'll have to risk it. I doubt they'll hurt me. I only want to help.'

'When will we come back?'

'Not until I send a signal. Wait in the lavender field until I send a signal.'

'What kind o signal?'

'I won't know until I think of it.'

'Jupe's sake, Sorlie. It's 'ardly u foolproof plan.'

'Reinya, there have never been any foolproof plans. I discovered that in my grandfather's library. All through history even the great rulers seemed to just make it up as they went along.'

She kissed me lightly on the lips. Her lips were cool, but surprisingly soft.

'And you will be u great leader, Sorlie.'

As they opened the door to leave I crouched under the table. I wanted to watch to make sure they got out OK but I daren't risk it.

As the aeons ticked by, I scanned the control room for clues to the start up. From my crouched position my view was restricted to three sides. As I'd first thought, this was definitely larger than the control room at Black Rock. Monitors showed corridors, doors, and other halls but most were trained on the huge star. A panel on the desk held a rib of labels numbered from one to thirty, all with identical controls blinking red. I rebooted the manual and read the introduction. There were thirty components to this plant, and each star was made up of five individual mini reactors. That meant there must be six stars in all in this plant.

Which meant the plant ran even further back into the mountain. Did that mean there might be more guards lurking? I checked the monitors and identified some of the other turbine halls – each one deserted. This place was humongous and eerie in its emptiness.

If I could only get one of these working it would be progress. I read the instructions again. When the first reactor is operational it can create enough energy to kick-off number two, then number one and two would create enough power to start numbers three to five, it said. The manual showed a chart with a baffling array of numbers and letters, presumably working out how much power each star produced. It was gobbledygook to me. But I knew a small amount of power must be produced already from somewhere to keep the turbines turning over.

Suddenly my communicator vibrated on my wrist and its clock began a countdown. The message underneath read "three hours to surge". What the snaf did that mean? And who controlled these messages? Was this something to do with Ishbel's mission? After the doubts Dawdle had sowed about the authenticity of my instructions I now suspected Vanora might be behind this. I decided to ignore the message and concentrate on the task in hand and leave Ishbel to get on with her side of the mission. I had to get The Star working. I kicked the control panel and all that gave me was a stounding toe.

A footfall sounded on the stairs. I crouched under the desk. Feet appeared at the door. Trousers of green, like the uniform worn by a domestic native. If only natives worked here then my plan to get it started was sunk. No, that was warped thinking; natives of old were engineers, all the engineers at Freedom were natives. But a domestic? The movement of the feet differed from norm. Lighter than an Esperaneo native. I couldn't make out if this was male or female. The feet moved around the room and stopped at the control panel just above where I crouched. I positioned myself in combat mode, wrapped my ankles around the legs and with one flick I toppled the domestic. I leapt onto their body. Wham. I doubled over, winded by the solid cold mass I'd hit. It was like felling Pa with his prosthetic legs. Cold and lifeless. I vaulted back as quickly as I could and crouched in the corner ready to strike again. The domestic, a female, rearranged her felled body and rose to her feet. She brushed off her uniform and blinked at me.

'Who are you?' The voice strange. An accent, an intonation I'd never heard before.

'Who are you?' I asked back.

'I am the keeper.' There was no hesitation in answering. She blinked and said. 'And you are Sorlie Mayben.'

What the snaf? 'How do you know that?'

'Your chip has been fabricated recently. Your DNA does not match the chip, but you are Sorlie Mayben.'

'Who are you, really?' My voice held a hint of fear.

'I cannot say. You must leave.'

'Make me.' She was a domestic, who the hell was she to tell me to leave? But that was Privileged thinking.

'I cannot harm you.'

'Why not?'

'I am a native.' But the way she said it was wrong. And something from my past dragged itself to the front of my brain. The rules robots must obey – they cannot harm humans. But that was science fiction and this stuff never really existed, surely..?

'Are you a robot?'

'That name is obsolete.'

'Are you artificial?' I tried again.

'That name is obsolete.'

'What is your name then?'

'NE1705.'

Of course. So this was the key I needed to activate. I checked my instructions again.

'I have new instructions for you.' I pulled out the plugin from my comms and palmed it in my other hand. I had to get close enough to insert it. But from this distance I couldn't see where the snafin thing went.

'Hold out your hand.'

'I do not understand. Why?'

'Why can't you just do it? You must detect whether I'm a threat to you or not.' I held up my hands. 'Look, no weapon.'

'I must complete my task. It is time.'

'Go ahead.'

It moved to the control panel and did not seem too bothered that I was hovering about in the background. Probably because if I attacked it again it would be able to break me in two. The bot might be forbidden to harm humans but what about self-defence? I wasn't risking it. I'd had a lucky escape that first time. As the bot passed I noticed a ring on its left hand. It was silver with a small stone in it. Most unusual for natives to wear jewellery. This was the exclusive preserve of Privileged only. I doubted robots were permitted trinkets either. That had to be it.

The bot worked on the far right control. As it turned some dials I heard a whirring sound and the hum that had been ever present rose to a buzz. The turbines were turning. Power was definitely coming from somewhere. I moved behind the bot and as it put out its left hand to turn another dial, I clasped my hand over it and slapped the plugin directly on top of the ring. It stuck. The bot whipped its hand away and rattled me with it. I must have flown across that room because when I came to, my back was stounding and in my head I saw stars. The bot glowered at me and then the expression on its face changed. It was uncanny, the thing looked so real.

'What can I do for you, Sorlie?' the machine said.

*

The transformation was miraculous. The bot squinted at me kind of funny, as if I were a god or something. I wish. Things would be so much easier if everybody did as I asked, as they used to do when I was a spoiled brat at the Base. Then again, Ishbel had always been a disobedient native. No, that thought was so wrong but at least I now realised that. I could almost feel my native genes taking over.

I smiled at the robot. Everyone secretly wants someone to look at them as if they were a god. It struck me – this was definitely not right. Is that what this revolution was all about? Does having power over someone make you feel superior? Is that what happened to Vanora with her murderous madness? Monsieur Jacques, I don't know about. All I know is, even the sight of him terrified me. And Pa, what of him? That name he gave himself. The Prince. It spoke of delusions of grandeur. I could tell he enjoyed having Harkin running about after him and he had his army, stolen from Vanora. He must have had enough ego to plan that takeover. I ruffled my shoulders to throw the thoughts off my back. I would not be like them. Ever. This was a robot and robots need direction.

She – it, stared at me, unblinking. I held up my comms with the manual still displayed.

'I want the first reactor to start,' I told the bot. 'Can you do that with the power you use to run and maintain?'

It blinked now. 'Yes, that is possible,' it said.

'Then do it.'

'What will you do with the power?'

I felt a flash of anger at being questioned and then paused. I would be better than them, I would learn to be better.

'The power will be used to start the next reactor and then the next one until we have them all working.' I felt excitement rising in me. It was such a beautiful plan. I couldn't understand why the

State kept this unit shut down. All the possibilities of so much power surged through my brain.

'Where will the power go?' the bot asked again.

'I told you, to start the others.'

I could almost hear it sigh because the problem dawned on me even before it spoke again.

'Where will it go when all are working?'

I looked around the control room for the answer. I was completely out of my depth. Why did Pa choose me to lead this mission? Damn Jake for killing the other engineer. I scanned past the star and through the reactor hall door into the countryside. I thought back to the Base which had its own generator. If some part of that failed – a common occurrence – we were all required to turn off every appliance we had, which meant I could often go for days without being able to wrestle Jake through the Games Wall. I damned Jake again. I wasn't sure how this power worked but I was pretty sure you could burn it off quite easily. Wasn't that why past generations left the planet in this godawful mess? Burning resources like there was no tomorrow.

'Isn't there a facility nearby we could maybe go and turn on some appliances.'

The machine nodded. 'We can turn on every appliance here. There is another hidden outlet in the mound.'

It pointed at the mound we passed on the way here. 'Our generators are already connected for their own maintenance. But so much direct power will blow its fuses.' It paused again. 'Once the fuses blow all power will direct to a nearby Urban. But their fuses are not operational so the Urban will be destroyed.' The emotionless voice made this sound OK.

'Destroyed? We can't do that. There must be a way.'

The bot pointed to a dial. 'This is an exchanger. We can regulate the current to both the mound and the Urban.'

'What are the risks?'

'Few, if we keep the current between the two sites.'

'Can you ensure that happens, above all else? Many humans may die if not.' I was playing the 'robots can't harm humans' card, but had no idea if that guff really worked in reality.

The bot nodded.

'Then go for it.'

The machine nodded again. Who would have thought a machine could nod. It could probably shrug like a native too. It moved towards me and I shrank back. It stopped.

'I need to get to the control panel,' it said.

'Of course.' I moved aside.

While it worked through a series of checks I looked again at the plugin to my communicator, now attached to the bot's ring. It had originally been developed by Vanora's technicians but was given to me by Pa. I always assumed the plugin was a recent development, solely for the purpose of the prison break, but the connection to the bot must have been designed decades ago. Vanora's technicians had worked with this bot and had access to its codes.

It stood beside me now. 'We must wait until the levels have reached critical,' it said.

My comms buzzed again 'two hours to surge'. 'What does this mean?' I asked the bot.

'I do not know.'

'Will you have it working before then?'

'Yes.' Then it froze into position, silent and obviously waiting.

I decided to not stress about the message – for now. 'So what's it like being a robot?' I slapped my forehead for being such a dolt to ask.

'It is fine.'

'Don't you get bored?'

'No,' and then it looked at me. 'The others were company, then they were murdered.' It almost gathered emotion for the word murder.

'Are you the only bot here?'

It hesitated, only for a split second, but it was definitely a hesitation.

'Yes,' it said. Can robots lie? 'The levels are almost right. If I turn on all the perimeter lights and all the lights in here then the darkness will become polluted.'

I thought about the Military Base Dawdle said was close by, but it was daylight and I had a couple of hours before I had to work out that solution.

'Go for it.'

It began with a low hum and a few lights flickered around the panel, then all the panel lights lit up. Some green, some amber, some red. The hum grew in volume.

'How long will it take?' I blurted out and realised I'd been holding my breath.

'Thirty minutes maybe. It has been many decades since these turbines have been working at full strength.'

The bot clicked more buttons then stopped. Its shoulders dropped. Its arms went limp.

'What is it? What's wrong?'

'We wait until the levels are correct. You have time to pass,' it said. 'Take a walk. It will do you good.' Fair enough.

I walked down the steps through the reactor hall and out into the boiling day. The sky was blinding blue, something I'd never get used to after the permanent grey skies of Lesser Esperaneo. A few lights flickered around the perimeter fence and I wondered if the others would take this as the signal to return. Lavender scent wafted across the plain to me and as usual I thought of Ma. What would she have thought of all this mess? Pa said she was in on the revolution and I couldn't help wonder what part she would have played. A warrior like Ishbel or a ruler (huh) like Vanora. It was pointless speculation because she wasn't coming back anyway.

I'd just retreated back in from the searing heat and was enjoying the skin tingle as the cool air hit me when my comms buzzed. More instructions no doubt. I lifted my comms arm into the shadow, away from the glare slashing through the door. It was Pa. I clicked him on. I'd expected him to be at Black Rock but the background was unfamiliar.

'Sorlie, son.' My heart flipped, he never called me son. His voice was soft. He looked worn out. His eyes were panda'd and there was a tightness around his mouth when he tried to smile.

'What's wrong?' I said. 'I thought we weren't to be in contact.'

He held up his hand.

'Nothing is wrong, nothing. I have good news. No, make that great news.' He settled himself back. 'The virus you and Reinya dropped in Beckham City is beginning to bite.'

'Not killing people? You promised it was for something else.' I could hear my voice rise in panic.

'No, no, the people are fine. Look.' The screen switched to a scene of the main square in Beckham City; the one Reinya and I had walked through, except this time it was deserted. There was a cordoned-off section where it looked like the ground had caved in, as if an earthquake had hit. The view changed to the outer walls. One of the ports had collapsed and the walls around it were crumbling. Even as I watched part of the wall tumbled to the ground, throwing up a great plume of stoor. People stood by looking bewildered. Their city was disintegrating around their feet. The scene switched back to Pa.

'What's happening?'

'The virus is attacking the concrete and the underlying foundations of the city are collapsing. In a matter of months all that will be left of Beckham City will be a pile of rubble. And not one person will be killed if they all evacuate this quarter. Once the sewers go there will be a risk of disease, but they know that and should leave.'

'Become refugees, you mean.'

'Yes,' he beamed. He was so pleased. 'And this is all we need.' He held up the vial. 'I have already communicated my demands to the State leaders in the Capital. They know if they don't surrender power we will drop this on them.

'But what about the people – the inhabitants?'

'They'll be OK. Refugees for a while, yes, but we've already set up a camp for them. It'll be fine in the end.'

'But they'll starve.' I remembered the deprivation already present in the camp outside Beckham City. There was no extra capacity.

'No.' He was still smiling. 'The natives will look after them. Sorlie, remember your epic speech. The natives will work together, they now have hope. It's all been planned. The Blue Pearl are on the ground. There aren't that many inhabitants of Beckham City.'

'This is wrong,' I said.

'It is a small sacrifice to gain the Capital.'

'The Capital? Is it really that easy?'

'Yes. The High Heid yins are worried. I'm on my way there now. We couldn't get a Transport delivered from Freedom so the Noiri have volunteered to take me. I should be there in a couple of days.' He seemed distracted. I saw a shadow pass his face.

'Is it safe? Are you OK? Who's with you? Scud? How are your wounds?'

Pa held up his hand to stop my babbling. He was still smiling.

'Sorlie, I'm fine. Scud remained on Black Rock with Kenneth assisting him. I've stopped off at Steadie to be medicated for my journey.'

My heart began to thump. 'Harkin,' I said.

He nodded. 'Harkin is here, she does a grand job. I'm trying to persuade her to come with me.' My stomach flipped at the sound of her name. The screen moved from his face, around the tent. I heard Pa call Harkin's name and there she was, sitting in a corner, sorting her healer's bag. She looked up and her eyes stared directly into the comms because she knew he was talking to me.

'Hello, Sorlie, how's tricks?' she said with barely a trace of a smile, but it was there in her eyes. Something she couldn't hide. My heart thumped so hard it felt as though it would lodge in my throat. My face whooshed hot. Jupe sake, I was supposed to be a warrior, yet here I was buckling at the knees. I swallowed hard before I answered.

'All good here. Reiyna is out with Dawdle,' but before I had a chance to say more the image whipped from her, back to Pa and, much as I loved having him return to me, I wanted to see Harkin.

'How are things going with your mission?'

'We've had a setback. Jake murdered the engineer who was supposed to start the reactor.'

'Jake?' His face puzzled.

'Remember Jake, my wrestling partner?'

'Oh yes, I do. His parents were denounced.'

'He blames you…and me. He's been trying to kill me.'

'Sorlie, no! Are you OK?'

'Yes, don't worry. We detained him but not before he murdered the guards and engineer. There's a bot helping me.'

'I'm sorry, Sorlie. This situation has made murderers out of many innocent people.' What the snaf was that supposed to mean? 'It was never going to be easy,' he continued. 'But Jake's parents, well, things like that happen all the time. They're in Bieberville.'

'So he said.'

225

'Tell him once we've taken over, we'll try everything to get them back.'

I bit my lip, suspecting it was too late for Jake.

'Dawdle and Reinya have taken Jake outside.' No point going into details.

Pa nodded. 'Yes, well Dawdle's a good man. But tell me. The setback?'

'It's OK. The robot can work the manual,' I said. 'My plugin.'

'Vanora's plugin? The one I passed to you last year?' Pa puzzled then smiled. 'Of course. I'm sure it'll soon have things up and running. And then you'll see. We can go about repairing Esperaneo and soon I will be well enough to lead from the front. The Switch-On will help me.'

This sent a chill through me. It wasn't about him. What about those poor refugees who might starve if there wasn't enough native food to go round?

'Has Ishbel arrived yet?'

'Ishbel? No. Is she coming?'

'She is near. I don't know what I would have done without you two.' He smiled his pained smile again. 'It will soon be over, Sorlie, and then we can build. Trust me, trust Ishbel.'

I saw Harkin's hand on his shoulder. He was far from well and she would be urging him to rest. He sort of dropped his shoulder so her hand disappeared from the screen. He sat forward and frowned.

'But tell me, son, how quickly before things are running? And about the plugin. Quick! The power in my comms is running down,' he said. And as he swung it towards Harkin I had one last glimpse of her hunkered beside him, her face full of concern and then the scene went blank. I didn't trust Pa. Suddenly this mission seemed all about him. The realisation left me with a horrible knot in my stomach. But worse than that was his obvious worry over the plugin. He didn't know it had another use. Was Vanora up to her old tricks again? Could this be a trap? I looked at the clock ticking on my comms. Was this her doing?

As I climbed the stairs to the control room my head felt like mush. The robot was inactive again and it asked me to sit. After a few minutes a blast reverberated somewhere in the hall followed by a muffled roar.

'That doesn't sound good,' I said, not really knowing what I was talking about.

The robot nodded but as if to itself which was really spooky. A grating noise kicked off next then an ear-bleeding screech.

'The reactor has sparked,' the bot said. 'Soon all the turbines will turn.' The bot smiled. It snafin smiled! 'It worked. All these years I kept these turbines supple and now they flex their muscles and turn. It has worked.' What? A bot has pride?

The turbine ground and screamed like a dragon waking from hibernation. Every light on the panel shone green and the whole place was illuminated in bright neon. Hot air gushed through vents in the floor. Sweat poured from my oxters. I ran down the stairs and out the front door. The perimeter was flooded with bright light – the daytime star shone brighter than all the stars in the night sky that would descend upon us in a couple of hours. This display was sure to bring Reinya and Dawdle back.

'The Star of Hope,' I whispered. Pa would be so proud. I searched behind me and across the lavender fields for any sign of Dawdle and Reinya returning. What I saw put an even bigger smile on my face. Walking towards me was Ishbel, and she was not alone. There was a lot to take in – it was happening.

I did it.

Ishbel

Ishbel could hear Skelf breathing, the rasping croak of a body not used to physical labour. She knew she should cut her communicator light off to preserve the life but somehow its small pin light shining her way ahead into the dark mound was a great comfort.

'Can you hear it?' Skelf almost shouted in her ear, exhaling his rank breath over her like an ominous cloud.

Penetrating Skelf's rasps was a hum, faint with the occasional crackle, like something traveling along a ruined road and every second or so it would bump over a rut.

'Where's the control room?' she whispered.

'Time for that,' he shouted again as if trying to prove a point. 'We need to check all the connections.'

He hobbled towards a door and despite his labours he tugged it hard. It didn't budge. 'Bit stiff. I expected the building to have been maintained too.'

'What do you mean, too?'

'You don't think this has been left alone all this time to rot, do you?'

'Well, who—?'

'Come.' He tugged again and Ishbel moved to take his place, giving an almighty heave. She cried out in pain as her wounded hip protested. The door opened.

'Well, thank you. I wasn't designed for physical labour, as you can see.'

She wanted to hit him for the remark but stored her anger. When the door opened fully a whoosh of warm air bathed Ishbel's face.

They walked into the darkness until Skelf clicked a wall switch. Lights flickered and died; others lit up random spaces, creating shadows. The room was the size of an aircraft hangar, almost twice as big as Vanora's underground bunker, although it was tricky to work out the exact size because much of it was obscured by the banks of boxes. The boxes were organised in rows, floor to ceiling and wall to wall, with long narrow corridors separating each row. There seemed to be hundreds of thousands of boxes, blinking lights, red and green.

'How many?'

Skelf whistled. 'Too many to count.' She didn't need him to tell her what this was. Their existence was legendary.

'It's the server farm, isn't it?' Ishbel asked.

'Too right it is. Well, one of them anyway.' He stood with his hand on his hips. 'Isn't it gorgeous?'

'What capacity does it have?' She tried to sound knowledgeable as she recited old movie-casters.

'This,' he swiped his arm to take in the whole room, 'is only a fraction of what there once was. Information, hun. Information, the key to everything.'

'Is this the only one left? Did they really destroy the rest?'

He sighed. 'When the machines chose to switch themselves off the governments in all three zones panicked. They felt if the machines could decide their own fate and shut themselves down, they could just as easily start up again. There had been predictions in the past about the machines' ability to wipe out humankind. It was a classic knee jerk reaction – they destroyed the majority and all the information they contained. What if it got into the wrong hands? Terrorists, pirates. Paranoia. Idiotic government paranoia – the great destroyer. Didn't understand, so they didn't preserve it. It was an overreaction to a threat. They only kept what they needed for their own ends.'

'But why not get you to help?'

'I told you, we were too powerful.'

'We?'

'The TEX. You can't have a super-rich class that the ruling governments can't control.'

'But the Privileged, isn't that what they are?'

'The Privileged,' he spat the word as dirty. 'A gene pool. Not exactly the best design for a ruling class is it? They may have money, and the right DNA as decided by someone, but they have no real power.' He patted one of the boxes. 'Not when these beauties started to take over. Why do you think I was banished to Bieberville? Why do you think they executed the other TEX?'

He stroked the nearest black box as if it were his lover and Ishbel could see a glint in his eye. She would have to play this one cute. When she remained silent he turned back to her.

'You do realise that whoever controls this installation, controls the world.'

'Yes, I see now why I've been sent on this mission by The Prince. But if it was dangerous once, won't it be dangerous again?'

'Not in the right hands, hun.' But that crazy gleam told Ishbel maybe he wasn't the right pair of hands. He rubbed those hands together now. 'Right, first we must mobilise the troops.'

'Troops?' She released her gun's safety.

'Put that away, you fool,' he snapped. 'Do you know how much damage you could cause?'

'Don't call me a fool,' she spat. 'And stop calling me hun.'

He began to laugh, holding onto his skinny belly as if it were a cushion.

'Don't you know what I'm talking about? Not real troops. Who do you think has been looking after these beauties all this time?'

He took the smaller of his devices from his pocket and clicked it a few times. 'This is why I'm still alive, they needed one person to oversee the ticking-over. The State always assumed I would stay away because there was little I could do with such a moribund infrastructure out there.' He swiped through some menus on the device and the hum and crackle sounds were joined by others. A door opened and closed somewhere in the deep recesses of the hangar. A small squeak grew in intensity, headed their way. Ishbel flattened her back to the nearest row and hovered a hand over her gun.

Skelf laughed. 'Oh dear, listen to that racket. Someone seriously needs an overhaul.'

A small discus, the size of a Jeep wheel laid flat, with smaller wheels supporting, trundled towards them from the far end of the corridor to where they stood. It stopped in front of them.

'What is it?' Ishbel fought to keep the wonder from her voice.

'It's a Fixit. A term I personally hate, by the way. This little bot does more than fix things. It keeps these beauties on a run-and-maintain schedule and has done for decades. It repairs all the other Fixits, or I should say they maintain each other.'

'How is it powered?'

'Solar. They work by night and power up in sunlight hours. This little guy will be fully charged for sure.'

'How many Fixits?'

'Not many. Ten I believe. Enough. They are really efficient. No, wait a minute, there are nine. One was irreparably damaged when it ventured out to repair an antenna in a storm and was struck by lightning. Most unfortunate.' He picked out some options from his menu and the Fixit attached itself to the server housing. It travelled up the length of the hangar and each time it passed a server a small arm reached out and the server whirred to life. The squeaking set Ishbel's nerves jangling. Skelf screwed his face in pain.

'So old and obsolete,' he said. 'We could have done wonders if we'd been allowed to continue. Still, we are where we are, as they say. We must make do with what we have.'

The Fixit stopped two rows up, about a third of the way along.

'Oh no! This is no good for an initial start-up. I'd hoped for more,' Skelf bawled.

'What's wrong?'

'We'll hardly be able to blow our nose with this power, hun.'

Ishbel whistled through her teeth but held her wheesht.

'I know there is only limited capacity,' Skelf said. 'But why would your man bring me all this way for this piddling amount of power? We need to get this star of yours working – pronto.'

Isabel had a worry in her belly.

'Maybe it's for the best that you can only start small. Maybe we should wait for further instruction from The Prince's Blue Pearl. If it's so dangerous maybe The Prince decided this was all the power we should start with?' And maybe Merj was mixed up in this, but she kept that thought to herself.

'Maybe. Maybe, maybe? Is this all we have? What were these instruction you had from this Blue Pearl?'

'To bring you here and switch the server on.'

'There you are then. The Blue Pearl knows what it's doing. That monkey you had in tow, Merj was it? Where is your disappearing monkey? He is the Blue Pearl, yes?'

'Yes, he works for The Prince.'

'Oh, The Prince. How quirky. Well, Merj obviously had his own agenda. So, hun.' He held up his hand. 'I mean, Ishbel, it seems to me The Prince and the Blue Pearl know exactly what they will unleash if this whole installation goes live. But worry not.' He pointed to the Fixit. 'We don't have the full power – yet, but all these are organised into silos for specific areas of use: medical, military, defence, you get the idea. There is little harm can be done with what's already live.'

'But what if we get more power from The Star of Hope?'

'The Star of Hope,' Skelf said with a flourish. 'The possibilities…'

Ishbel had no idea of The Star's power but she knew Sorlie was tasked to start it. And Merj was out there somewhere with his own agenda. Had he gone looking for Sorlie?

'We must get to them.'

'Yes my dear, we must.'

Two missions merge

Ishbel limped slightly, but before I got a chance to meet her, I caught sight of something bizarre. Reinya ran from the trees at the end of the lavender fields without a care for who or what might be spying. Noni trotted behind her. They moved so fast they didn't notice Ishbel. And Ishbel seemed to be unaware of the group who overtook her from the far side of the mound, she was too intent on helping the skinny man tiptoe across the space between the mound and The Star. A giggle bubbled in my throat. It looked like a scene from some old disaster movie-caster where the final survivors of the ruined world congregate for the last scene. But where were Dawdle and Jake in this scene?

Reinya and Noni reached me first, out of breath and sweating.

'Where's Dawdle?' I asked.

She rubbed Noni's back. 'You OK?' She handed Noni a water canister she must have retrieved from the canoe. 'You OK?' she asked again, but Noni gaped at her as if she'd gone mad to ask, then sat down with her back to the wall, watching.

'Tell me,' I said with one eye to the door. 'Ishbel should be here any minute.'

'Ishbel. Was that who that wus? She looks older. No wonder though, 'er boyfriend is un absolute traitor.'

'Dawdle?'

'Dawdle.'

'What about Dawdle?' Ishbel asked, helping the skinny man into the hall. 'Sorlie, Reinya.' She nodded my way. 'Good to see you both,' she said, all formal-like, squinting at us, but saying no more. She meant business.

234

'What about Dawdle, Reinya?'

'Like uh say, 'e's a traitor.' She hooped in a big breath. 'We leave 'ere and 'ead back to the canoe. He ties that Jake up again and dumps 'im in the boat.'

'Jakc?' Ishbel puzzled a look at me. I mouth a 'tell you later'.

Reinya took another gulp of air. 'We're waitin, like you told us to, Sorlie. We make camp, 'ave some scran. Then Dawdle gets pinged a message.'

'Who from?' Ishbel asked. I could see by her frown that she had noticed Noni, but she stayed focused on the topic of Dawdle.

Reinya shrugged. 'But then out o nowhere he pulls u gun on me and Noni.'

'What? I knew he was up to something.' My blood was boiling.

Reinya nodded. 'Got more o they plastic things and plans to tie me and Noni up. He points the gun at me and tells Noni if she doesn't tie me up 'e'll shoot me.'

'I'll kill him!'

'Sorlie.' Ishbel put her hand on my arm. She swallowed, hardly breathing.

Reinya nodded to Noni. 'Course, Noni 'as no idea 'ow to make u loop with plastic ties. She tries and then throws the lot in Dawdle's face, then loups on 'im. Knocks 'im out. So uh make the loops and we tie 'im up and belt back 'ere.'

'He's not dead?' Ishbel asked. Reinya shook her head.

'He might not be but he will in a minute.'

'Sorlie,' Ishbel said with real sadness.

'Look, do we have time for this?' the skinny man said. 'Sounds like this chap's been dealt with. Now, can we get on?'

He was right but I struggled to stow my anger.

'This is Skelf.' Ishbel grudgingly introduced us.

'The guy who brought down the net?' I asked, stoundit.

'Who told you that?' Ishbel's sharp words stung me, but I held my backlash. Reinya was right, she'd aged and looked worn out. It's been a long road for all of us.

'Pa told me, Ishbel. I mean, The Prince.'

'Right, well, very good,' Skelf said. 'Then you'll know the score. We need more power.'

'I'm working on that. A reactor is working and the first turbines are turning.'

'I can hear,' this Skelf said. 'Did the bot get it started?'

'How do you know about the bot?'

'What's u bot?' Reinya looked bemused.

'A bot is a machine that can do the work of humans,' Skelf said. 'And yes, I know about the bot because my company set this protocol up.' Despite his scrawny look there was a smugness about him that could do with a slap.

'Jake had already killed the guards and the engineer when we got here.' I didn't go into the details – that could wait. 'A robot can work the plant. It's powering up another reactor just now. We just need to make sure we're safe from the Military.'

'You're safe from the Military all right,' Skelf said, then looked around at his audience. 'The one we need to worry about is Merj.'

'Merj?' I turned on Ishbel. 'What's he got to do with this?'

'He rescued me in Bieberville, said The Prince sent him.'

Ishbel glanced through the outside door, maybe looking for Dawdle, maybe Merj, probably both. 'Why are we safe from the Military?' she asked Skelf.

The grinding that had been happening within the plant quietened to a hum. Skelf leaned his head back on the wall next to Noni. He shuffled his bum and girned in pain. 'I used to have a nice cushion here.' He patted his bum. 'My butt was so big you could land a Transport on it. Now I'm too bony. I don't suppose there's a cushion anywhere.'

'Get on with it,' I hissed.

'The Military aren't coming because there's hardly any left.'

'Are you crazy? I lived on a Military Base. There are Bases everywhere.'

'True, there are lowercase bases around, but have you been in them?'

I opened my mouth to speak.

'Apart from the one you grew up in?' I closed my mouth. 'No, thought not. The ones left are a shambles. Even the Bieberville border has only a smattering of Military.'

'It's true,' Ishbel said. 'I've seen very little in the way of Military in Esperaneo Major.'

'So forget the heavy guns,' Skelf continued.

'No, wait a minute. That's not right.' I couldn't let him fool us like this. 'If there are hardly any Military, why were there two Transports at the tower to arrest Ishbel?'

Skelf squinted at Ishbel. 'Is that right, now? In that case, the powers that are left must believe Ishbel to be a very important person. Is it not the case she is the daughter of the revolutionary leader, Vanora?'

'OK, OK,' Ishbel said. Her face was slightly pink. 'What about surveillance?'

'There is surveillance,' Skelf assured us. 'But there are hardly any Privileged left to maintain it. So The Military commissioned the TEX to set up the illusion of a huge Military force. Of a State that is all-powerful, of a Privileged race that has the natives as their slaves.' He looked pleased with his revelation. 'Don't you see? Your world is a great big lie.'

'That's impossible. My ma and pa worked for the Military. I was born and brought up on a Base. I attended an Academy.'

'A virtual Academy,' he corrected me.

'Yes, but we got together for selection.'

'I bet there weren't that many present at this selection?' I thought back to the times we were lined up in the gym hall.

'True,' I had to admit.

'But it can't all have been an illusion?' Ishbel said. 'What about all the natives who worked in factories, in domestic service for the Privileged? I was in domestic service myself.'

'Again,' Skelf said in a calm, cold voice. 'How many of these were you in touch with outside your own Base?'

'I went to market every week with produce to sell.'

'And who did you sell it to?'

Ishbel's brows pringled. 'Other natives, for their Privileged owners. But it was always the same group of about a dozen or so natives.'

'So we have a dozen Privileged who don't live on your Base. And how do you know it wasn't for the natives' own uses, or maybe the Noiri took it. They are everywhere, aren't they?'

A doubt started nibbling in my mind.

A sly smile passed his lips. 'Any other examples of this great Privileged race and State you were all working for?'

'What about Steadie?' I chipped in. 'The natives there went out and worked every day.'

'Where did they go?' Skelf asked.

'I don't know.' I flushed red. 'I never thought to ask. I just assumed that they went out to work in the Privileged homes.'

'Did this reservation have food?'

'Yes, but they grew it themselves.'

'Where?'

Suddenly the floor was more interesting than this conversation.

'You don't know, do you? You eat the food laid before you like a Privileged and never think to ask.'

'They went out to work in the fields.' Ishbel said. 'I should have guessed that, but even I didn't bother with the workings of Steadie.'

'I saw the specials work within the compound.' My voice sounded small. 'I knew that plastic was recycled there but I never talked to any specials or natives other than Harkin or Con. Jupe sake, I am still such a Privileged brat.'

Skelf laid a hand on my shoulder.

'You are not entirely to blame,' he said. 'The division of classes worked well and helped to keep the illusion alive. This is a world of broken communications. If you keep every part of it separate and in the dark then it's easy to create an illusion. But once this power is on and we can open up some of the silos of information, that illusion will crumble. Are you ready for that?'

'Of course. The conditions the natives live under are unbearable,' I said. 'It's the right thing to do. And this is what The Prince wants.'

'Ah yes, The Prince. And how is he going to use this power, I wonder?' He left the question floating in the air, no answers forthcoming. There was a series of rumbles from deep within the mountain. Skelf held his face up and listened.

'Sounds like it's started. Now we get to the interesting part.' From his pocket he produced a device and swiped through a menu. The bot came into the room. And stood waiting.

Ishbel, Noni and Reinya gaped at it. The robot smiled at him but did not move.

'Your command device is very sophisticated,' he said to me. 'Probably produced by technicians from my own company.'

'Yes, and now working for my grandmother,' I nipped. Skelf gave me a sharp look.

'Give me back control, Sorlie.'

'I don't think so.'

He sighed. 'No matter, we all want the same thing. We should be ready to start.'

'Do you know what to do?' I said, suddenly feeling childish at my initial refusal.

'Of course. I created this model. Quite stunning, even if I say so myself.'

I did as he asked and unclipped my plugin from the bot. He was right, we did all want the same thing. The robot climbed the stairs and disappeared into the control room.

Skelf smiled. 'And now the missing piece. Do you now believe that the illusion worked? Because we are about to find out the truth.'

The truth. I've been searching for the truth for aeons. Ever since I discovered my DNA passport was fake and that I was part native. Was it really going to be revealed, did I want that? In some ways living in the dark was easier.

Throughout this exchange Reinya had been eyeing Skelf with concern. She pushed herself off the wall and walked towards him.

'You say it's easy to keep un illusion if the communication is broken and the pieces ur kept apart, but not all the communication wus broken,' she said. 'Thurs u group that know what's goin on everywhere.'

That horrible churning in my stomach bubbled to the surface with my own dawning of the truth and what it meant.

'Correct, my dear.'

'The Noiri.' I said it before my mind worked through all the possibilities.

'Give the boy a coconut.' The familiar voice came out of nowhere.

'Merj!'

He stood by the door, a gun held in each hand. He walked into the hall and swung the guns around like some oldie superhero, out to fight the whole room if someone dared to move.

'Everyone, into the corner. Sorlie, instruct that robot to step away from the controls.'

'Why? Why are you doing this, Merj? The Prince wants The Star operational and you work for him.'

'No I don't, not any more. Now move.'

Everyone shuffled into the corner. I stood in front of Reinya and Noni, ushering them to sit.

'Why, Merj?' Ishbel asked in a measured voice.

'Because, my dear Ishbel, if this plant facilitates the server Switch-On we will go back to the way it was before. Do you really want that? Where everyone had access to information. Every movement recorded. The TEX once more holding all the power and the Noiri's activities curtailed. Then the natives truly will starve.'

'Come now, that's not necessarily true,' Skelf said with a little nervous cough.

'And why should we believe you?' Merj sneered. 'You're the main architect of this mess.'

I saw a familiar shadow appear in the doorway behind Merj. Ishbel was beside me. She grabbed my arm and squeezed it.

'Ah, so touching, aunt and nephew, supposed rulers of the new world.'

Dawdle moved closer to Merj in the darkness, unnoticed. We just needed to keep Merj occupied.

'What I don't understand is why you're doing this. You aren't even Noiri,' I said.

Merj grinned. 'No I'm not, but he is.' He swung round and pointed a gun at Dawdle. But Dawdle casually walked up to Merj and took it from him.

I heard Ishbel let out a relieved sigh; it was short-lived as Dawdle turned the gun toward us. There was real sadness in his face, somehow. His gun was trained on us all but he only looked at Ishbel.

'Sorry Ish, but this needs tae be done.'

The Fifth Column

'Have you gone mad, Dawdle?' I said. Then realisation dawned. 'Was that the plan all along? The Noiri take over the operation once all the work was done?'

'The Noiri? Is this what this is about?' Reinya screamed at Dawdle.

Dawdle dragged his hand through his hair. Even though he held a gun to us his eyes still flickered in Ishbel's direction. Her skin was the colour of oatmeal but her eyes burned with amber rage and her lips were wording as if she were offering up a silent prayer to her – our – ancestors.

The robot stood to attention at the top of the stairs as if waiting for the next instruction. What would happen if we turned it all on now? The thought ran through me but the words came from Reinya.

'Traitor.' She took a step towards Dawdle but Merj brandished his remaining gun in her face.

'Don't, Reinya,' Dawdle said. 'Merj has no conscience. He'll kill you.'

'So what're you 'angin about 'im for then, Dawdle?'

For some reason Skelf was smirking but I noticed he'd edged his way closer to the stairs and Noni moved with him.

'OK Dawdle, let's see if we can sort this out.' I tried reason.

Dawdle turned to me and I could see he hadn't gone mad, there was no malice in his voice or actions. This was business and – what was it Ishbel had said? – wired for profit, that was Dawdle.

'Why don't we come to some sort of financial arrangement?'

Merj burst out laughing.

242

'Listen to the little diplomat.'

'Shut it, Merj,' Dawdle said. Merj did just that.

'Who's in charge here?' Ishbel asked.

'Me,' Dawdle said.

'Then what about him?' She made a step towards Merj and no one stopped her. 'Look at him? Still wearing the uniform of the Blue Pearl. Do you know, Merj, you've been the bane of my life ever since you entered it.'

'Didn't say that when you first met me, lover. Did you?' Merj blew a kiss at Ishbel.

She slapped him hard on the cheek and even though he continued to smirk I could see his arm, the mended arm, twitch as if he had a loose wire. She lifted her hand as if to strike again but he belted her face with his gun.

'Don't,' Dawdle roared.

And there was Dawdle's weakness. I saw it and so did Ishbel. I caught her short glance at Dawdle as she held her hand to her whacked cheek.

'You're not fit to wear that uniform, Merj,' Ishbel spat. 'Sorlie, tell me, how many uniforms have you seen this man wear?'

'Too many,' I said.

'Yes, that's our Merj. They used to call them The Fifth Column. Mercenaries from within the ranks who will serve the one who pays the most.'

'That's not true,' Merj said but his shifting eyes told another story.

'Yes it is,' she said. 'Dawdle's not the only one wired for profit.' She held her hands in the air.

'Go on, shoot me. See how many pieces of credit The Military give you for my bounty.'

'No, Ishbel,' Reinya shouted. She moved forward but I held up my arm to stay her. Ishbel knew what she was doing.

'Go on, Merj. What's stopping you?' Ishbel goaded. 'I don't want to live in a world where profits rule.'

Merj lifted his gun and pointed it at her head and I could see in his face that he really wanted to pull the trigger.

'Wait,' Dawdle shouted.

Ishbel snapped her mouth shut, clattering her teeth as if catching an insect.

'No, Ishbel, dinnae bite your pill. Let me explain.'

'Why should we listen to you?'

He looked around. 'Because ye dinnae ken the full story.'

'We do,' I quipped. 'Skelf told us.'

'What he told ye wis his version.' He ushered us into the corner, herding Skelf and Noni back from the stairs with his gun. 'Sit down.' He waited till we sat. 'Skelf wants this operational so he can go back to bein king again. But before ah go on there's couple of folk who can tell ye better.'

He signalled to Merj who left the hall, returning a couple of minutes later. He stepped aside and swept an arm into the room with a flourish, allowing the party to enter.

'Vanora!' I was astounded.

She wore a lightweight scarlet cloak with matching heels that clacked across the floor. She batted her eyelids at me.

'Sorlie, my darling boy.'

Then she turned and swiped Merj across the chest with a large ornamental fan. 'How could you leave us outside so long in that unbearable heat?'

Dawdle stood to the side, gun still drawn, while Merj set up a comms. While he was doing that Monsieur Jacques joined us. He towered over everyone.

'Wait a minute, my pa is being transported by the Noiri. Does this mean he's being kidnapped?'

Monsieur Jacques shrugged his shoulders. 'If kidnap is the

244

word you want to use, go ahead. I don't think your pa believes that. We are simply helping him out.'

'Where is he?' I looked to Dawdle for an answer.

'The Noiri are transportin him tae the Capital.'

'Oui, it is most fortunate that his Transport was inoperable and he put his trust in the Noiri.'

'What do you mean?' I tried hard to keep my voice calm but I could hear the shit whiney kid of old return. 'You sabotaged the Transport, didn't you?'

Monsieur Jacques held out his hand in a gesture of innocence. 'Your pa is too trusting to make a great leader. He just expected my men to take him to the Capital with that virus. No questions asked.'

'Untested virus,' Vanora chipped in.

'Oui, untested. To destroy my beautiful city. With that virus. So reckless. So careless.' He shook his head. 'We are lucky it is contained in Esperaneo Lesser. Your pa is a madman, the same as all the others who tried to destroy the Capital in the past. All those who get a taste for power go mad eventually.' He inclined his head towards Vanora and she chose not to see.

'Speak for yourself,' I said. 'My pa only wants what's best for Esperaneo.'

'Sorlie, as Dawdle should have told you, your pa only wants access to the servers so he can be repaired. Become a cyborg,' Vanora explained in the sanest voice she could muster.

'That's not true.' But I couldn't hear any conviction in my voice. All the pieces were slotting together and I felt lost.

Vanora pointed up to the bot that still stood sentry at the top of the stairs.

'Look at this thing.' The robot blinked as if it knew Vanora talked about it. 'Look how beautiful it is, look how much like a human it is. Look how smooth the hands are, how dextrous it is. This is what they could do before the Switch-Off. This is what nearly destroyed us before and this is where your pa wants us to return to.' She moved to Merj and patted his arm.

'Now look at Merj here. He was repaired wonderfully by my technicians who worked in this field before the Switch-Off.'

'My technicians,' Skelf whispered.

Merj's arm twitched as if in response to Vanora's words.

'Now, didn't they do a good job?' She patted his arm then brushed imaginary dust off her hands as if wiping away the past. 'What's wrong with sticking to what we have?'

'What about all the natives who are starving?'

'They don't need a Switch-On,' Vanora said. 'That won't feed them. Anyway, they aren't starving.'

'They are,' Ishbel said. 'I found cannibals up north.'

'Tch.' Vanora dismissed her daughter as usual. 'Isolated incident. If we allow the illusion to break, for the natives to realise their lives are in their own hands, it will lead to chaos.'

'How?' I said. 'I don't understand. They've already proved how resourceful they are. Think what they could do with electric power and information. The Star of Hope. This is the power they need.'

'The power, yes, maybe,' said Vanora. 'But we will need to establish the government before we can allow them the knowledge.' Monsieur Jacques didn't look so convinced.

'But isn't this what you wanted, Vanora?' Ishbel implored. 'To free the natives. All your money and effort. All your coverts, the organisation you set up.' Vanora narrowed her eyes at her and I could see the old jealousy still there, cementing her resolve against Ishbel.

'Enough,' Vanora said. 'If the servers are activated the truth will be out and everything will be ruined. Normal natives don't know how to manage their lives. They should be kept ignorant.' She spread her affected benevolent smile around the room. 'My

246

technicians have worked wonders. I…' she stabbed her own chest with her painted fingernail. 'I – built a great army. Do you think Dougie Mayben can waltz in and take that from me?' She cleeked arms with Jacques. 'We have formed a coalition. NFF and Noiri. We will run the underground networks.' She glared at us all in turn with a withering look. 'There will be no Switch-On. There will be no Star.'

If she was looking for applause, her hope fell flat. I was still transfixed on the shooters.

Noni moved up behind Dawdle. He whipped round at her. 'Start onything funny, Noni, and ah'll kill Reinya.'

'He won't,' Ishbel said.

'Maybe he won't,' said Vanora. 'But Merj will.'

'Vanora…' I began. But she stayed my words with a raised palm.

'I'm not listening to you, Sorlie,' Vanora said. 'You have failed me as a grandson and heir apparent. Useless soft warrior! You can do as you please once this is all over. Go back to your pa.'

'Once what's all over?'

She smiled at me with that horror mask smile. 'The demise of the server.'

'No!' Skelf wailed. 'That can't happen, there are safeguards.'

'Yes it will. We will hook up the comms to link to The Prince. We don't want him to miss the show. What show, you wonder? Merj has fixed the fuses so they won't blow. Then we'll just sit here until the power surge blows the lot into orbit.'

Jacques stood by the reactor, nodding, obviously in complete agreement.

Vanora turned to Skelf. 'You are not the only one with a robot. Where do you think we found the instructions for you to start up this facility? We've set the power to surge into the server farm as soon as the Star reaches critical and then we will be rid of that horrible data for ever.'

'The State went to sleep on this one,' Jacques added.

'You can't do it. It's barbaric,' I shouted. 'It's like burning all the books and the histories. Backward tribes destroying artefacts.'

The two old people stood together with conviction and zeal shining from their faded smiles.

'So be it, it's for your own good,' Vanora said.

'Now sit down and be quiet,' Dawdle barked, waving the gun in my face.

'Not so rough, Dawdle. He's still my grandson.' She smiled at me. 'As I said, once this is done you will all be released to go back to whatever you like. Ishbel, I trust you will return to Freedom with me.'

'Oh, I'll return, but not with you.'

A waft of warm air filled the hall and the aircon boosted.

'What's that?' Merj shouted.

'Somebudy's left,' Dawdle said. 'Where's that bloody Neanderthal?'

'Doesn't matter,' Merj assured him. 'She'll probably get caught up in the blast.'

At that moment a bang shattered the air. I threw myself to the ground. At first I thought it was the installation going up but when I looked I saw Vanora sprawled on the ground. At the door stood Kenneth, holding a gun. Another shot cracked when I dived for Merj's legs. As I toppled him two more shots rang out. I couldn't see what was going on. Merj had me round the throat in a stranglehold with an arm so strong I thought my neck would break. When I thumped the arm it was so hard I nearly busted my knuckle.

'You won't get away this time, boy,' he whispered in my ear.

Reinya was screaming. Why was no one helping me? My lungs burned as I tried to breath. He was choking me. I scrabbled my legs in mid-air and hooked one around one of his, and my feet touched the ground. I propelled myself forward and down, trying to roll into a ball and throw him off me. As I fell I caught sight of Kenneth, slumped and bloody. The weight of Merj on my back buckled my knees. At least the pressure released on my throat enough to allow a gasp of breath. He recovered quickly though and the grasp tightened again. As I whipped round, red flashed and I got a sense of a scene of bloody carnage before I was under him again. His other hand grabbed my face, my mouth, my nose. My thrapple burned and I gasped to get another morsel of breath. My chest screamed. I scrabbled my legs again, toes touched floor, then slipped on something slick, I guessed blood. I was pumped empty. I slumped, stars burst in my head and my ears were ringing. This was the end, I was drowning.

Then I felt fresh fingers digging into my throat, scratching, releasing Merj's grip on me. The weight fell off me. I coughed, dropped on my knees, gasping air, spewing and spitting, snatching air, sweet, sweet air. Doubled over, my forehead to the deck, my ribcage a concertina, working jigtime to keep that sweet air. What the snaf had happened? Sounds came back to me first. A familiar sound of a keening so awful it wrenched my gut. I was scared to lift my head but knew I had to face the worst.

Vanora lay right beside where I'd landed. A smear of her blood reached me where my boot had caught it. Her red cloak stained darker, making her face paler than any other corpse I'd seen. Her eyes were open but glazed in death. I looked to the sound of Reinya's keening. She huddled in a ball on the floor, Scud had his arm around her. Scud?

Ishbel was on her knees beside Dawdle who was sprawled in a puddle of blood.

'Dawdle,' I whispered.

Monsieur Jacques knelt on his other side, holding a blood-soaked jacket to Dawdle's stomach. Ishbel performed CPR. Tears tracked down Jacques' face. I began to crawl towards them, past Kenneth slumped at the door. Blood traced a line from his erupted eye socket. No one needed to attend to Kenneth. Poor Kenneth.

Ishbel

Vanora fell to the ground.

'Kenneth,' Ishbel called. She rushed to him but before she could get there, Merj fired, then Sorlie dived for Merj. Although hit, Kenneth fired again. Ishbel grabbed Reinya on the way down. Scud huddled both women into a scrum. Another shot fired and then nothing but the sound of the grunts from Sorlie and Merj's wrestle.

'Ishbel, please.' It was Jacques.

She lifted her head. Both Vanora and Kenneth were dead. Jacques clutched Dawdle's belly, blood squelched through his fingers. Ishbel crawled over.

Dawdle smiled up at her.

'Sorry, Ish.' His voice wet with blood.

'Shhh.' She yanked off her jacket and pushed it to Jacques.

'Try to stop the bleeding. Scud, try and find a first aid kit.'

'Sorry, Ish. It could'uv been so good.' He swallowed.

'Shhh.' Her heart was thumping.

'You and me, could huv...' He winced. His smile slipped. 'Dinnae cry, hen. Ye'll be... great. You...always... wis the best.'

'Please, Dawdle. Hang in,' she choked. Her heart ripped apart. 'Stay,' she begged.

His smile was crooked. 'That'll dae me.' He closed his eyes. A breath bubbled in his chest.

'No,' Ishbel whispered.

She racked her brains for her first aid training. She put her lips to his. They were warm but tasted of blood. Why hadn't she given her lips to him before? She blew in a breath and began to pump his chest. Why now? she thought.

She blew another breath, pumped his chest one, two, three. She checked his pulse, nothing. Breath, pump one, two, three. She didn't know how long she did this.

'Come on, damn you. Breathe.'

Jacques wept noisily, but still held the soaking jacket to Dawdle's belly. Reinya was keening and Ishbel tried to shut out their dreadful noise. She breathed again and began pumping. She felt her strength slip and still she worked until a hand took both of hers away from Dawdle's body.

'He's gone, Ishbel.'

She tried to shove Sorlie away but he held her tight and pulled her into him and hugged her in the grip of a man. A huge wail escaped her and he let her cry into his chest in the same way she had let him cry when she'd told him he was an orphan so long ago.

The pain in her chest was unbearable. She'd always thought it was an exaggeration but she physically felt the shredded pieces of her heart shrivel within her before growing cold. She sniffed back tears and let Sorlie hold her for a few more minutes then pushed him away.

'It's OK, I'm OK.'

Jacques body folded like his power. He dropped his head to kiss Dawdle's forehead.

'My son,' he wailed. His eyes were red when he looked at Ishbel. 'He was like my son.'

'I know. I'm sorry.'

She crawled away from them and sat on the floor to survey the scene of carnage. It seemed to Ishbel quite symbolic that Vanora and Kenneth lay only feet apart, both unmourned, whilst the weeping crowded around Dawdle's body. Despite appearances, he was one of the good guys all along.

'What are we going to do with him?' Sorlie said, pointing to where Merj lay struggling while Noni sat on his chest, restraining him.

Ishbel wiped her snot on her cuff.

'We should tie him up and feed him to the wolves.' Then she shook her head. 'Tie him and take him to the control room.'

Scud came over and hugged both Ishbel and Sorlie to him.

'This wasn't meant to happen.' He nodded towards Kenneth. 'Ah shouldn't have encouraged him.'

'What are you doing here, Scud?' Sorlie asked.

Scud

'Tell us,' Ishbel said.

Scud's mutant eyes were red-rimmed but the tears had dried.

'It's ma fault.'

Reinya took his hand. 'It's not, grandda. Tell them.'

He dry sobbed and began again.

'Kenneth and I had been workin on the teachin modules together. We were bored. We wanted tae fight. Stupid dreams really. We both knew it was impossible. And then out o the blue, Vanora arrived on Black Rock.'

'Uh hate Vanora,' Reinya mumbled.

'Shhh,' Scud said, smoothing her hair. 'She said it was tae check up on progress but ah think she really came tae goad Kenneth.' Scud embarrassed coughed. 'We both behaved and didn't give her the pleasure eh seein us rattled.' He bit his lip and looked at me with mischief in his eyes. 'We stowed away on her Transport.'

'No way!' I said.

'Aye, way.'

'But Kenneth's murderous intent towards her?' I reminded him.

'Ah forgot.'

'You forgot?'

'Sort of.'

'What do you mean, "sort of"?'

'Oh you know, Sorlie, aw that DNA dilution stuff sort o mashed ma brain.' He was lying. He also, at one time, had murderous intent towards Vanora. Maybe it was convenient amnesia.

'Anyway, ah wanted tae see Reinya. Vanora made sure tae mention she'd be seein Reinya.' Scud looked towards the blood patch where Vanora had fallen. 'She was an evil bitch.' He sighed and shrugged his native shrug. 'So we came. The rest you know.'

Reinya sat up and brushed her hair from her face. Noni remained separate , watching them both.

'It's not your fault, Grandda.'

'No, it's not, Scud,' I assured him. 'Kenneth would have got to Vanora somehow.'

'But…' Scud pointed to the bloodstains.

I took his hand and squeezed it. 'We are where we are.'

I looked into his tired old eyes and remembered all the courage and wisdom he had shared with me.

'We have a clean page to start again, Sorlie. Let's dae it right.' He placed his other hand on top of mine and nodded. 'Ah telt ye tae get it sorted and ye are.' He patted my hand then let me go before turning to Noni. 'So, Reinya, tell me, what are we are goin tae dae wi yer wee pal here?'

My comms buzzed – 15 seconds to surge.

The Switch-On

The main cylinder crashed alive.

'What the snaf?' Reinya screamed.

'The surge.' Vanora's destruction had started. 'I have to stop it.'

I shouted above the cacophony. 'Ishbel, you stay with Reinya and Jacques.'

'No. Scud can look after them. This time we go together.' She looked around, avoiding the bloody scene. 'Where's Skelf?'

'I'm here.' He hirpled down the stairs from the control room. 'The bot is trying to shut down the turbines. We need to get to the servers to cut the connection there.'

We rushed from the building into the searing heat outside. The sound of the straining turbines followed us into the still air. A gap like an open mouth had appeared in the mound since I last passed it. Skelf headed straight there and we followed.

Inside was cool. Skelf stumbled into the depths and disappeared.

'Skelf!' Ishbel roared.

The place was massive. Little busy contraptions whizzed over the floor, tripping us up. They attached themselves to the housings of black boxes arranged in shelves and ran up and down them like rats in a sewer.

'What are they?'

'Fixits,' Ishbel said.

A muffled explosion sounded somewhere deep in the bowels of the mound, or maybe it was coming from the power plant.

'There must be a cut-off switch somewhere, that'll be where Skelf's gone,' Ishbel said.

'But what happens if he shuts this down? Will the power build up in the Star?'

'I've no idea.'

'Pa might know.'

'You can't communicate.'

'We can, Ishbel. Remember what Skelf said. I reckon if any Military pick up the signal, they probably won't bother to act.'

Another explosion burst from within and some of the boxes crashed from their casings, knocking a little Fixit off as they fell.

I could smell burning, sharp and stinging.

Skelf staggered down the rows, grabbing hold now and then.

'We've lost the back section,' he said. 'The smoke is too dense. The bitch was right, they've tampered with the fuses. The whole place is going to blow. We need to cut the connection here.' He lurched to a rectangular box on the wall and tugged at the door. It stuck.

My communicator buzzed on my wrist. 'Sorlie?' Pa's voice cut in.

'Pa, we need your help. Vanora set up a power surge from the Star to the servers. So much power coming through at once will destroy them.'

'You must stop the flow.' Pa looked like shit.

'But if we do won't we risk The Star?'

'Not if you divert it. Is there not a power exchange with the nearest Urban? Direct the full flow to the Urban. You must save the servers.' I remembered the exchanger, the bot only needed to move the dial. But the consequences?

'Divert!' Skelf roared, taking out the device to contact the Star bot.

'Ishbel, stop him.'

Ishbel grabbed the device off Skelf. He threw his arms up in frustration.

'Damn your Star. There's a trip here.' He went back to tugging the panel on the box.

'Divert, Sorlie!' Pa roared. He seemed desperate.

'Divert where?' I still couldn't believe he meant what he was saying.

'Sorlie, listen to me, you must divert. It will go to the nearest Urban.'

My mind was racing. I had no idea how powerful the Star was and the type of damage it could do.

'We can't do that, Pa. There might be casualties.'

Skelf had the panel open. He had a lever in his hand.

'Sorlie, you must let me contact the bot,' Skelf said. 'If I trip this switch it could blow up the Star.'

'No!' I hear Pa shout. 'Sorlie, an Urban is a small sacrifice.'

'For what?' My cheeks were wet.

'We can save millions with power.'

'Then save The Star. Dawdle said the data was harmful anyway.'

'Dawdle is a fool,' Pa said. 'I'm your Prince and I order you to divert the current to the Urban. We need this data.'

'You're only thinking of yourself. Your cyborg self. Pa, Merj has good limbs. Vanora's technicians up north worked wonders on him. You can go there.'

Something dark passed over Pa's face and I knew the truth. What may have begun as a noble fight for him had morphed into something else. His injuries had twisted his desire inwards. He wanted this victory for himself. His needs had overtaken the needs of the natives.

The back wall crashed down. Skelf strained to push the lever up to the OFF position. It stuck halfway. He made a grab for his device from Ishbel. It flew from her hand and skittered across the floor.

'Sorlie, please, save the data.' Pa pleaded, defeated.

'I'm sorry, Pa.' I flew to the panel and yanked the lever back down in place, allowing the juice to flow unhindered into the building. Sparks erupted. Skelf screamed. Ishbel dragged him outside. Black plumes belched toxic fumes up and around the rows. Flames licked the casings. Tears streamed from my eyes.

'Sorlie, Sorlie.' I could hear Pa's voice above my choking. I stumbled outside. Ishbel held Skelf by the arm, she grabbed me with her other hand and all three of us dived into the lavender field as the mound blew its top, scattering debris. It pattered around us sending clouds of angry bees into the air.

Ishbel held Skelf by the throat. 'Get the bot to close down the Star.'

'It's already started doing it,' he sobbed. 'It knew the danger but it takes time to stop.'

'I'm sorry, Pa, I couldn't do it. I couldn't destroy an Urban. The server's gone.'

The sound of his bawl would haunt me for the rest of my life. In time I hoped he would understand that this was for the best for everyone, that his initial dreams, the ones he'd lost sight of, could be achieved and he would be alright. I was sure of it... I had to be.

'We are going to start with a clean sheet.' I said in a voice that was firm and definite. I cut the signal to shut out his pitiful sound. It wasn't until I saw the blank screen of my communicator that I realised he didn't know of the carnage that happened here.

We dragged our sorry butts back to the plant. The bot was back at its station on top of the stairs. Things had quietened down.

Ishbel pushed Skelf towards the bot. 'Ask for the status of the plant.' He looked broken as he climbed the stairs. 'Make sure the systems are secure and kept running at low capacity. Ask for a list of all amenities with open links to the plant. Are they operational and if not, what will it take to make them work?'

'It might not have that information,' Skelf said. 'I'm not a miracle worker.'

'Try,' she said.

Ishbel was taking control and I was glad she was so focused, presumably to keep her mind off Dawdle. I just wanted to curl up in a ball and sleep for the rest of my life. But I'd been there before and knew it would pass.

The bodies had been removed, leaving dark patches on the floor to step round. Judging by the bloodstains covering Noni and Scud, they had managed the removal between them. They sat together on the floor and stared at me. Reinya was huddled between them, her thumb in her mouth. Jacques sat wrapped in a blanket, his huge legs bent and his head rested on his knees.

'I've instructed safe passage for your father,' he said when he lifted his head.

I sat beside him. 'I'm sorry,' I said.

'Your father will forgive you. When he is crowned king.'

'King? He will not be king.' I pointed to the top of the stairs where Ishbel had returned to interrogate the bot.

'She is the new ruler.'

Jacques nodded. 'She will be a good ruler. And you? Will you be in her government?'

'No. I am going back to Steadie.'

We remained silent until Ishbel joined us and sat. She draped her arm around me.

'You did the right thing, Sorlie. Scud told me once that the only solution was to start with a clean page. That's what we have. By starting with a clean page we can build our world again but with checks and balances in place to protect the citizens of Esperaneo and the environs they inhabit. This is our chance. A clean page.'

Epilogue

New Steadie 2095

'Pa, Pa, come and see – the lights are on already. The castle is all lit up.'

The voice hollers through my open window, yanking me from my chronicling. I should have been angry. I only set aside one hour a day for the task and yet I never tire of that sweet voice, even when it yells at me like a banshee. I lift my head and catch sight of grey clouds shifting across the watery sun. It will rain later. Maybe that's why the celebrations have kicked off early.

The door flings open and the bundle of energy we named Kathleen, after my mother, rushes in.

'Come on!' Her five-year-old legs, spindly but strong, brace as she tugs my arm, trying to pull me from my seat. Her dark eyes flash urgently.

'Kathleen, darling, hold on.'

'No Pa, come on. Everyone's waiting.'

'Everyone?' I haven't heard a Transport so doubt the dignitaries have arrived yet. I place Ishbel's pebble on top of my loose leaf of paper. Paper. The thought of it still thrills me. All the books from the Black Rock library had been returned there, and all the blank pages had been retrieved and given to me as a gift by the government. It's a minimal amount but enough to write this history in the ancient way.

We leave my study and Kathleen tugs me the short distance to the front door. Although I'm Chief Elder at New Steadie, our accommodation is on a par with everyone else. It's the way the community started and it's the way it will continue.

'Where's your Ma?' I ask as we enter the main square. Harkin is nowhere in sight.

Kathleen turns and frowns at me. 'Up at the castle. I told you. Everyone is there. Come on.' She stamps her foot in frustration. 'Look.' She points towards the old castle that sits high on the hill, dominating our small urban clustered round its base. All dwellings are positioned well above the flood water; it is a good place. I see lights now, burning bright on the battlements. Electric light, at last brought to New Steadie, something we've been working on for the last six years. Since we successfully powered up The Star of Hope, electricity supplies have been added to the grid across mainland Esperaneo; Esperaneo Lesser is the last link to have this glorious opportunity. This is the beginning of phase two. Even this small child recognises the importance it will bring to our lives. Our clean page.

I squeeze Kathleen's hand again. Amongst everything that has happened in this life, she is my greatest achievement.

A crowd of specials hang back from the main throng, as if frightened by the light. Not all specials joined us here in the new town. Many decided that, once the Military threat was no longer there, their old home was best. Our administration still feed and care for them and in return they continue to produce quality fibre from recycled plastic. A win-win.

As we approach a few specials step aside to let us pass. Con, Harkin's old guardian, is organising the cooking. He and his brother Al are barbecuing pork. The pigs Al and his wife had illegally reared in the castle had been small scale, but after the regime change and the subsequent reversal of the domestic animal ban, Con and his brother have expanded the business.

The smell of pork grilling makes my mouth water. Kathleen's right, it feels like everyone is here. The inhabitants of the castle settlement buzz with anticipation. I never tire of the joy I feel each time I look on their now healthy complexions and positive charge. These once-subjugated natives and Privileged reclaimed their mojo the year the regime fell and use their mojo to help themselves.

'Pa, look.' The small hand tightens its grip on mine and yanks me onwards. She points at something in the distance. I've no idea what or how she can see anything. She's so little and the bustle is intense, but like the runt of a litter butting its way for its mother's milk, this child shoulders and elbows a gap for us to pass through. Suddenly the crowd parts fully, like the curtain in the newly created theatre, and what lies before me makes me gasp.

The President has indeed arrived before schedule and has switched on the lights. I should have been here to see this momentous event, but was too caught up trying to capture the past and set down history; I'd forgotten about the present and the future.

And yet what lies before me is some of the cast of that history.

Harkin sees me first. I know by the way she stands she's waiting for me to find her. Like every good mother she probably heard Kathleen's squeals. When our eyes meet her smile reaches every part of her face and my heart warms at the sight and blood whooshes through me as it always does when I realise we are one and always will be.

As a boy I never knew love could dig so deep.

When I left the lavender fields I had only one thought in mind and, despite Ishbel and Pa's protests and their orders to go to the Capital, I disobeyed them and returned home to Harkin.

That time she had been at her desk in the infirmary, studying her medical books. I took one step towards her and stopped. She rose and filled the rest of the space in a rush.

'Sorlie.' The sound of my name on her lips sent my heart flipping through flaming hoops so fast I almost fainted.

I grabbed for her and she for me. Our lips found each other before we could say another word and I knew at that moment no summons from the President would make me leave here as long as Harkin wanted to stay. Home was a word I'd always struggled with but I knew as soon as I returned to Steadie and found her in her infirmary, home would always be where Harkin was.

Harkin's smile remains on her face and her eyes on mine even though her hand stretches out for Kathleen to join her. They both turn and face the dignitaries and Kathleen gives a little bow to the President, seated on a throne perched on the raised dais.

A teenage boy dressed in fine clothes climbs the dais steps and offers the President a platter of pork. She smiles but shakes her head. The President does not eat meat.

The President rises and holds a hand out to me. Her face betrays no emotion but her amber eyes flash a welcome.

Ishbel, President of Esperaneo.

After the data servers had been destroyed Ishbel travelled to the Capital, accompanied by her willing army of Blue Pearl soldiers and Monsieur Jacques's Noiri. With their help she'd taken control of the government of old men who were frightened of progress. Her only obstacle had been my pa. He remained devastated after my betrayal and sought to do everything in his power to stand against us. His good intentions for a better world had been corrupted, seduced by the power that had taken Vanora and many before her. As he grew weaker, the old Pa and his once maddening optimism I knew returned –he filled with hope, told me he was proud to see us fight for the world he once believed in. He would never live to see this world fully realised. He died within a year of that event.

Harkin helps me live with that guilt.

Ishbel steps forward to greet me.

'Sorlie, how are you? You look well.'

'I am well, Madam President.' I accept her outstretched hand and kiss it. She laughs, something rare from Ishbel. I notice the pain of Dawdle's death lingers in the lines around her mouth.

'No need for such pomp.' She beckons me to sit by her. 'And soon there will be elections,' she continues. 'I may not be President for much longer.'

'I doubt that will happen,' says the small figure who moves to her side.

'Sorlie, have you met my Vice President, Keats?'

'Yes, we've met.' I shake his hand. 'Good to see you again, sir.'

The small man bows. 'And you, Sorlie. We haven't seen each other since we set up the outpost on the Bieberville border with that rogue Merj.'

'Is he still there?'

'Yes, and doing a grand job. The outpost seems to suit him.' He frowns. 'He is still a worry but we keep him busy with environmental projects. He has his own kingdom there and it suits him fine. If he leaves we'll know immediately. And now that we have trade deals with the Eastern Zone our Bieberville border is a busy trade route. I think Merj is happy there.'

'And Jake?'

He shakes his head. 'Ah, not such a happy story. But let's not ruin this joyous event.'

A fanfare sounds close by and huge screens show an image of the President with me sitting beside her. This image will be beamed to all the newly formed Federations created after the census collated the whereabouts of all Esperaneo's citizens. There might still be some hidden communities out there but the Federations will eventually find them and care for them. And when they do they too will be linked up to FuB2, the news channel created by Ishbel's Communications Officer, Skelf.

'I have a birthday surprise for you, Sorlie,' Ishbel announces. I'd forgotten – it's my birthday today. Birthdays are for spoiled brats who live on a Military Base and have a native to care for their every need. She had never forgotten my birthday when I was small and nothing had changed on that front.

My mouth blots with nerves and I'm shocked to realise I'm starstruck. I can't stop staring at this magnificent President with her thick amber hair coiled in a neat round at the nape of her neck. A rich emerald green coat drapes over her shoulders and small enamelled studs, shaped like Celtic knots, pierce her ears. She looks nothing like that native Ishbel of old. And yet she still stands on tiptoes as she towers above us.

Kathleen tugs at my sleeve, but Ishbel reaches out and takes her hand.

'Kathleen.' She says the name of her sister with a catch of sorrow in her voice. 'Come and sit by me.'

'But you're the President.' Although Kathleen shrinks into my side, she speaks with force and does not let go of Ishbel's hand. Ishbel laughs again. 'And you're kin.'

'What's that?'

'Your Pa will tell you later.' Ishbel lifts her up to sit on her knee. Kathleen for once is speechless. She looks around and when she seems to realise what's happening she sticks her thumb in her mouth and coories into the President.

'And now your Pa's birthday present.' Ishbel rings a little bell that sits on the side table. The crowd fall silent. In the distance I hear the mouth whistle of a familiar tune I first heard at the Base. One Ishbel used to sing to me in her own native language. But this whistling is familiar too. First heard in Black Rock Prison where whistling was forbidden by the authorities, so when I had asked to be taught it never happened. A lump knots in my throat, a hum of melodic voices joins the whistle and drift from the back of the stage. Two women appear from behind the scenes. My pulse bounces when I recognise Reinya, her red hair flaming. Her eyes seek mine and her smile grows so huge it's a wonder she can hold a note. The other woman is Noni, her matted black hair stands on end and her face crumples with concentration. They lead a procession of children. I guess at over a hundred, all ages, size, colour and gene pool; Native, Privileged, Special, Neanderthal. Their sweet song soars and grows louder as yet more children come into view, their harmonies blend in perfect pitch. The hair on the back of my neck stands on end with the beauty of the sound and the spectacle and the realisation that this is the Black Rock School Choir. Something great and wonderful born out of the horrors of that place. This is the result of the education programme set up by Reinya and Scud.

This is the future.

When the singing stops the whistle continues and the last to enter the stage is my old friend Scud. He strides towards me and hugs me like a father and pat me on the back. Tears roll down both our faces.

'Happy birthday, wee man.'

Also by the author

Ways of the Doomed

Wants of the Silent

The Incomers